Sojourner

Janalyn Voigt

Sojourner
COPYRIGHT 2018 by Janalyn Voigt

All scripture quotations, unless otherwise indicated, are taken from the Holy Bible, New International Version(R), NIV(R), Copyright 1973, 1978, 1984, 2011 by Biblica, Inc.™ Used by permission of Zondervan. All rights reserved worldwide. www.zondervan.com

The Author is represented by and this book is published in association with the literary agency of WordServe Literary Group, Ltd., www.wordserveliterary.com.

Harbourlight Books, a division of Pelican Ventures, LLC
www.pelicanbookgroup.com PO Box 1738 *Aztec, NM * 87410
Harbourlight Books sail and mast logo is a trademark of Pelican Ventures, LLC

Publishing History
First Harbourlight Edition, 2019
Paperback Edition ISBN 978-1-5223-0203-2
Electronic Edition ISBN 978-1-5223-0202-5
Published in the United States of America

Dedication

To my sweet daughter, Zemier, who sneaks behind me
while I'm writing to read over my shoulder.

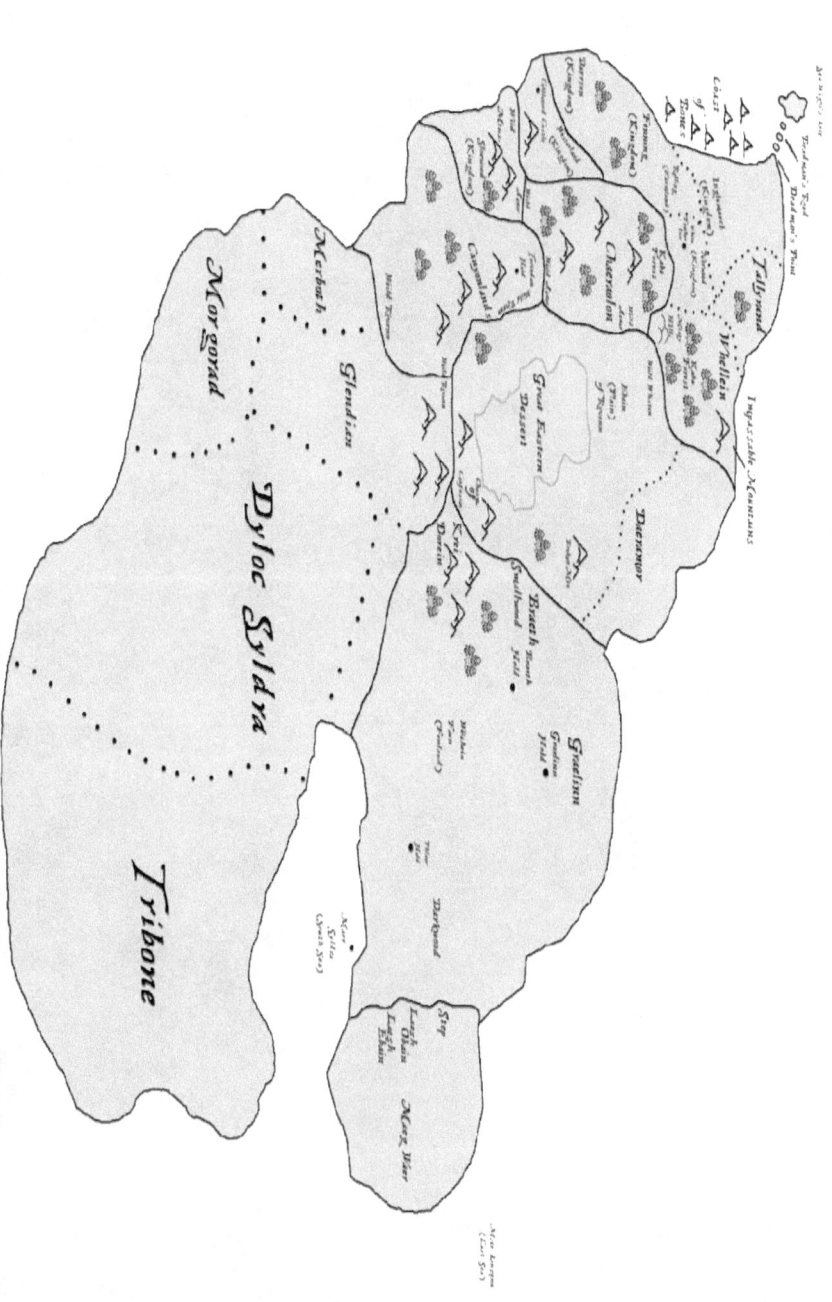

What People are Saying about DawnSinger

Janalyn Voigt is a fresh voice in the realm of fantasy. Her writing is crisp, her verbs muscular, and it's all wrapped up in a lyrical style. Blending action and romance, DawnSinger is a journey through fear, failure, and faith, and I look forward to its sequel. Eric Wilson, NY Times bestselling author of Valley of Bones and One Step Away

In DawnSinger, Janalyn Voigt has penned a novel full of surprises. With adventure, mystery, and an unlikely romance, this beautiful, epic fantasy debut will leave you scrambling for the next book in the trilogy. Jill Williamson, Christy Award-winning author of By Darkness Hid

DawnSinger is a delightful fantasy spun with bardic prose and threaded with danger and intrigue. Linda Windsor, author of Healer, Thief and Rebel, Brides of Alba Historical Trilogy

Janalyn Voigt builds an exciting world, tranquil on the surface but filled with danger, ancient enemies, and a prophecy yet to be fulfilled. DawnSinger leads you into a land only imagined in dreams. I can't wait to read the second book in the Tales of Faeraven trilogy. Lisa Grace, bestselling author of the Angel in the Shadows series.

Part One
Secrets and Lies
1

A tiny creature leaped from beneath Mara's foot and splashed into the nearest pool. She jumped back, flailing. Ripples circled outward from the place the creature had entered the water. An iridescent frog emerged and cleaved the surface with strong strokes as it swam away from her. She tucked her skirts at her waist and crouched to see it better, but she already knew it for a grillon. The frog emerged onto one of the rocks, the river flowing behind it, and from that point of safety, watched her with sides puffing. She stared back at the beautiful creature whose venomous bite could end her life.

A fish jumped, the splash it made jarring her nerves. The grillon flicked into the next pool. Mara let out her breath and straightened. Sun heated her skin, pleasant after the cold of winter, but she forsook it for the shifting shade of the path beneath the trees.

Her father should know about this. Da wouldn't say or do anything to alarm the inn's guests, but he'd want to search the pools for others of its kind.

She put a hand to her back and rubbed away an

ache. Youth and a lifetime of working at the inn favored her with strength, but she'd spent all yesterday afternoon bent over while picking dewberries and most of today stirring vats of jam. When her mother had urged her to slip away for a break, she'd ignored a twinge of guilt at leaving Mam alone with such a hard task. The inn gave them much to do in the days of fair weather. A weary traveler wanted to stop the night where a comfortable bed offered rest and a plentiful board satisfied the belly. The inn offered both, which meant that it did not lack for customers.

"Mara!" A tousle-haired stable hand called to her.

She waved to Hael, and he grinned in return. A sudden lift of heart sent her to meet him before he could leave the stableyard. It was an old game, one they'd played since she could remember.

Hael slowed his pace, grinning. He'd taken to letting her win of late. She arched her brow to tell him she knew this, but a smile tugged her lips. "I suppose Mam looks for me already."

"That she does." He ducked his head, an unruly brown lock escaping his cap.

"I shouldn't keep her waiting, but I need to find Da." She swept a glance to the inn yard, where insects turned lazy spirals in the air.

"Your father be in the common room. What's amiss?"

"I saw a grillon at the river."

His brows met in a scowl. "Did you take harm?"

"Of course not. I know to be careful."

He tapped her under the chin, a smile warming his brown eyes. "A grillon can bite even the careful."

"It wouldn't let me near."

"If grillons did not fear people, more would die

from their bites."

"Don't grillons prefer the bog? I've never seen one in the cove before this."

Da and Hael always returned from cutting turf for the fire in the bog lands with tales of the strange creatures they found. Last summer, Da had brought home a grillon trapped in a jar. Mam had been none too pleased about that. He'd explained that he meant to take Mara along next time and wanted to warn her about the grillons. Mam made him promise to put an end to the grillon, but had it somehow escaped?

"Sometimes they stray. Don't be afraid. I'll search him out for you."

He'd never gazed at her with such a soft look on his face before. What did it mean? She stepped backward. "I'm not fearful, only concerned about the lodgers."

She kept to the the edge of the stableyard, lifting her skirts as she sidestepped puddles left by the night rains. Ignoring the inn's wide front steps, she went around to the back door and found it hooked open.

Everything seemed the same as when she'd left. Aunt Brynn's face, red as her hair, glistened above several large roasts she turned on metal spikes. Their drippings hissed into the flames flaring below to haze the air with smoke. Ardel, the kitchen maid, her curly brown hair covered by a muslin cap, slid loaves of bread into the oven. Mam stirred a pot of stew and wiped her brow with the back of her hand as fading red tendrils strayed from beneath the brown kerchief knotted at her nape. She glanced up as Mara came in.

"There you be, and none too soon."

"I'm sorry, Mam. I shouldn't have gone to the river."

"That one!" Brynn shot a venomous glance to Mara. "Idling about. Take her in hand, Heddwyn, or she'll bring you grief, and no mistake."

Mam waved a hand. "She can't help being lively, just as you were in younger days. Come, Mara, and stir the stew."

Brynn fell to grumbling.

Mara gripped the wooden spoon and stirred the steaming pot with more force than necessary. Mam bent with Brynn over the meat, perhaps more to distract her sister than to check for doneness. Ardel crossed her eyes behind their backs. Choking back laughter, Mara stirred the stew.

When the rush to serve began, Mam shoved a tray into Mara's hands and thrust her through the swinging kitchen door into the common room. The fragrance of bruin stew from the bowls she carried made her mouth water. If any food remained after the guests took their portions, the kitchen workers could eat it. Otherwise, their evening meal would consist of bread and cheese. Aunt Brynn usually kept back a share of the guests' food for herself despite the rule, but Mam observed it.

"Quinn, where be my ale?" A burly man in farmer garb called.

"Here, Calib." Her father pulled a tankard of foaming ale from one of the barrels behind the counter and plunked it down on the farmer's table. He tossed a smile Mara's way before returning to load a tray with more tankards of ale. Mara delivered the bowls she carried and started back for more.

The swinging door burst open, and she sidestepped to avoid a collision with her aunt, who scowled at her. Aunt Brynn's dislike seemed to have grown of late, although she had no idea why. Pushing the thought away, she flung herself into the task at hand and hurried toward the common room balancing more bowls on her tray.

The swinging door burst open. Mara's tray flew from her grasp. Stew splatted the wall and ran down into the floor rushes. Mara gasped. . Hadn't Brynn heard her coming as she had her? The servers always yielded to the one carrying food.

"Watch yourself!" Brynn snarled as she passed. "Look what that wretched child has done now." She spoke so loudly that her voice carried from the kitchen.

Heat crawled into Mara's cheeks. No one in the common room could have missed what Aunt Brynn said.Tears stinging her eyes, Mara turned to go into the kitchen.

The door rocked open, and Da caught her arm in a firm grip. "Never mind." Da said close to her ear while handing her a rag and a bucket of water.

She summoned a smile. "Thank you."

He nodded and turned away.

Her father's kindness heartened her, and Mara bent to clean the mess with a better heart. Ready to throw out the water in the bucket, she went through the kitchen toward the back door.

Ardel stepped in front of her. "Let me."

Giving her a grateful smile, Mara surrendered the bucket. She held her head high as she returned to the common room with fresh bowls of stew. A man with black hair came in the front door. Dark eyes sought hers, and she pulled in a breath. What brought their nearest neighbor, Rohan, from his homefarm? Not hunger, for he made no move to sit at one of the trestle tables but remained standing in the small entryway. Her father rushed to him, and Rohan spoke near his ear. The two stepped outside. She could see them talking on the porch through the greased oilcloth window. Da came back in without Rohan.

She put the matter out of her mind. Whatever business her father had with Rohan had nothing to do with her. As the level of bruin stew lowered in the pot, the babble in the common room rose. Even after the kitchen workers had scrubbed down the kitchen, the travelers still made merry.

Da pulled her behind the counter and peered at her in the light from the lanthorn hanging from a rope overhead. "What brought that frown to your face? Not Brynn?"

"Nothing, but a grillon come to visit." She kept her voice low.

"Where?"

"At the cove."

"All right, then. T'will probably leave again on its own."

She nodded, all at once weary.

He tilted her face to the light. "You're growing up quicker than I realized. Off to bed. You've a caller come morning and will want to look your best."

"A caller?"

"Rohan asked to see you."

Alarm jangled through her. "And what would Rohan want with me?"

"He'll tell you that himself, I'm certain."

આ

Mara turned over, yet again, and pulled the covers about her with a sigh. Neither sleep nor morning seemed likely to arrive any time soon. A pity, since her thoughts made ill companions. That she was old enough to court had somehow escaped her notice until now. The idea knotted her stomach. Rohan seemed nice enough, but she'd never thought of him or anyone else as someone to marry. A bar of moonlight crept past the edges of the wooden shutters and into her chamber. It had stretched all the way to her bed before sleep claimed her.

A knock dragged Mara from sleep. She moaned and pressed a hand to her throbbing head. All she wanted to do was sleep. At least she had an excuse to avoid her caller. Surely Mam would send word to Rohan that she wasn't in health today. The knock came again, and she forced herself from bed to crack open the door.

Mam pushed into the chamber. "What's this? Lingering abed?"

"My head aches."

"Hmm…" Mam's eyes narrowed. "I'll brew an infusion. You'll recover before Rohan arrives."

"But Mam—"

"Stir yourself. He means to ask you to marry him." She took herself off to make the remedy.

Mara swallowed against a lump in her throat. She'd never thought Mam would be happy to see her gone. There seemed nothing to do but drag herself from bed and endure today's ordeal. Rohan wanted a wife, did he? Maybe she could persuade him to look elsewhere. She pulled her coarsest tunic of brown linsey over her linen chemise, braided the sides of her hair and wound it on top of her head. Her mirror glass told her she looked as she'd intended, tidy but not festive.

Mam brought the headache infusion and Mara breathed in the scents of lavender, rosemary, feverfew, and mint in its soothing steam. She sipped the sweetened liquid, and its warmth uncurled within her stomach. She rested the cup against her forehead and closed her eyes. She would let Rohan speak, then remind him that an inn-keeper's daughter could not count herself an equal match for a gentleman farmer of his caliber.

She made it to the kitchen on shaky legs, where she managed to swallow a crust of bread and drink a dipper of water.

"He's here." Da called in through the doorway.

Looking up from peeling yellowroot at the scarred work table, Ardel bolstered Mara with a smile.

Mam stopped in the middle of spreading fresh rushes to peer at her. "Ach! Could you not have worn your fine scarlet? You're pale as a new lamb's wool." She came to pinch Mara's cheeks.

Brynn slapped the bread she was kneading. "Leave her be. Rohan's a farmer and will want a plain wife."

Maybe she should have worn her finest garments and stained her lips with beet juice.

Rohan, feathered cap in hand and wearing a belted tunic of rough wool, leather leggings, and sturdy boots, waited beside Da in the entry.

Mara came from the kitchen, weaving between the tables in the common room with slow steps.

"It's nice to see you, Mara." Rohan held her hand a little too long in greeting.

"Hello, Rohan." She resisted the urge to snatch her hand away and freed herself more gently.

"Come, sit in the parlor." Why did Da have to

sound so cheery?

"Thank you, but I'm a man of the soil, little given to parlors," Rohan forestalled him. "Will you allow Mara to walk with me?"

She'd rather walk beside Rohan in the fresh air than cast about for words in a stuffy parlor. On the other hand, being alone with him might make walking worse.

Da nodded. "All right, but stay near."

Mara said little as she kept pace with her unwelcome caller in the spring sunshine. They left the stable behind and followed the path beneath the trees to the river bank. For a time, they watched in silence while the White Feather River hurried away on its journey to the sea.

Rohan turned to her. "Tell me of yourself."

She lifted a shoulder. "I was born and raised here at the inn."

"You're no stranger to hard work, then."

"I help with the cooking and serve the food."

"Do you tend crops as well?"

"Aye."

He nodded approval. "You'll have a strong back."

Something in his tone made her uneasy. "I'm an innkeeper's daughter. T'would be strange if I didn't."

"Have you traveled?"

"Almost never."

"Do you wish to see the world?" Rohan asked in forbidding tones.

She shrugged. "I've not thought much about it."

"That's answer enough, I'd say."

Glancing at him, she found him smiling. "And what of you? Are you happy with a farmer's lot?"

"I am." The corners of his eyes crinkled. "I'd be

more content, had I a wife."

"Then I hope you may find one."

His eyes warmed. "I think I have done so."

She looked away. "That is a matter to know for certain."

"Obtaining a wife need not weigh upon a man of means. He has only to find a worthy maiden."

"You say nothing of love."

"That emotion comes later, if it wills."

She shook her head. "Wedding vows made without it can prove themselves a snare."

"Bah!" He folded his arms. "I have no patience for matters of the heart."

"Have you not?" Hope lifted her voice. Perhaps he would leave her alone after all.

"What does a farmer know of romance?"

"I want nothing to do with it myself." There. She had let him know how she felt.

"It seems we are agreed."

Relief washed over her. He had come around so quickly. "I believe so."

"That's well then." He nodded. "I will ask for you."

She stared at him. "You must not!"

"Why, pray tell?" A note in his voice hinted of wounded pride.

"Forgive me, but I should not have spoken so sharply. It was only dismay at having to confess that my dowry is not large."

He waved a hand. "What do I care for a dowry? A wife with a strong back ready to bear my children and able to keep my hearth and home is all I require. You'll do well enough."

"I'm certain you should continue looking for a

bride more suited to your station."

"What do I care for that? The man who marries Quinn and Heddwyn's only child stands to inherit the Whitefeather Inn and its lands. That expectation can replace a dowry."

His interest took on new meaning, all of a sudden. "But I want no husband."

He smiled. "Only consider what I'm offering, and you'll change your mind."

She wouldn't but didn't tell him so. From the set of his jaw, he meant to ask for her no matter what she said or how she felt.

Surely Da wouldn't promise her to this smug man against her wishes.

2

THE STRANGER

Seated at a scarred table in the inn's common room, Rand did his best to ignore the hostile stares from more than one pair of rounded eyes. He'd chosen a dark corner away from the lanthorn light in the hope of escaping notice. As a Kindren among the Elder, he'd expected to encounter suspicion. From the look of this crowd, he'd better keep watch to avoid being knifed in his bed. He couldn't let anything happen to him, not with his father's errand to carry out, although the thought of it made his stomach churn.

Almost as soon as Rand sat down, the man with silver-threaded black hair who had greeted him at the door brought a tankard of ale and called into the kitchen for service. He seemed eager for his Kindren guest to eat and leave. If so, in this their desires matched. A long day in the saddle had sapped Rand's strength and left him eager for sleep.

He lifted the tankard with his left hand, favoring his bruised side, acquired courtesy of his half-brother's ambush. The sudden memory of Draeg standing victorious over him, and looking far too much like their father, tightened Rand's jaw. He banished the image, unwilling to let himself think of defeat at a time that called for courage.

A maiden pushed through the swinging door from the kitchen, balancing a tray of small pies. She glanced about the room, and her clear green eyes fastened on his. He'd never seen such beautiful eyes. Hair black as an eberec's wing crowned her head in a braid and also rippled down her back. Her face showed no blemish, so youthful he might take her for a child save for the female form her kirtle failed to hide.

A shy smile touched her lips as she lowered the tray before him. He accepted her offering and, diverted by hunger, crammed his mouth full of venison pie. She stepped back and away, all the while watching him. He must look rough after days on the road, or perhaps she'd never seen a Kindren before. He stared back, as fascinated with her as she seemed with him.

He'd known her at once from the description given him, but he'd never expected to find his quarry so quickly.

❧

Mara felt the Kindren looking at her out of long eyes a strange hue between green and amber, deepened by the dim light in the far corner. He had a look she'd seen before, that of a care-worn sojourner. How far had he come, and what errand thrust him upon the mercies of the road?

The front door opened and the lanthorns suspended from overhead beams swung in the draft that fanned her face. Light flared across the stranger, turning his hair red-gold. She'd taken him for older than he now appeared, but guessing a Kindren's age wasn't easy. His kind hardly ever stopped at the inn these days, and she'd forgotten how intriguing she found them.

She dragged her gaze from his, breaking the slender thread that had stretched between them, and turned away in time to see Rohan and Da shut the door to the porch behind them. Her mouth went dry. Rohan had wasted no time.

She didn't have to look to know that the Kindren still watched her as she pushed through the swinging doors into the kitchen.

"What troubles you?" Mam asked, making her jump. "You be pale as a specter."

"T'is but a passing mood." Mara gave Ardel the empty tray to load with more venison pies.

Brynn paused while forming dough at the work table. "Mayhap one of the Fieann whispers enchantments in your ear."

Mara could almost believe it. Had the Kindren traveler snared her with magics? Even now she felt a strange pull to return to him.

"Careful..." Ardel peered about as if one of the smallfolk might lurk in a corner. "Don't speak of such things."

"Why not?" Brynn pushed wisps of hair off her forehead with the back of a flour-covered hand. "For all we know, Mara herself might be a changeling come to steal our breath as we sleep. She might—"

"Brynn!" Mam cut across her sister's words.

Brynn shut her mouth but her eyes continued to speak.

"Specters and Feiann, indeed!" Mam scoffed. "I should know better than to while my time in idle fancies. Let's leave this talk."

Ardel finished reloading the tray and held it out for Mara to take. "It's best to say nothing of fell creatures that can ride in on uneasy talk," she warned.

Glad to leave the kitchen, Mara carried her tray into the common room. With Rohan and Da still pacing on the porch, she had more than specters and smallfolk to worry about. The Kindren traveler had vanished. He must have been in a hurry to seek his bed, assuming Da had allowed him to stay. He'd once turned Kindren travelers away in favor of peace at the inn, but in these quieter days he might tolerate them.

She emptied her tray, went into the kitchen for more, and came back into the common room to find Da shutting the front door behind him with Rohan gone. Her skin prickled. Why did Da look so pleased?

Pushing the puzzle from her mind, she went about her work, but then Da pulled Mam aside in the kitchen while they were cleaning up for the day. Ardel washed the last of the crockery in the long sink with water piped in from the river. Brynn had long since retired for the night. While Mam and Da talked in quiet voices, Mara stopped scrubbing the work table and strained shamelessly to hear. She could make out none of their words.

Da went out to the last guests lingering in the common room, and Mam beamed at Mara. "Rohan has asked for you."

She set her jaw. "I'll not have him."

"What's this?"

"He wants not a wife but a servant to tend his house and bear his wretched bairns."

Mam frowned. "Don't speak amiss of a man willing to take you without a dowry."

"I'll just finish in the morn." Ardel, her face flaming, sidled past them and out through the swinging doors.

Mara used the small interruption to gather her

thoughts. "He wants the inn and lands. He said as much."

Mam's nostril's flared. "And what of that? If the man takes care of you and yours, he'd deserve them."

"Am I such a burden?"

Mam's face softened. "Nay, child, never that. But can you not see that to wed our neighbor would keep you near?"

"Not marrying at all would leave me closer."

"Foolishness." Mam shook her head, her brow puckered. "You'll want to marry."

"Why?" Mara said in desperation. "Why can't I stay here with you and Da?"

"Hush, child. T'is the way of things, and naught to be done about it. Fledglings fly the nest." Tears stood in Mam's eyes.

"And what of Da? Does he want me to leave as well?"

"Da agrees that you should marry Rohan."

Mara had nothing more to argue after that. She left her mother, care weighting her steps, and escaped into her tiny chamber. Despite her exhaustion, sleep came in restless bouts that did little to ease her.

Weak light was outlining the wooden shutters at the window when she dragged from bed. Dawn after a bad night came as unwelcome, but her work would not wait. This early, quiet shrouded the inn, save for soft voices behind closed doors. Mam and Brynn would be in the kitchen, stoking fires and planning the day's repasts. Mara slipped out the front door just as a cock's crow rose above the rushing of the river. The moon hung low, refusing to fade from the pewter sky.

She lifted her skirts, her feet swishing in the dewy grass, a basket for gathering eggs in the crook of her arm. The stableyard mud had hardened enough to travel a straight course to the hen house. The pastures gleamed in the dawn, but the stable hunched over in darkness with only a faint bar of light reaching from the open doorway. The thud of hooves and a familiar whistle carried to her, and on impulse she turned aside to enter. She felt her way along the rough wall boards to the tack room.

The whistling stopped. "Good morn." Hael greeted her in altogether too cheerful a voice. Rubbing a saddle with a cloth he dipped into a crock of neetsfoot oil resting on a stool beside him, he looked all at once familiar and safe.

She made a vague sound, not quite trusting her voice.

His smile faded. "Mara, what's the matter?"

He knew her far too well. She should never have sought him out while tears pressed at the back of her eyes. She shook her head.

His brow puckered in a frown. "Is that aunt of yours causing trouble again?"

"'Tis nothing so simple." Her voice quavered.

"So then." He set the cloth down next to the crock and rubbed his hands together. "Tell me."

At the quick sympathy in his voice, tears slid down her face.

"Faith!" He stared at her with a look of helplessness. "What can be so bad?"

"They want me to marry Rohan." She gasped the words between sobs.

He looked at her without expression. "And what do you want?"

"Not that."

He took up the cloth again and bent to rub the

saddle with force. "Then you must not."

"You make it sound so easy."

"Have you no say in the matter?" He threw out the question without turning his head.

"Little, it seems." Her voice sounded as shaky as she felt.

He looked back to her. "Are you certain?"

"Mam has her mind set on it."

Hael straightened away from the saddle. "And what of your Da? I can't think he'd want you unhappy."

"Mam said he liked my marrying Rohan."

"Tell him how you feel. Could be he'll change his thinking."

She dabbed her eyes with the corner of her sleeve. "If you weren't full of oil I'd give you a hug."

"Just my luck." He scowled, then winked. "Go on with you."

ᏀᏃ

Rand sat up in bewilderment, but then remembered he slept in a cramped attic chamber beneath the gabled roof of the Whitefeather Inn. He stretched, groaning at the pain in his bruised muscles. At the memory of the black-haired maiden who had served him in the common room, he groaned again. He didn't want to harm anyone, and especially not someone who had looked at him with the very eyes of innocence.

What could his father have against her?

Not for the first time, he cursed his birth. Were he a son of Amora like Draeg, he'd not have been sent to prove himself on such a mission. At the disloyal thought, a shaft of guilt lanced him. His mother had nurtured him as well as she could, given the limitations of her position. His father should have married her as he'd promised instead of making Amora his lof raelein instead. Then he, and not Draeg, would be the favorite son.

He looked out the tiny window and sucked in a breath. The black-haired maiden, as if summoned by his thought of her, walked toward the inn carrying a basket of eggs. He backed out of sight.

She must gather eggs every morning, a good thing to know. He would saddle Taelant, ride east, and hide in the ruined homefarm he'd passed yesterday. When she came to gather eggs on the morrow, he'd be waiting.

A wave of sickness crashed over him at the thought.

3

An Agreement

Mara paused partway up the stairs as the inn's front door swung open. Da stepped onto the porch and smiled at her. "You're awake earlier than usual this morn."

She didn't often see him on his way to check the fish traps. "Da, may I have a word with you?" Her voice sounded breathy.

His smile faded. "Aye. What troubles you?"

"I don't wish to marry Rohan." The words rushed out on a breath.

His forehead puckered. "T'would be a shame to turn down a good offer you'll never see the like of again."

"I don't love him, Da."

"Sometimes love comes later in a marriage." His gaze searched her face. "Take just a wee more time for thought."

"I already know my mind on the matter, thank you."

"Your Mam sets her heart on having you near." He rubbed his chin. "You'll want to settle this with her."

The ache in her fingers reminded her to ease her grip on the basket. She gave him her best smile. "You could speak with Mam yourself, if you would."

He sighed. "Marry Rohan and you'll want for

nothing."

From the set of his jaw, he'd given his final word. Brushing past him with tears stinging her eyes, she flung herself into the inn. Da wanted her gone, too. She leaned against the wall in the common room and breathed deeply, trying to calm herself.

Mam and Aunt Brynn's voices from the kitchen rolled over her, soft at first, but then more fervent. Mara tilted her head to listen and caught her name. "I don't know why you've kept her all this time." Aunt Brynn spoke with venom. "I say give her to Elcon and be done with it, assuming her father still wants her."

"Mara's the only child I have. Not having birthed yourself, I don't suppose you can understand mother-love."

"Bah! Don't pretend Mara is your own child when we both know she isn't."

Mara put a hand to her mouth to hold back her gasp. Mam had never told her she didn't belong to her.

"That's not what I said, Brynn, and well you know it. I *have* birthed. Even if my babes didn't live, bringing children into the world stirs a woman in deep ways. Mara be all the more dear to me because of it."

"*Dear?* That wayward snip? Speak no more of this foolishness."

"If love be foolishness, then I own to it."

"And who is this child you love? A babe what you stole from the Kindren high king."

"We thought she wouldna be safe with Elcon!" Mam protested. "Look what happened to her mother, after all. How were we to know peace would follow?"

"If I've told you before, I'll say it again. You should have given her up when he came looking for her."

"Once the lie be told, 'twas too late."

"And what of Rohan?" Aunt Brynn went on. "Should he not have a decent Elder wife rather than a wretched Kindren half-blood?"

"Quiet yourself! Mara will wake soon, and I'd rather she not hear things she shouldn't."

Mara shook her head. They'd lied to her. She wasn't their daughter or even an Elder. Everything about her life was a lie. No wonder they wanted to foist her onto Rohan. The basket over her arm tipped and eggs splatted to the floor. She stared at them, soaking into the rushes. Boots thumped on the stairs warning her she was no longer alone. The Kindren traveler, wearing his cloak and carrying a saddlebag, smiled at her from the stairs. "Good morn."

She couldn't answer, but stared at him.

He came down the stairs and offered her a smile. "You've had a bit of trouble, I see."

Was her upset written on her face? But, he was looking at the broken eggs on the floor. "'Tis a small thing," she said in a husky voice.

He smiled then, his eyes warming.

She examined the stair rail as if she'd never seen it before. "You're on your way, then?"

"I am."

He'd taken too long to answer, and she risked glancing at him. Why did he look sad? Perhaps his journey came as unwelcome. "Health and happiness to you?" The usual parting she gave lodgers came out a question.

His fleeting smile did not warm his eyes. "It is to be hoped."

"What road will you travel?" As soon as the words left her mouth, her cheeks warmed. That was none of her business. Why she'd asked she couldn't say, except that he'd sparked her curiosity.

"I'm headed into the wilderness that lies between here and Torindan."

Her breath caught. She'd heard tales of the wilderness, and also of the fabled high hold of Faeraven, the place where the Kindren king Mam had named as Mara's father lived. "What will you do there?"

He raised an eyebrow. "You ask a lot of questions."

Her face burned. "I-I'm sorry…"

"Don't be." He smiled again. "Only let me trade my answer for your name."

"I'm Mara."

"Mara." Her name sounded musical when he said it. "I'm Rand, a tracker hunting for my shraen."

"Shraen?"

"Your people call such rulers kings."

"Why have you come so far? Has your king no game near his stronghold?" Why question him further? She should let him go on his way.

"He would have the tender meat of a spring ibbera kid from the Maegrad Ceid."

"I don't know of such a place."

"I referred to the range called the Crystal Mountains by the Elder."

A king might command a hunter to travel afield to please his tastes, she supposed. Did he know of her father, Elcon? She couldn't bring herself to ask. "Well then, may God grant success to your hunt."

"Thank you." The light in his eyes died. "But I'm not sure I hope for Lof Yuel's favor." He opened the door and left her.

Puzzling over his last remark, she retrieved a broom from behind the counter in the common room and swept the soiled rushes into a bucket. If the dogs were allowed in the inn, they'd have made short work of the mess, but Aunt Brynn couldn't tolerate them near or she'd start sneezing.

The door to the kitchen opened with a rattle of crockery, and her aunt came in carrying a tray of empty tankards. "There you be." She tossed her head. "Wasting eggs, I see. Well, don't be idle. There's work to do." She set her burden down on the counter and swept back through the doorway.

Mara carried the bucket outside to empty it. The Kindren traveler had disappeared, but she heard voices from the stable. She tipped the eggshells and fouled rushes in a pile of kitchen scraps that would decay to feed the garden. Rand came out of the stable leading a chestnut horse of undeniable beauty, his cloak flaring in the breeze that ruffled his tawny hair.

As he turned to mount, she hurried toward him. "Wait." She'd called too softly, but he seemed to hear and wait for her. "I need your help, if you would give it." She said to his leather boot.

"Mara, look at me."

She lifted her head, and her gaze collided with his. "Take me to Torindan." The words rushed from her.

"Torindan!"

"The High Hold of Faeraven."

"I know what Torindan is, but what does a maiden like you want—"

"I will pay you — well."

His brows shot upward. "What of your parents? Do they approve of your making such a journey?"

"They don't know about it."

He whistled. "Do you have any idea how far away Torindan is from here?"

She shook her head.

"I didn't think so." He pointed at the tallest of the snowy peaks rearing above the kaba forest in the south. "By horseback it lies several hard days' ride beyond Maegrad Ceid."

"*Please*." Tears stood in her eyes. "You have to help me."

"What are your reasons for leaving home?"

"They are sound."

His gaze traveled her face. "All right. There's an abandoned homefarm just east along the river. Do you know it?"

"Aye."

"I'll wait there, but only a little while. Mind you come in secret." He stepped back, still holding her gaze. Rand mounted with agile grace and sent his horse into a trot that carried him along the river road and out of sight.

Misgivings hissed through Mara. How easily the Kindren had agreed to her request. Shouldn't he have refused or at least taken longer to convince?

Hael came out of the stable and stood beside her, solid and comforting. She'd forgotten him. How long had he watched her with Rand? He angled a questioning glance at her. "What sort of words were you having with the Kindren?"

She almost thought—could that be jealousy in his voice? Surely not. His brown eyes searched hers, and suddenly she wasn't so sure. *Not Hael, too. Isn't it enough that Rohan has lost his wits?*

"Why so sad, Mara?"

"'Tis nothing." Her shaking voice betrayed her,

but he didn't press for an answer. She turned away without looking at him. "I should get to work or Brynn will go on about my laziness."

Mara slogged through the day with her body weary and her mind elsewhere. She went to bed certain sleep would elude her, but exhaustion tugged her into oblivion at once.

She woke with a start. Something—yes, there! The gentlest brush–a touch almost–but not of a mortal hand. *What*—no *who* could this be? The quicksilver touch faded, leaving an ache. It felt as though she woke from a lovely dream never to return to it again.

The possibility of sleep now gone, she left her bed, pulled on clothing, and braided her hair. Afterward, she pulled the blue velvet pouch from beneath the bed, untied its strings and tipped out the doeskin band with a sapphire at its center that Mam—*Heddwyn*—had given her two summers ago to mark her sixteenth birthday. She'd trimmed her lanthorn's wick, but the star-shaped jewel at the gem's center sparkled even in dim light. She hated to part with the one thing of value she owned. Mam had wanted her to save the band to wear at her wedding. The memory brought a lump to her throat. She couldn't think about that now or she might change her mind about leaving. What was the use? If she stayed, Mam and Da would only pressure her to become Rohan's wife. However pretty their arguments, she knew they didn't want her around any more. Brynn's criticisms must have turned them against her. Since she had to leave the inn, she'd rather do it without a husband.

Swallowing against tears, she slipped the band back into its velvet pouch and tugged the strings tight. She would use the band to pay the Kindren tracker.

She sheathed a hunting knife in one of her elkskin boots and, gathering the rough wool of her cloak about her, brought her horse bow down from its peg. With nothing more to delay her, she lifted the lanthorn from its hook, its swinging sent shadows jumping.

Her chamber door creaked as she opened it, loud in the quiet. She listened with ears straining and pulse beating in her throat.

Nothing stirred.

She tiptoed down the corridor dividing the sleeping and living chambers, passed through the family parlor, and let herself out the back door.

Moist air slapped her face, and the scent of water bespoke a gathering storm. She might not reach the homefarm before it broke, but she wouldn't turn back now. The kitchen windows gaped sightlessly as she skirted the back of the inn. She turned the corner and crept to the root cellar door. As she pried it open, a musty odor arose. The narrow steps took her downward, and she filled several pouches with yellowroot, jerked elk, and apples. A Kindren tracker should have no trouble feeding them both, but she couldn't be sure he would still be waiting. Besides, she'd rather rely on herself as much as possible. With that in mind, she pulled a small hand net from its hook before climbing the steps again. She'd used it many times to catch fish. A quick glance into the inn yard showed no one about. She slipped inside the stable, comforted by the familiar shuffling of horses. Hael would soon wake and come to feed them. She must hurry. As she neared her mare's stall, Lilthe whickered. Mara fed her an apple to quiet her, and then went to collect her saddle and bridle.

It was darker in the tack room, and she

immediately stubbed her toe. She sucked in a breath to keep from crying out and managed to keep hold of her lanthorn. Why had she forgotten that Hael had pulled that saddle out from the wall to oil it? Blinking away tears of pain, she forced herself to keep moving.

Lilthe's tack hung in its usual place. She gathered it in her arms.

"Mara?" Hael called from the doorway, watching her with his eyes too alert for someone who had just awakened. She tried to speak, but nothing came out. She tried again. "I'm to go to Havenhoe. Mam promised Verda I would show her my way of netting fish." She held up the net she'd taken from the cellar as proof. It wasn't entirely a lie, she persuaded herself. Mam *had* told the new mistress of Havenhoe homefarm she'd send Mara along to teach her to fish. Hael lifted an eyebrow. "Today?"

"Aye." Heat crept up her neck at the lie.

He gestured to the net dangling from her hands. "You might have called me to help you."

"I didn't want to wake you."

"You must know I rise early." He rubbed his neck. "But why must you make such an early start?"

She cast about for a reason. "I-I wanted to get back in time to gather more dewberries."

"Did you not get enough the other day?"

"That was for jam. I want to make some pies."

He stared at her as if to see inside her mind. "Well, then. I'll saddle Lilthe for you after she feeds."

"All right." Mara kept her voice calm, although she chafed at the delay. Lilthe whinnied, as if aware of her owner's moods. Mara stroked her neck to soothe her.

"Mara?"

"Aye?" She didn't turn her head.

"You'd tell me, wouldn't you, if something was bothering you?"

She swallowed. "If I could." There! She hadn't lied.

"You always can."

Her lips curved in a smile. Dear Hael would say that. At the thought that she might never see him again, a lump clogged her throat.

Lilthe stomped and snorted.

Hael laughed. "Be still, I'll feed you!" He took up a pitchfork leaning against the wall and delivered hay into Lilthe's trough. "If only all fair maidens spoke as plainly."

He moved down the stalls and soon all the horses lipped hay. Mara gnawed at her lip, and fought the urge to tell him the truth. He'd never let her go if she did, not that she blamed him. Going off into the wild lands with a Kindren tracker could only be called foolish.

After Lilthe finished her hay, Hael saddled her and led her into the stableyard, where he helped Mara onto her back.

Hael stepped back. "Shall I see you safe?"

"No need. Havenhoe's not far."

He squinted at the sky. "Looks like a storm may blow up. Sure you want to go?"

"Rain makes the fish bite."

"Well, then, guess I'll look forward to some dewberry pie."

She rode away feeling lower than one of the stableyard puddles for tricking Hael into helping her run away.

4

STORM AND FURY

Rand startled awake. Silence hung heavy in the darkness, and yet the touch of a hand had jerked him from sleep. He would swear to it. Watching the shadows, he pushed to a crouch, his dagger steadier than his breathing. "Who's there?" He sounded strained, frightened, weary. A faint shuffling answered him. The hair on his arms rose with his certainty that the entity that had summoned him from sleep did not cloth itself in flesh and blood.

A creature loomed black against the pewter sky. He knew the flapping sound its wings made from his early days at Pilaer. He'd loathed the giant raptor birds but had pretended to admire their savagery to please his father and avoid Draeg's mockery. This one was a long way from its roost in the east of Elderland. The rider on its back provided an explanation for that but roused other questions. On what errand would his father send a welke rider? And did it have anything to do with his own?

Rand held himself tensed and still, until the flapping faded into the night. The walls of the burned-out homefarm crouched against the underbrush threatening to consume it. Nothing stirred. Whatever uncanny creature had awakened him seemed to have retreated, perhaps frightened by the welke rider. However Rand doubted sleep would visit him again.

He sat with his back to the wall in the caved-in section of the homefarm, feeling safer beneath the open sky. Walls hid him on all four sides, except where the collapsing roof had pulled down a section and moonlight streamed into the ruined building. Through this breech he watched the road that would deliver Mara to him.He should rejoice that she had fallen into his hands like a ripe sweetberry. Killing her here, away from the inn, would be easy—far too easy. Once he fulfilled his errand, he could silence his brother's laughter and finally win his father's respect. Maybe then his father would look on Mother with more kindness. Dread constricted his chest. The truth stared at him, real as a jaggercat stalking the forest. He couldn't bring himself to crush her throat beneath his hands and watch the spark of life die within her. Nor could he bear seeing her face change when she realized his betrayal.

Ignoring his weak thoughts, he hardened his heart. Becoming a warrior meant following instructions without question. But then the image of Mara looking up at him with sorrow yesterday morning arose to torment him. He groaned, and the dagger shook in his hand. His father would be angry. Draeg would batter him without mercy. It didn't matter. He couldn't bring himself to harm the maiden who had snared him like a fish trapped in a net. He'd heard tales of witches who with a glance could bring a warrior to his knees, but he'd never expected to fall prey to one. Now he saw why his father wanted her dead. He should want the same thing, if only to free himself from her enchantment.

CR

Thunder boomed above Mara, and the first raindrops pelted her face. Lightning jagged, sending Lilthe sidestepping.

"*Whsst*, now," Mara murmured. She guided her mare back onto the road.

Hael had tried to talk her into remaining home to avoid the coming storm. If she had listened, right now she'd be safe and warm but no closer to solving her problems. She might be making a mistake. If, as Brynn said, Mam had stolen her from the high king of the Kindren, revealing the truth to him might cause trouble. She didn't want to tell on Mam, but she couldn't ignore that her rightful father had searched for his daughter and might still want her to live with him in Torindan.

She had to believe she belonged somewhere.

The road straightened out of a bend to reveal the abandoned homefarm haunched over like a hump-backed hermit, unsightly even when shrouded by rain. She couldn't remember the whole story of why it had been abandoned, but according to Da, Kindren wingabeast riders had set it on fire during raids from Torindan. The unprovoked raids had happened long ago, but echoes of the anger they'd roused still separated the Elder and Kindren nations.

A thunderclap sent Lilthe skittering. Mara reined too sharply. Her mare snorted and tossed her head. "Sorry, dear one." Her thoughts made poor traveling companions while she needed to rely upon her wits.

The heavens opened full force, hurtling rain into her face. She clutched her cloak at the throat and sent Lilthe into a gallop. The mare's hooves kicked up a spray of muddy water but Mara didn't care. The homefarm neared, and she slowed Lilthe even as the beating of her heart picked up its pace. Did the Kindren tracker wait within? The breech in the structure opened like a monster's maw before her. She reined in Lilthe, all at once uncertain.

A dark figure hurried toward her through the breech, Rand with his head bent against the rain. Lilthe shrilled and pranced. Mara called out to her mare, but the wind snatched her voice away. Lilthe's hooves left the ground and pawed the air. Mara fought to stay seated. Rand rushed to the mare and Mara brought her down. Long shudders ran along the mare's sides, and she needed convincing to follow Rand into the ruin. Mara could sympathize. Why had she ever agreed to meet in such a place?

The Kindren led Lilthe beneath the roof. His horse nickered and extended a muzzle to the mare. While the two horses greeted one another, Rand offered his hand to help Mara dismount.

She glared at him. "You startled my horse."

"You needed help."

"I can handle my own horse." Lilthe was normally docile, but Mara could admit that hadn't been how it must have seemed.

"Come now." He spoke in the same tones he'd used to gentle Lilthe. Moonlight softened his face as his head tipped beguilingly.

She took his hand and let him help her down but held herself poised against an uneasiness she couldn't shake. Water dripped from her cloak and hair to pool on the remnants of a wooden floor. This must have been the parlor, for it was too large for sleeping quarters. Sadness touched her. The man and wife who had once made this their home had borne no children, so Mam had said. After their deaths, relatives in Westerland had squabbled over the homefarm, agreeing only to leave it neglected and alone.

Rand released her hand and stepped away from her. "Did you come away from the inn without interference?"

"For the most part," she hedged. Something in his voice disturbed her, although she couldn't name the reason.

"Might someone have followed you?"

"I don't think so, but I'm not certain." She added the last part to appease her nerves. Letting him wonder whether Da or Hael would follow her couldn't hurt.

He strode toward the opening in the wall and stood looking out with rain drenching him. He turned back, water glistening as it ran from him in rivulets. "Would any think to look for you here?"

There it was again—that strange note in his voice. "The stable hand might." Hael would never look for her here, not after she'd informed him how much this place unnerved her. She wouldn't let on about that to the Kindren, though.

He joined her beneath the roof again. "Then we must leave."

"In a thunderstorm?"

He pushed back his wet hair. "It seems so."

She gnawed her lip. This was what lying brought. "There should be time enough to wait for a break in the storm. Only a fool would stir in this downpour."

He folded his arms and leaned against the wall, relaxing his posture for the first time since she'd arrived. "I suppose you're right."

She sent him a suspicious glance. Had he seen through her ruse? With his face in shadow, she couldn't tell.

Dark clouds passed overhead, cutting off the light. Rain pounded the roof. It must be full morning now. She wrung out the hem of her cloak and pulled the hunting knife from her boot. She straightened, hiding it in the folds of her cloak, just in case.

He pushed away from the wall. "Tell me something."

She tried not to cower as he walked toward her. "What?"

He kept coming.

She stepped backward but fetched against the wall.

With a deft movement, he caught her hand and twisted the knife from her grasp. "When did you think to use that?" he gritted out.

"Let me go!" She kicked at him, wincing as her foot connected with his shins. He released her without warning, and she stumbled.

Her knife, cradled in his hand, pointed at her heart. Shadows hid his features still, but the tilt of his head had her easing backward. "What are you doing?" The breathiness of her voice betrayed her fear.

"Tell me why you seek Torindan."

"'Tis my own concern." She tossed her head in a show of bravery she didn't feel.

"I beg to differ. That I'm to deliver you there makes it mine as well."

She wasn't certain she wanted to go with him any longer. "Stop pointing that knife at me and I might tell you." Not that she would betray Mam's secret by giving the whole truth when a part would do.

"All right." He lowered the blade.

"I'd rather keep my own counsel, but since you

insist on knowing…" She let the silence stretch to breaking before going on. "I'm half-Kindren."

"That…changes things." He turned the blade and offered it by its hilt.

Mara stared at the knife, struck dumb by surprise.

He gestured with his head. "Go on. Take it. But remember I can relieve you of it again, if called upon."

"Point taken." She slipped the knife into her boot.

"You've skill with a knife." He crossed his arms. "But why did you feel in need of one just then?"

She settled on the truth, or at least part of it. "I've never liked this place."

He leaned against the wall again. "Might I expect an attack whenever your surroundings displease you?"

"All right, *you* frightened me."

Whatever he had expected her to say, it must not have been that. The surprise on his face showed even in the feeble light. "You have nothing to fear from me, as it happens."

What did that mean? And why did he speak with such irony? It made no sense, but somehow, she believed him. He'd given her back her knife, after all. "Well, then. You're hired." She drew the velvet pouch from her cloak and tossed it to him.

He caught it with one hand and upended it into his palm. He gave a low whistle. "How does an innkeeper's daughter come by such a treasure?" He held up the band, and its star sapphire glistened in the moonlight.

"Honestly, of course." She made no other reply. She would trust him no further than necessary.

5

AFTER THE STORM

The storm passed, but another kind of tumult raged within Rand at the sight of Mara, her damp hair bound in dark braids that fell to her waist as she fed apples to the horses in the soft early light. Last night she had faced him at the point of a knife, utterly beautiful in her defiance. When he'd trapped her in his arms, he hadn't expected the desire to keep her safe that sprang within him. Nor had he anticipated the strange sensation that a knife thrust into her side would pierce his own. He'd told her the simple truth when he'd said she had nothing to fear from him.

After she'd mentioned having Kindren blood, her longing to reach Torindan had made better sense. The pull between them that he'd attributed to witchcraft could have been caused by the shil shael, the hereditary soul touch he'd only just begun to experience as a son of Rivenn. If so, this meant Mara was his distant kin. Did his father know this?

He saddled the horses, his mind occupied with the problem of what to do with Mara now. She wanted him to deliver her to Torindan, but as the son of Elcon's mortal enemy, he could not approach the high hold of Faeraven and live. He dared not remain away from Pilaer much longer, for his mother's sake. She would bear the brunt of his father's wrath if he failed to return. Rand frowned at the unhappy consequences that returning with his errand unfulfilled would bring down on him. Accepting his father's displeasure, Draeg's scorn, and whatever punishment came seemed the lesser of two evils. He would rather lose his own life than take Mara's. She glanced up looking startled, for all the world as if she'd heard his thought. He jerked his gaze away. "We should set out."

"Aye."

On her lips the word sounded infinitely sad. He didn't inquire again into her reasons for leaving home. She'd made it clear they were her own. She lifted into her horse's saddle before he could offer his help. How serene she looked, but her thoughts must be in turmoil. He vaulted onto Taelant's back and rode through the breach ahead of Mara. They traveled eastward in the mud and fitful daylight, on a road broad enough to allow him to ride alongside her. His attention kept straying sideways. The curve of her cheek, sweep of her eyelashes, and even her hands, gentle on the reins, attracted his notice. A curious sensation of joy assailed him at the simple sight.

At the old ford they crossed the stone bridge with the horse's hooves ringing. They passed into a tunnel formed by kaba branches tangling into a green roof, and the forest swallowed them. The day warmed, and even in the weaving shadow beneath the trees, their damp garments steamed. The way narrowed, becoming a rutted track. This did not slow them for they met no other travelers, not surprising since it was too early in spring to cross the passes. The road climbed, turning the river into a gleaming silver ribbon below.

They stopped for the night in a meadow with enough daylight for Rand to draw his bow and fell a deer. He dressed it, cutting part of the meat into strips to smoke over the fire. They roasted chunks of venison on sticks while the horses grazed on new grass and drank from a sparkling stream. He ate his fill, but Mara took little. She did not speak, and her eyes shone with tears.

In the gloaming, that uncertain time between day and night, she unrolled her bedding beside a fallen log and lay down. He placed his own bedroll at a small distance, even though it was too late to save her honor. The Elder held their maidens less closely than the Kindren, but she'd never escape the shame of spending a day and a night unchaperoned, let alone traveling alone with him.

He could tell that leaving home weighed upon her, and yet she had parted with something of great value to do so. Had she stolen the star sapphire band? It seemed too fine for an innkeeper's daughter. She'd claimed to have acquired it by honest means, but could she have stolen it from a guest at the inn? He picked up a stick and poked at the fire. It was hard to imagine, but what did he really know about her? She might be hiding a small horde of ill-gotten jewels that could bring pursuers.

Once she slept, he would search her belongings.

ଦ୍ଧ

Mara fought to keep her eyes open as the track beneath Lilthe's hooves angled toward the bleached sky. Here in the lower reaches of the Maegrad Ceid, the air thinned, seeming not quite to fill her lungs, while the air radiated the heat of midday. The horses broke free of the kaba forest, entering an alpine meadow where stunted pines twisted and bellflowers waved above lingering snowbanks.

Rand reined his horse in and waited for her to catch up, a frown marring his forehead. "Are you unwell?"

Did he really care about her or was he wondering how much farther he could push her? She drank from her elk skin water bottle before answering. "I need rest."

His gaze assessed her. He gave a curt nod. "We'll stop at the cascade just ahead."

She caught the distant splash of water. It seemed so far away, but she made no protest, for the stunted pines and boulders alongside the track offered no shade. Lilthe must have smelled water, for her pace quickened. Her hooves rang against the stones littering the trail and sent some of them clattering over the drop. Dizziness pressed Mara, and she dared not look downward.

Regret stabbed her. If she'd remained at home, she could have avoided this ordeal. She wouldn't let herself think about Da and Hael searching for her with Mam worried sick while waiting for news. She'd acted rashly, but it was too late to change anything.

The track crested a rise and crossed a bridge built of ancient timbers over a plummeting stream. Rand dismounted to lead his horse over the rickety bridge, and Mara did the same. Although Lilthe balked at first, she finally clopped across.

The road bent in upon itself, ready to climb again, but Rand turned aside onto a trail forged by game. She followed him into a canyon where ferns clung to sheer walls of blushed stone, their fronds waving in the breeze that cooled her face. Water misted the air, a spray sent up by the force of the cascading streams. Over time, the torrent had worn a hollow in an otherwise flat-topped shelf of rock, and the sides of the pool thus formed canted at a reckless angle. The game trail ended at the shallowest edge, farthest from the waterfall, where better footing could be had.

Lilthe and Rand's chestnut steed lowered their heads and drank of the frothing water. Mara followed Rand to a ledge behind the cascade, where they both cupped their hands to gather water from the shining streams. Its coolness soothed her parched throat.

Rand ducked his head beneath one of the streams and came to stand beside her again with a wolfish smile. She surrendered to the urge to stare at the water running in rivulets down his neck, the firmness of his jaw, and the way his tawny hair glistened when wet.

With a teasing glint in his eyes, he pushed her forward.

Cold water poured over her, making her gasp, but then she lifted her face and let it cool her. She stepped out of the waterfall refreshed. Rand's laughter surrounded her, an attractive sound. Forgetting her earlier constraint, she smiled at him.

His laughter quieted, and he turned back to the horses, now grazing on brambleberries. Rand rummaged in his saddlebag and brought out several small bundles tied in kaba leaves. He tossed her one. Struck by the charm of his smile she almost missed it.

She sat beside him with her legs dangling over the edge into the pool and gave her attention to the smoked venison her bundle contained. After tearing at the meat like a ravenous pup, she glanced up to find him watching her in amusement. Heat blossomed in her cheeks.

He chuckled. "It's good to see you feeding yourself. I wondered if you meant to starve."

At the reminder of her earlier upset, she had to blink away tears.

"Mara, why did you run away?" His soft tone barely rose above the splashing of water, but she heard him.

"Because I'm lackwitted."

"I doubt that."

"You hardly know me well enough to form an opinion."

"I'm certain you wouldn't run away without cause."

"I didn't want to marry." She hadn't meant to blurt that out.

"And now you are on your way to Torindan? Something's missing from your story."

She shrugged. "There's not much else."

He touched her arm, and a tingle ran down her spine. "I've an idea you've left out the important part."

She gazed at him, helpless to look away, drowning in emotion. Was this how Hael had felt when he'd looked at her so strangely? If so, he had her pity. Oh, but this made no sense. Why should a stranger stir her when Hael did not? Rohan had said love might grow between them, but if this was indeed that tender emotion, they'd never have found it together. She couldn't imagine feeling this way about Rohan nor picture him allowing himself to fall prey to this aching restlessness.

Rand lowered his head, his breath feathering her cheek. His lips brushed hers.

She quivered, torn between delight and outrage.

He shouldn't do this, nor should she let him. A sigh escaped her.

Rand deepened the kiss, and the hand she put to his chest to push him away clutched him instead. Rough wool slid across her palms, and her fingers curved into his surcoat, drawing him nearer. A flame flickered to life between them, warming her from within, growing...

He groaned and pulled away. "I shouldn't have done that."

Mara pressed the back of her hand against her lips, looking anywhere but at him. The regret on his face made plain that he despised himself for kissing her.

CR

Rand shifted away from Mara. Had he lost all sense? He was not his father or brother, to take all he desired from a maiden. His mother, despite her failings, had taught him better manners. She had never spoken of her own ruin, but he could guess her story. His father had seduced her, playing on her weaknesses until she'd surrendered. Afterwards, she had lacked the will or means to save herself from his ill treatment.

Rand had promised his mother he would never abase a maiden. He wanted Mara beyond reason but would not take her by force or persuasion and should not have stolen so much as a kiss from her.

Restraining the impulse to offer his hand to help her rise, he picked up his saddle bag. Touching her presented too much of a temptation. "It's time to leave." His voice grated in his own ears, but he didn't trust his ability to ease her look of pain without losing his head.

She brushed past him, going at once to Lilthe. From her posture in the saddle, he had offended her. He sighed. There was but one solution he could think of that would protect her purity, but she might never forgive him for what he was about to do.

∞

A dark figure sprang from nowhere, knocking Mara to the ground. She tried to cry out but could barely draw breath. Gritting her teeth, she shoved with all her might. The weight of the monster pinning her shifted, and she gulped in blessed air. Her attacker returned, crushing her with brutal force–

Mara bolted upright, bathed in sweat, heart hammering, and peered into the shadows around her. Where had her bed at the inn gone, and how came she to be sleeping in a moonlit meadow? With the return of memory arrived another realization.

The dream again. 'Twas only the dream.

She laid down again, although sleep would not return with the horror lingering. It could haunt her for days. She'd once woken screaming in the dead of night, and Aunt Brynn--*Brynn*--had afterwards warned Mam that the blackness of her soul called forth evil.

What if Brynn had been right about her?

Running away had been wrong, Mara could admit that now. She'd given little thought to the grief that leaving would cause others. No, that wasn't quite right. The truth stared her in the face, condemning her. She had *meant* to hurt her parents and make them regret lying to her. A chord of sorrow throbbed within her. If only she could turn time backward and spare them the pain she had wrought.

Her anger had hurt no one worse than herself. Now she could see that if she'd held her ground, she might have avoided a betrothal to Rohan. Even after discovering the secret Mam and Da had kept from her, she should have given them a chance to explain. Now it was too late. She could never go home, nor would she marry. No one wanted a half-blood, and a ruined one at that. If she ever doubted the truth, she had only to remember Rand's rejection.

The sky lightened, blushing at the horizon. The forest remained in darkness, so still it seemed to hold its breath as it listened for the mourning doves to utter their first laments. Mara sat up, clasping her knees for warmth.

Something moved in the meadow.

She started but then recognized Lilthe. She scolded herself for giving in to nerves. But wait...where was Rand's horse? Taelent never strayed far from Lilthe. Mara scanned the meadow.

The grass was still flattened in the place where Rand had lain. Where was he?

The question brought her to her feet. Something might have happened to him. She wanted to call out, but a remnant of caution from her dream held her back. A shiver ran over her, and she pulled her cloak from on top of her bedding and settled it over her shoulders. Her hands sought the woolen pockets for warmth, and her fingers closed over a familiar shape. She withdrew her hand and brought out her velvet bag. Although she already knew what it would contain, she opened the bag and tipped out the contents.

Her hand fisted around the sapphire band Rand had returned to her.

6

LOST PASS

More than anything, Mara wanted to lay her aching body down. Every gasping breath burned her lungs. Tears trickled from the corners of her eyes to chill her cheeks. She could barely feel her feet any more but trudged upward, forcing a path through the snow. Her strength deserted her all at once, and she stopped to gather herself, putting up a hand to shield her eyes against the glare. The wind whistled, and heavy clouds swallowed the surrounding peaks.

With a sinking stomach, she admitted the folly of going on.

She should have stayed with Lilthe. When the mare had started limping, it had been all Mara could do to turn her loose. Lilthe had tried to follow, and it had broken Mara's heart to drive her away. Maybe, if she could return below the snow line, Lilthe would hear her call. Mara would build a shelter to protect them both from freezing to death or becoming food for a jaggercat or a bruin foraging in the lean time before berries clustered in the thickets.

Rand had left packets of jerked venison in her saddlebag, but she would have to replenish her food supply soon. Da had trained her in forest skills, and she had her horse bow and net, but first she needed to climb down from the pass. She started back, following the tracks she'd made in the snow. They hurtled a long way down. Why had she pushed herself to go so far? She retraced the path made by her footprints, but lost her balance partway down and stepped into soft snow that gave beneath her feet. She went down, flailing, and slid toward the edge of the cliff.

This then would be her death.

A rise bumped her upward, knocking the wind from her. She flung out her hands and clawed at whatever they caught—snow and more snow, but also something that lashed her palm. She gripped it now, but her slide continued to the length of her arm and wrenched her shoulder. She jerked to a halt, her feet dangling in thin air.

Her chest hurt as she panted to breathe. Black dots stood before her eyes. She fought to stay awake and pulled herself to more level ground. The temptation to sleep tugged at her with more force.

Why not surrender? Life hardly seemed worth living any more...

"No!" She lurched to her feet with the world spinning. Her legs trembled as she started back down the hillside. Halfway down, her knees betrayed her, and she sank into the snow. After a brief struggle, she fell back, utterly spent, and drew in her breath on a sob. She'd been an utter fool to leave home, but even more so to let pride keep her from returning.

Now she would die in the wilderness.

ʘ

The thought of Mara alone in the wilderness almost turned Rand around He hadn't been thinking clearly when he'd left her. His haste to protect her from his own desire had blinded him to the fact that he should have escorted her home. He reined in, torn over whether or not to turn his horse around but then remembered her skill with a knife and fishing net. She didn't have far to travel before reaching home. Surely his withdrawal would force her to go back where she belonged. What else could she do? He, on the other hand, had better return to Pilaer. He frowned. Whenever he irritated his father, Mother always suffered. He preferred that any punishment for his actions should fall only on him.

Leagues passed beneath Taelant's hooves as Rand journeyed through Whellein and Daeramor. At midday, he hid himself in a stand of trees in the outskirts of Graelinn's grasslands and waited for nightfall. Only a lackwit would travel in broad daylight through the plains with welkes flying out from their roost within Maeg Waer, the gloomy pinnacle in the east. Rand also sought to avoid those who might question the direction he traveled. Journeying south and east toward Pilaer would mark him as one of Freaer's rebels.

He set out again with the road before him shining blue in the moonlight except where the wheels of countless wagons had cut dark ruts. He followed it into the shadows of Weithen Faen before emerging in a place where marsh reeds formed a thicket on either side of the verge. The reeds rustled in stray drafts and a night bird whistled an alarm.

His father had mended the broken places in the road and now watched and waited, gathering strength for the attack he planned. Rand had only been a babe in arms during the siege of Torindan. His father didn't like the rout his forces had suffered spoken about, but

Rand had heard enough whispers to piece together what had happened that day. Torindan had been near surrender when the one called Emmerich stood on the barbican with his arms raised, as if to call down all the forces of Lof Yuel. The darkness that followed had confused his father's armies. They'd slashed at one another, and then broke and ran.

The clouds parted, and moonlight flared across Pilaer, floating above the drowned lands in the distance. Broken marble pillars flanked the edges of wide stairs as the ghostly fortress hovered over the rooftops of the remains of the town it had once protected. Even as he drew closer, Pilaer receded, but he counted that as a trick of the faen.

The back of his neck prickled. Who knew what darksome creatures lurked nearby? He never liked traveling through the drowned lands at night, although reaching the ruined town was little better.

He rode through the moonlit streets with shadows crouching at the edge of sight, ready to spring. He'd grown accustomed to these wraiths, although he would never call them pleasant companions. They'd plagued him without mercy in his early days. Once he'd understood they could not attack the body but only the mind, his terror had lessened. In this understanding he found an imperfect peace, but whenever he relaxed his guard, the wraiths would run at him. Draeg laughed at the fell beings and even danced with their shadows, but his movements would become frenzied as if driven by fear, and he'd soon run away with wraiths pursuing.

Rand skirted Pilaer's marble steps and followed the path to the gatehouse. He hailed the watch, and a pale face looked down at him from the battlements.

"Traveler, state your name." He recognized the voice of one of Draeg's friends.

"It's me, Lutz. Rand, son of Chaeldra." As Freaer's illegitimate son he lacked the right to call himself by his father's name.

"Stand forth."

Rand urged Taelant out of the barred shadow cast by the lowered portcullis and into full moonlight. The screech of metal gave way to a steady clanking as the portcullis lifted. He rode beneath the iron fangs and waited at the wooden door that formed a second barrier until it gave with a rasp. Lutz peered around the opening and gave a chuckle. "You look a mite better than last I saw you."

Rand stiffened. That had been immediately after Draeg's last beating, with him writhing from repeated blows to the stomach. Lutz had been one of those urging him to get up and fight again.

Lutz grunted and edged the opening wider. "I suppose you want inside."

He didn't really, but there was no help for it. Taelant's hooves rang on the ancient stone path that cut through the outer bailey toward the stables. Weariness clouded Rand's mind, but he'd rather not rouse the stable boy in the dead of night. He dismounted and fumbled for the lanthorn tied to his saddle. Shadows climbed the stable wall as he raised it. The door creaked as he pushed it open, but nothing stirred within. He led Taelant into the low building and tended him with quick skill.

When free to seek his bed, he hesitated. Passing through the ruined hold at night could lead to misadventures. It might be better to risk being bitten by rats in the stable loft. And yet...he wanted his own chambers.

He extinguished his lanthorn, familiar enough with Pilaer to walk its corridors without its comfort, and let himself into the keep through a side door. His footsteps echoed as he traveled the corridors. Pilaer had once housed the fathers of his people, but after their defeat at the hands of garns, the Kindren had forsaken the stronghold, and with the passage of time its grandeur now crumbled into decay. His father had repaired the road but had made few restorations to the abandoned hold beyond those needed for ease and readiness for war.

Long flights of stairs delivered him without event to his quarters in the south tower, but as he reached his door, the one across from it scraped open. Light from the candle his mother clutched made hollows in her face and gleamed in the silver-threaded hair of gold that tumbled past her waist. She waved for him to enter, and setting aside his need for sleep, he obeyed. She shut the door and turned partway toward him to stand in profile, the simple tunic she wore hiding her thinness. "Your footsteps woke me, not that I sleep much these days."

Mother tossed upon her bed for reasons he knew well. But why wouldn't she look at him? Cupping her chin, he felt her wince. He tilted her face to the light and caught his breath. Angry welts marred her jaw, scratches that had drawn blood. His own jaw tightened. "Amora goes too far!"

She jerked away and covered the telltale marks with her hand. "Pray don't concern yourself. There's nothing you can do."

She answered as she always did. How he hated that she spoke the truth. If he tried to defend her, she would step aside from his protection and suffer greater harm. He sighed. "Why do you endure it?"

She shrugged and made no reply, but then he needed none. She suffered the cruelty of Lof Raelein Amora, High Queen of Pilaer, because she had nowhere else to go–or so she said. He'd long pressed her for the reason why she remained, but she'd refused to speak of the guilt that kept her chained to the hardships of an ill-favored concubine. After a while, he'd stopped asking her to explain, not certain he wished to know the answer, after all.

She placed her candle in its stand on the mantle of the marble fireplace. Looking down into the flames that guttered in fitful drafts, she spoke with her back to him. "My son, you were gone too long."

"Why do you say this?"

She turned, but only slightly, still hiding her injuries. "Freaer looks for you each day." Her brow creased. "What errand did he give you?"

"Something I am not fit to do. I failed utterly."

"Then you should not have returned!" Alarm throbbed in her voice.

"Don't concern yourself, Mother. There's nothing you can do."

Her eyes widened. "Do you mock me?"

"I only repeat your words to help you understand. He will punish me, but I must accept what I cannot change." He spoke with confidence but his voice cracked at the last.

"No!" Fear stamped her features. "I'll not sacrifice you to him. I've kept you too long from what you should know."

"Then tell me now."

"Your father is evil, Rand. He will prey upon your

weaknesses to corrupt you. He drove me to madness for a time, and I committed acts that forever cursed me. And now he seeks to destroy you also, because you are mine. If you cross him, he will crush you. You must leave at once and never return!"

He paced before her. To hear his suspicions spoken as fact saddened him. For his mother's sake and, if he could admit it, for his own, he'd tried and failed to please his sire. But his father hated him. Killing Mara would have come straight from the hand of evil. How could he have thought otherwise? He'd deceived himself, wanting so badly to believe in his father he'd turned a deaf ear to the pleadings of his own soul. Otherwise, he would have seen the truth for himself. In declaring it, his mother freed him.

He caught her hand and kissed it. "Escape with me."

She pulled away, her expression shuttered. "I cannot."

"Cannot or will not?"

"What does that matter? Either way I am bound to my fate."

"Don't ask me to leave you!" But he spoke without hope.

She touched his face. "Taking me would serve you ill."

"I don't care. Whatever your shame, I will bear it."

"My son, always remember that I love you." Her voice broke, and she turned away with tears trembling in her eyes. When he would speak, she held up a hand. "I beg of you—go."

He hesitated. How could she ask this of him? In his early days he'd first noticed the disrespectful way others spoke to her, and he'd vowed to protect her with his life. Now it seemed he could not save her at all, for whatever choice he made would wound her.

A thudding came at the door. "Open in the name of Lof Shraen Freaer!" They gave his father the title he strove to steal from Elcon.

Mother swung around to clutch his arm, her eyes wild. "Hurry! You must escape through my maid's chamber."

The maid's door burst open as several guards, the gold and red Rose of Rivenn on their surcoats, swarmed into the chamber. They surrounded Rand. "The Lof Shraen summons you."

How had they found him so quickly? And then he remembered Lutz at the gate. Of course. Mother's gaze clung to his as they shoved him out the door. Flanked by guards, he stumbled down the tower stairs and along torchlit corridors toward the presence chamber.

His father sat on his throne with Amora beside him, the two much alike in their golden beauty He waved his cup at the guards, sloshing wine. At this time of night, he would be enjoying certain pleasures rather than sleeping. "Leave us."

Urwan, a garn dressed in chainmail and leather, remained beside his master on the carved marble throne, but the strongwood door thudded shut behind the other guards. Rand stood motionless at the edge of a faded gryphon inlaid in the marble floor, waiting to learn his fate.

His father pierced him with a glance, the expression on his face unreadable. "You have failed me."

How could his father know this? He'd spoken to no one but Mother. Could her maid have overheard their conversation and reported it? The guards had come through the maid's door, after all. And yet, there would have been little time for her to relay information to them. Perhaps his father knew nothing but hoped to trap him into revealing the truth. Well, he could have it. Rand had no intention of adding to his sins by lying. "I did not complete my mission."

His father's face snapped into lines of anger. "I will have obedience from my subjects!"

Rand ignored the pain that always sliced through him when his father refused to acknowledge him as a son. Even after what his mother had told him, it stabbed him. He knew better than to question or explain and so returned silence.

A cord stood out in his father's neck. "Have you nothing to say for yourself?"

For the first time in his life, Rand faced his father's wrath with composure. "I have no defense."

His father's eyes searched his own. "You think it only a matter of accepting punishment, but I promise you it will not be that simple."

Uneasiness stirred within Rand. Mother had called his father evil, and a force by that name now throbbed through the chamber.

"By disobeying my will you stand guilty of treason, a crime punishable by death. I will have my due, make no mistake, but it pleases me to let my lof Raelein choose your fate." He bowed to Amora.

Her eyes glinted, and she lifted her wine goblet in a salute. "Let his mother take his punishment." The soft words pierced him, each an arrow.

"*No!*" Rand shouted.

Urwan stepped closer.

Rand's hands fisted at his sides, but he knew better than to attack a garn without a weapon.

Father arched a brow. "You object?"

"The fault is mine alone. Take my life instead."

"Gladly." A small smile accompanied the words even as Amora scowled. "You have only to return and complete your mission and return, and then I'll allow you to die in your mother's place."

Part Two
Torindan

7

IN THE WILD LANDS

"Wake up, Mara." A masculine voice dragged Mara out of darkness. The warmth of a blanket covered her, and strong arms cradled her. It seemed a dream, almost, but the aching breath she drew felt real enough. Mustering her strength, she tucked herself against her rescuer's chest. How long had it been since she'd felt so small and defenseless? Not since her father—Quinn—had carried her as a child. If only she could lift her head enough to look into his face. The voice was not Rand's, but she seemed to know it."Who are you?" Her whisper barely stirred the air.

"Someone unwilling to let you die, although you seem given to the notion."

"I deserve that."

"You shouldn't have tried to cross the passes alone."

"My guide left me."

"Rand thought he was protecting you."

"How come you to know his name?" For that matter, how had he known hers? She craned her neck but only glimpsed a strong jaw and black hair before her strength died. She sagged back against him, thankful that he seemed bent on helping her.

"Let yourself rest." His murmur lulled her into a kind of half-sleep.

She woke to the rattle of empty branches as the trees surrounding her swayed in the wind. Her feet burned as if on fire. Memory rushed over her in a tide, leaving a different kind of pain in its wake. She tried to sit up but gasped and fell back again.

"Have a care."

She turned her head and found a black-haired man watching her from dark eyes. "My feet..."

"I'll try not to hurt them." He raised her with an arm at her back. "Will you drink?" He picked up a cup.

The rim pressed her lips, and she opened her mouth. Cool water slid down her throat, easing its dryness. She drank her fill. "Thank you for saving my life."

"I'm glad to have found you." He set the cup aside.

She stared at him, intrigued. The lift of his head bespoke nobility, but he wore a humble woolen tunic and ragged cloak. "Who are you?" she asked.

"I am called Emmerich."

"My name is Mara. How long have I slept?"

"The better part of a day."

"I want to go home." The words slipped out of their own accord. Well, she would not take them back. If only she could return to the inn, but it was too late to start over.

"Stop telling yourself what you can't have," he

scolded her.

She narrowed her eyes. "How is it you know my thoughts? Do you use magic?"

He smiled and shook his head. "Your face gives away every thought."

Something moved at the corner of Mara's eye. She turned her head. "Lilthe! I thought I'd lost her." Her joy gave way to sorrow, and she shut her eyes on tears. "She's lame."

"Not any longer."

Her eyes flew open. "How did my horse heal so quickly?" Mara tried to rise but the bindings on her feet prevented her.

"Don't try to walk." He unwrapped the bandages on her feet to reveal blackened and swollen skin.

She winced. "Will I ever be able to use them again?"

"They will mend in time. Until then, you'll need to ride or be carried."

"How will I manage?" she wailed.

He gave her a gentle smile. "You must rely on me."

"But I don't want to keep you from wherever you are going."

"You can come along." He bandaged her feet again. "Although you may not like the journey."

ᴄᴿ

Rand pushed open the door to his mother's outer chamber. He shouldn't have come, but he had to see if she was really gone. Despite all, he still wanted to believe his father would not do so horrible a thing, that this nightmare was not real, and that he would find his mother within her chambers, engaged in music or some other pleasant pastime.

Carved images of wingabeasts, gryphons, and unibeasts cavorted across the face of the yawning fireplace. Wax drippings marred the mantle where the candle Mother had left there only the night before had burned low, the spreading pool of wax extinguishing its flame.

He pushed away from the door and came more fully into the chamber. Mother must have fought the taking of her liberty, for signs of a struggle could not be mistaken. A small table lay on its side, a crack across its marble top, the woven rug twisted beneath it. The mirror glass on the wall behind the table had fallen and shattered.

A wave of sickness rolled over Rand, and he sucked in a breath. He couldn't think of his mother in the rat-infested dungeon. She had always feared the dark.

Footsteps sounded in his mother's inner chamber. He'd been quiet out of habit, not expecting to trap an intruder, but now he went still.

The connecting door swung inward.

He waited, tensed and ready...

Mother's maid, wearing one of her mistress's jeweled coif headdresses, preened herself as she stepped into the inner chamber. Her eyes widened at sight of Rand, and she tried to slip past him.

He grasped the maid's arm. "Thief!"

She dug her nails into his hand. "Let go of me, or I'll scream for the guard!"

What was he doing? He'd never harmed a member of the fairer sex and would not start now.

"Let her go." The voice Rand least wanted to hear intruded. He released the maid, who spat on him before fleeing, but he barely noticed her, so intent was he on his half-brother. Clad in the green and scarlet surcoat that marked a member of Pilaer's high guard, Draeg stood in the doorway, his posture deceptively casual. He wore no sword, but a dagger waited upon his belt. With hair of gold springing from his brow and eyes of lightest silver, he had the beauty of both his father and mother.

Rand adopted the defensive stance he usually had to call upon in Draeg's presence. "What do you want?"

"Such a greeting you reserve for me, *Misbegotten*." Draeg fixed his wolf-like stare on Rand. "I've a mind to instruct you in manners."

"You'll have to learn them first." Rand snapped, past caution.

Draeg's eyes widened, and he barked with laughter. "Your temper has improved little since the last time we met. Never mind. I'll teach you to fear me, yet."

"You're the better fighter. We both know that. Must you prove it again?"

The wolf eyes narrowed. "You need a reminder."

"I assure you, I do not. I well remember the last one."

Draeg laughed. "I can well imagine you do. But I've a mind to finish the lesson. You're as good as dead, anyway, or so Mother tells me."

"Then perhaps *you* should fear *me*."

Draeg raised a brow. "Oh?"

"What does one already dead have to lose?"

"I'll teach you the answer to that!" Draeg unsheathed his dagger.

"What's this?" Rand's half-brother had never pulled a knife before but had always punished with his fists.

A smile spread across Draeg's handsome face. "Mother will have her way."

Rand hissed in a breath. *Of course.* Amora preferred him to fail in his mission so his mother's life would be forfeited. She must have sent Draeg to kill him. Did his father know of this? He couldn't bring himself to ask. "We're unequally matched. The guards took my dagger." He'd have been unwilling to use it against his half-brother, in any event, except to ward him off.

Draeg shifted, readying to spring, and the dagger in his hand glinted. He feinted left but spun right. Deceived by the move, Rand winced as the blade sliced his sleeve. Warmth ran down his arm. Before he could recover, the blade slashed again. He thrust himself backward out of range and slammed against the wall.

Draeg launched at him like a coiled spring.

He flung himself to the floor and rolled into his half-brother's legs.

The dagger clattered out of reach as Draeg went down. They both struggled to stand. Draeg recovered first. With a roar, he went for the throat, his hands cutting off Rand's air.

Rand broke Draeg's hold and twisted free, ignoring the pain that shot through his wounded arm. He lurched to his feet, panting.

"I always win. This time will be no different." Draeg's gaze flicked about as he spoke.

Rand also searched for the dagger, but it had slid out of sight. Draeg did not know that to spare his mother any backlash, Rand had sometimes let him win. He could not match his half-brother's strength but had the advantages of agility and quick thinking.

A glint beneath a side table gave away the dagger's location. He felt Draeg tense, and they dove for the weapon together. A chair in the way crashed on its side, ramming the side table and rocking the ironstone vase on its top. Draeg shoved Rand away, and he slammed into the wall. With the breath knocked out of him, Rand watched with horror as the table teetered above his half-brother. He rasped in a breath. "Watch out!"

Draeg thrust his arm beneath the table just as the ironstone vase walked off the edge. It thunked against Draeg's head, and he went limp.

Rand bent over his half-brother, motionless in the wreckage. Only a little blood trickled from the lump on his head, and his heart still beat. He would live. Rand snatched up the dagger but had to wait for the room to right itself before he could bind Draeg's hands and feet with the cords tying back the window hangings. He cut strips from the hangings to bandage his wounded arm.

Draeg stirred and moaned, so Rand gagged his mouth. He wouldn't do worse than that when all he needed was a little time to escape.

ॐ

Mara gripped Lilthe's saddle. "Where are you going?"

Emmerich reined in his horse and looked at Mara from the narrow track leading to the passes. "I'll keep you safe."

"I have no wish to return to the snow." Skittish, Lilthe seemed to share her sentiment. She patted the mare's neck to comfort her.

His dark eyes warmed. "Trust me."

She could barely frame an answer. "You ask too much." Trust him? She knew almost nothing about him. Well, only that he had saved her life, rescued her horse, and treated her with kindness. She'd given herself into Rand's keeping for less. Emmerich's gaze rested on her while she fought an inner battle and, defeated, gave a quick nod.

Winter had eased its grip on the passes. She saw it in the first earlyflowers pushing up through the snow and in patches where blades of pale grass glistened in the sun. Before they reached the ascent to the passes, Emmerich cut westward, leaving the path behind.

He led them into a hollow where stood two ice sculptures shaped like a Kindren and wingabeast. Uneasiness stirred within Mara. What business could he have in such a forsaken place? The air felt flat and dead. Fear lodged in her spine. "Something is wrong here. I feel it." Her voice echoed strangely.

Emmerich dismounted in front of the Kindren statue. Did tears shine upon his face? "Kai!" He strode to the wingabeast statue. "Flecht!"

Had he lost his mind? Or was she losing hers? He spoke to the ice carvings as if they could hear.

The Kindren statue trembled, the movement increasing in intensity until a crack ran through one of its arms. All at once the statue shattered, raining sparkling shards of ice in rainbow colors.

How could this be? Mara blinked, but a living and breathing Kindren *had* replaced the statue. Clad in warrior's garb, he peered at Emmerich with long eyes more silver than gray. More ice flew, and then a winged horse tossed its mane beside him.

The Kindren knelt in the snow before Emmerich with tears sliding down his cheeks. "Thank you for freeing me."

"Kai." Emmerich's voice broke. "I longed to do so but had to wait for the right time. Will you help me free another?"

The Kindren sprang to his feet as if he had never stood frozen. "Gladly. Who would you have me serve?"

Emmerich glanced toward Mara.

Kai turned his head and started. "Aewen?"

"She looks like her mother."

"Is this the snow maiden? So much time has passed…" Kai seemed lost in thought.

"You knew my mother?" Lilthe gave a delicate snort, and Mara loosened the reins she'd gripped too tightly. "Tell me about her, if you will. I know very little." She addressed them both.

Kai's brows drew together. "Why does Syl Marinda need to ask about her mother?"

Mara frowned. "What name did you call me?"

"She grew up an innkeeper's daughter and was kept hidden from her father," Emmerich answered.

Kai scowled. "Kept from Elcon? How could such a thing come about? I left the babe in her nurse's arms with her promise of protection."

"After you went away, Syl Marinda's nurse gave her into Heddwyn's care and traveled to her sister in the north to beg shelter for herself and the babe. During the journey she lost her way in the bog lands and drowned. When guardians came searching for the child, Quinn and Heddwyn hid her. When Elcon came himself, they informed him she had died with her nurse."

Sorrow spasmed across Kai's face. "How Elcon must have suffered."

Pain twisted through Mara. "Why would Mam and Da do such a thing?"

Emmerich shook his head. "The natural mind often clothes acts of selfishness in garments of love."

"I must return to Elcon at Torindan..." Kai angled a glance at Emmerich. "If it still stands."

Emmerich smiled. "Both Torindan and Elcon remain."

Kai drew a deep breath and released it. "That is well, then. And what of Freaer?"

Emmerich's face saddened. "He rebuilds Pilaer...and seeks to take Syl Marinda's life."

"Then I will protect her with my own."

"I don't understand." Mara broke in. "*Who* is Syl Marinda?"

Two pairs of eyes, one pale and one dark, turned toward her. Kai gave a tender smile. "At your birth, your mother named you Syl Marinda, which means 'snow maiden' in the Kindren tongue. Do you not know that you are Elcon's daughter? Once told that you live, he will want you to stay with him in Torindan."

"But, I have never so much as met my father, and I know little about Torindan."

"I would find it an honor to remedy both omissions. We should start for Torindan at once." Kai whistled, and the silver wingabeast came to him. He caught its bridle and patted the arching neck. "Flecht, I've missed you."

"Mara must first return to the inn at the White

Feather," Emmerich said.

Emmerich saw far too much and understood her too well for comfort. Emotions warred within Mara, too many to name. She felt joy but also dread, reluctance because of the way she'd left, but also anger over her reason for leaving. If she asked why Emmerich wanted her to return to the inn, his answer might be too hard to bear.

"That may put Syl Marinda in danger."

At Kai's sharp tone, Lilthe flinched.

Mara restored her sense of sanity by stroking her mare's neck to quiet her. "Why?" she asked the question that throbbed within her in a quiet voice.

"Freaer has long coveted the high throne of Faeraven." Emmerich took up his horse's reins but paused with his hands on the saddle. "He will stop at nothing to win it for himself. You could stand in his way."

"Who is this Freaer?" Mara didn't like anything she'd heard about him.

"Your father's sworn enemy, and your own."

"Mine?" Memories of the nightmares she had suffered and the evil she'd sensed searching for her returned, and Mara shivered.

"You are Elcon's only child."

Mara frowned. "I don't understand..."

Emmerich levered himself into the saddle. "He will name you heir of Faeraven."

8

RELUCTANT JOURNEY

Mara sat on a boulder jutting into a stream that flowed into forest shadow. Daylight lingered in the mists hovering above the water. After the journey from the passes, exhaustion dragged at her, but with so much to think about, her mind did not welcome sleep. "Why do you want me to return to the inn?" she asked.

Emmerich looked up from bandaging her feet. "You forgot to say goodbye."

How did he know so much about her? A greater question was how he had rescued Kai, but she didn't want to ask. When it came to Emmerich, she could only manage one disturbing question at a time. She shook her head. "They wanted me gone."

Emmerich tied off her bandage and sat back on his heels. "Do you really believe that?"

"Why must you answer with a question?"

"Let me put it plainly then. I thought you wouldn't want to leave those who love you wondering whether you live or not."

She clasped her arms about herself. "They don't care about me."

He leveled a gaze on her that she couldn't quite meet. "Come, now. You don't believe that."

"They lied to me."

"You speak with bitterness but also truth. Tell me, have you ever lied to someone who trusted you?"

She opened her mouth to deny it, but remembering her last conversation with Hael, closed it again.

He stood to his feet and looked out over the water. "Wronging those who wrong you will not bring peace."

She sighed, having noticed that very thing. "You are right about that."

"I think you will find your parents ready to forgive." He turned to face her. "Can you say the same?"

CR

Flecht dipped his head to drink from the stream near camp while Kai stood on the bank drinking in air scented by the kaba trees that towered overhead. He threw a rock into the water and watched its shadow pass below. What joy to move again, to truly live — sweet and yet bittersweet without Shae.

Daring to ponder his reflection in one of the pools, he discovered he had not aged. And yet, those he loved must have. His life resembled the rock he'd flung, sinking as the stream flowed on. Life had gone on without him. The infant he'd left at the inn had formed into the likeness of her mother. Emmerich, then but a youth, had become a man. Elcon would have reached his prime by now.

The trees soughed in a rush of wind that tasted of rain. Nature itself seemed ready to weep. The new leaves of a white whispan tree bent over the water whispering secrets. The stream hurried on.

"You are lost in thought." Emmerich stood nearby

holding a loaf of bread. Kai had not heard his approach.

He sighed. "I wonder what I will find when next I return to my homeland."

"Don't concern yourself about your mother and father. They are well, although grieved over your loss and that of Shae."

Kai drew breath. "So you have visited Whellein? And what of my brother, Daeven?"

"He never returned from the sea."

Kai closed his eyes as he absorbed this news. Pressing duties at Torindan had always prevented him from searching for his missing brother, and now so much time had gone by that any trail Daeven had left would have vanished. "Did my parents speak of my other siblings?"

"They mentioned nothing amiss."

"Tell me of Elcon."

Emmerich broke the bread and offered him a portion. "He held Torindan against Freaer's siege and afterwards mourned Aewen and his lost child. Eventually he took Arillia to wife, but they have borne no children."

"And what of Freaer?"

"He retreated to Pilaer, where he has readied for a renewed attack on Torindan."

"Has Elcon strengthened its defenses?" Kai took a bite of bread and found it sweet.

"Elcon has grown too comfortable. You must warn him that war is at his door."

"I'm loath to carry ill tidings, but I will tell him."

"There is one name you not speak."

He looked past Emmerich into the flowing water. Here and there the stream swelled around rocks before smoothing again. "Fear prevents me."

"Shae is well."

The tension went from Kai. "I'm thankful. She came to me even after Erdrich Ceid cast her spell on me, or so I imagined."

"She comforted you, and in so doing took her own comfort."

"How long must I wait for her?" The cry came from deep within his soul.

"Time will give the answer. Meanwhile, eat and drink. You must recover your strength for what lies ahead."

All Kai wanted was Shae in his arms, but he bit into the bread. "Tell me the fate of Erdrich Ceid."

"What if I told you there is no Ice Witch?"

Kai blinked. "Then who held me bound all this time?"

"No one."

"I don't understand."

"That is true, nor should you seek the hidden knowledge, but I will tell you there are places where time stops."

"How can that be?"

"All worlds were built as pathways to Lof Yuel, but the weight of evil now tilts them out of balance. They rub against one another, trapping time between them."

"I stumbled into a time trap?" That would explain why he hadn't aged. The idea of an Ice Witch bent on trapping unwary travelers seemed less frightening, somehow. "Can the worlds be brought back into balance?" Surely Emmerich, who had delivered him from such a place, would say they could.

Emmerich set a leaf upon the water and

straightened as the current spun it. "Such a thing comes at a great price."

CR

Rand bent over Taelant's back as his horse's hooves pounded in a numbing rhythm. Mara would have returned to the inn at the White Feather by now. He turned his predicament over in his mind, as he had countless times already, searching for a way out. The thought of harming her made him sick to the stomach. If he spared Mara's life, his father would send someone less merciful to take it, and his mother would still die. The only course left to him was to save his mother's life. He'd not see her sacrificed for a life already forfeited. His feelings for Mara didn't matter. As Draeg had said, he was already dead.

This time he must not fail.

The road followed the banks of Weild Whistan, the waterway that became the White Feather River in Elder lands. At the cove where a road split off toward the inn, he hesitated. Mara might tell her parents of his part in her disappearance, but to save her reputation, he thought she would not. It would be safer to hide and wait for her to go about her chores outside the inn, but he needed to know whether she'd returned to the inn. With Amora plotting to end his mother's life, he'd have to risk approaching the inn to find out without delay.

Taelant huffed, his sides heaving, and Rand's conscience smote him a heavy blow. He'd driven his horse beyond endurance. He turned aside and led Taelant to the pools trapped by large rocks at the water's edge. While Taelant lipped the surface of one pool, Rand cupped his hands and brought cool water to his own mouth from another.

A flash of color caught his eye. *Could it be?*

A grillon, its sides puffing, watched him from a flat rock at the pool's edge. He crept backwards to where Taelant stood and pulled a hand net from his saddle bag. The tiny creature tried to hop away, but he captured it with skill from his early days in Weithein Faen. With a flick of his knife, he ended the tiny creature's struggles. Stripping the frog of its poison sacks, he bathed the tip of his knife in the liquid within, careful not to let it touch his skin.

At the inn he tossed his reins to the stable man and, taking the porch steps, flung open the door. He stomped into the entry. "Have you lodging?"

The innkeeper turned to him with a look of surprise but then schooled his expression to politeness. "Aye, but 't'will be the attic."

"That will do." Rand climbed the stairs and at the end of the upper corridor gripped the rough ladder that took him into the attic loft, favoring his bandaged arm as he climbed. The room's small window overlooked the inn yard and gave a view beyond the stable and pasture, all the way past the kaba trees to the river.

Mara, if she was here, would venture outside at some point. The poison would act at once, ensuring she wouldn't suffer.

He could give her that much.

CZ

The great wings rose like a silver curtain about Mara, then beat downward as air rushed over her. She clutched the saddle with one hand and held onto Kai with the other while gripping the wingabeast with her knees and feet. The ground shrank away below as a lump rose in her throat. Flecht lifted in a graceful spiral, and then Kai turned the wingabeast south and east, toward the inn at the White Feather.

Loath to part from Emmerich, she'd taken comfort from his promise to find her again. That would not be soon. Although he would take Lilthe back to the inn, by the time he arrived she would have left with Kai for Torindan.

The wild lands passed below, the kaba canopy a tangle of green threaded by blue streams. The wingabeast followed the river with wind rippling through his flight feathers. The swollen flood waddled between rocky banks in deep channels before spreading to comb through rocks. They passed over an islet where flocks of croboks nested, wings glinting blue above the weilo trees that bent to wash their curling tresses in the river. Mara smiled at the familiar sight of the birds while tamping down the worry that plagued her. What sort of greeting might she receive at the inn? What kind would she give?

The abandoned homefarm came into view, and then the cove with the inn beyond. How different this place that had been her home seemed now that she no longer belonged here. As the wingabeast spiraled downward, her heart beat faster. Hael came out of the stable and stood with his hand shielding his eyes. The great wings beat the air, and then the wingabeast's hooves touched the ground. Hael rushed forward. "You' live!" He spoke to them both with equal wonder.

Kai dismounted and grasped the stable man by the shoulder. "You've grown into a worthy youth."

A grin stretched Hael's face. "I never thought to see you again. We searched and searched but finally gave you up for dead." His smile faded. "Did you come to harm?"

"Lof Yuel kept me."

Hael flicked a glance to Mara. "I see you've remembered you have a home." He turned away to gather the wingabeast's reins.

"Hael..."

He walked away, leading Flecht toward the stable.

Mara sighed. "I don't blame him for being angry."

Kai gave her a sympathetic look. "Perhaps you'll find a better reception inside. No, stay put," he warned as she moved to dismount. "It still pains you to walk." He lifted her into his arms and strode with her toward the inn. His boots thumped on the porch steps, and he reached for the latch.

The scarred door swung open.

Da must have been coming to open the door but now stopped in his tracks with a thunderstruck look on his face. "You've come back from the dead, have you? And brought Mara along with you."

"Quinn." Kai glanced into the common room, not yet filled for the evening repast. "We have much to discuss."

"Aye." Da turned his head. "Heddwyn!"

The doors from the kitchen swung open, and Mam came through with a questioning look on her face. "You're shouting to raise the...who be this? *Mara!*" Mam's face went white as she stared at Kai. She put a hand to her throat. "Not you!"

"Seeing me comes as an unpleasant surprise, I'll

warrant." Kai's voice rumbled close to Mara's ear.

"Why do you carry Mara?" Mam asked on a rising note. "Is she harmed?"

"Mam, it's all right." Mara's spoke past tears. "I hurt my feet, but they're healing."

Brynn burst through from the kitchen but stopped so abruptly the doors thumped into her. "What's this?"

"Never you mind." Heddwyn snapped in a tone Mara had never heard her use.

Brynn glared at Kai. "I thought we were rid of the likes of you."

How strange to hear Brynn attack someone else. She'd never been good at protecting herself from Brynn's judgments, but remaining silent as she railed at the Kindren seemed a betrayal. "Kai is my friend." She spoke with quiet firmness.

Brynn stared at her in obvious shock.

"No more of that, Brynn!" Da rounded on her. "Set aside whatever you have against the Kindren."

"Hmpfh!" Brynn turned on her heel and thrust back into the kitchen, leaving the doors swinging angrily behind her.

Mam's face pinked. "Brynn can be...thoughtless. Of course, we thank you for bringing our daughter home."

Kai stiffened. "She's not your daughter, and well you know it."

Mam's gaze flew to Mara. "Have a care what you say."

Da gestured toward the door leading to the family's quarters at the rear of the inn. "Let's keep this matter dark."

In the small parlor reserved for the family, Kai lowered Mara onto a bench and pulled up a stool beside her. With his nearness bracing her, she could speak her mind. "Mam, you told me the truth yourself, although you didn't know it. I overheard you talking about me with Aunt Brynn the morning I left home."

"Is that why you ran away?" Mam's eyes filled with tears.

"That and the fear of marrying Rohan."

Da sat next to her on the bench. "But you had only to refuse him."

"It did not seem so." Did he really not know how he and Mam had pressured her?

"T'was my fault." Mam's voice shook with the force of her sobs. "I pressed you to wed Rohan, telling myself I meant to keep you near for your sake when t'was for my own."

Mara forced words past the tears clogging her throat. "I shouldn't have gone off the way I did."

"Whsst now!" Da slid his arms around her, and she rested her head on his shoulder. "That be the past."

Mam stood watching while twisting her hands together. Mara flung herself into her arms. "I'm sorry."

Mam stroked her hair. "Never mind, child."

Kai stirred. "I intend to escort her to Elcon."

Da turned a wary gaze his way. "How do we know you will keep our daughter safe?"

"You are bold to claim Elcon's child as your own."

Da opened his mouth but closed it again.

"Never mind, Quinn," Mam stepped away from Mara. "We both know I'm to blame for this."

"Nay, Heddwyn—"

"Please!" Mam's outcry silenced Da. Mara sank to the bench as Mam went on. "At least now I can free myself from guilt. I thought to take what life would not give—a child of my own. After Mara's nurse died, I went against my husband's wishes and kept her for myself."

"Don't say any more, Heddwyn—" Da protested.

Mam shook her head. "Nay, don't stop me when you know it's true. 'T'was a bit more complicated than that in the living, but I persuaded myself I was the best person to watch over the babe. With the Kindren at war, how could I think of giving her up? Elcon couldn't save her mother's life, and he'd driven his own people to rebellion. Why should I think he could protect my wee bairn?"

"That choice was not yours." Kai's words throbbed through the chamber.

Mam drew a ragged breath. "It didn't seem so then. My only ties to Mara were those of the heart, 'tis true, but I counted them as stronger."

"And yet, living apart from her father, she remains at risk."

Mam's brows drew together in a frown. "We told none her secret."

Kai lifted an eyebrow. "If Freaer learns Elcon's daughter lives, he will stop at nothing to take her life. Are you certain no one knows her identity?"

Mam nodded, but Da cleared his throat.

"None save Brynn."

9

ENDINGS AND BEGINNINGS

Kai quaffed cider while waiting for his meal to arrive. The inn's common room was only just beginning to fill, a fact that well suited him. Mara had refused to join him, wishing to avoid questions about her disappearance from those who made the inn their gathering place. Her reluctance spared him the dangers of sharing a table among the Elder with one who did not show her Kindren blood.

He sat with his back to the wall in a corner where the light from the lanthorn did not reach, thus avoiding suspicious glances from those seated at other tables. Although Brynn did not serve his food but waited upon others, whenever her gaze swung his way it hardened to a glare. He sighed. Some things had not changed.

It would not be wise to linger. After the journey and with an early start on the morrow, he could use an early night anyway. The thought of flying over the route across Maegrad Ceid he'd followed when he'd vanished, made his skin crawl. Delivering both Syl Marinda and Emmerich's warning to Elcon by the fastest means possible demanded he retrace it. He would ask Lof Yuel to guide their flight.

Guests entered the inn and seated themselves at a long table. That they bore no packs or trunks marked them as locals. An apple-cheeked man with dark brown hair springing from his head struck up a lively melody on his lute, to the delight of all.

A cloaked figure crept toward the door behind them but paused to glance back. The light picked out tawny hair not quite hidden beneath a hood and fell across a face that stirred Kai's memory. How came this Kindren to the inn and where was he going carrying a laden saddlebag? He looked much like the servant, Chaeldra, who had vanished after taking Lof Raelein Maeven's life.

Kai sprang to his feet and followed the figure into the inn yard. "Wait!"

At his call, the other Kindren spun about.

Kai searched for words. "I am glad to find another Kindren among so many Elder. Will you not stop to talk?"

The Kindren shifted into the balanced posture Kai knew well from his own training, the stance of a warrior ready to defend himself. "I'm sorry, but I was just leaving."

"I won't keep you except to introduce myself, then. I am Kai of Whellein."

"Well met." The other Kindren moved off without giving his name.

"Which road takes you on a journey this night?" Kai called after him.

The stranger half-turned. "A lonely one." He continued toward the stable.

"Do you go to Torindan?" Kai called after him.

The stranger gave no response.

Within a few paces, Kai stepped in front of him. "I asked you a question." He didn't bother to hide his suspicion.

The stranger lifted his brows. "State your interest."

"You are acting oddly, I think," Kai challenged him. "Have you something to hide?"

"My affairs are no concern of yours."

"I'm making them mine."

The stranger's eyes narrowed. "By what right?"

"As a guardian of Rivenn." Kai held his ground.

The stranger swept Kai with a glance as if taking his measure. "Kindren rule does not extend to Norwood. However, I will answer your curiosity. My homeland is in the east of Elderland where most Kindren travel by night to avoid welkes."

His story made sense, on the surface. "Why didn't you tell me this before?"

The stranger smiled. "You did not inspire my trust in the asking, I'm afraid."

The stranger's change in manner didn't entirely convince Kai of his innocence. "You also withheld your name."

"I'm not sure why you want it, but I am Reinwald of Graelinn."

Kai relaxed a little. His zeal to protect Mara might be making him overprotective. One question remained, however. "What brought you to the Whitefeather Inn?"

"The need to break the journey from Torindan. And to save you another question, I visited a cousin there."

"Name this cousin," Kai rapped out the demand.

The stranger dropped his gaze then slanted a look upward. "Faelric of Rivenn."

Kai did not recognize the name but his knowledge of Torindan was not current. He stepped back. "Safe journeys."

CR

Mara took another footstep and her skirts swayed around her ankles. Hammer blows rang out from the stables, telling her she'd find Hael there. She hobbled onward on the dark path, ignoring the pain from her bound feet, driven by the need to beg Hael's forgiveness. He'd only ever treated her with kindness. In turn, she'd lied to him and left him to worry about her. She reached the stable doorway at last, and found him mending the gate in one of the stalls by lanthorn light.

The hammering stopped, and he lifted his head. "On your feet, are you, and walking about by evening?"

"This seemed important."

"This?" He folded his arms across his chest.

"Saying goodbye. I...missed doing that before."

His jaw set. "You leave on the morrow, as I am told. Where are you bound?"

"I'm not to say where."

"Such mystery." He gazed lingered on her face.

She bit her lip. "I'm sorry, Hael."

"Save it." He turned back to his task.

"Wait!" Her voice shook.

He paused but didn't turn.

"That night...I should have told you the truth."

"Never mind. I'm nothing but a stable hand." He started hammering again.

She sucked in a breath and raised her voice to be heard. "Don't speak so. Surely you know what you mean to me."

He glanced at her over his shoulder. "Maybe I don't."

Heat rose into her cheeks. "You will always be my

dearest friend."

He laid his hammer down and came to stand before her. "That will have to be enough, I suppose."

"I'm sorry." She spoke just above a whisper.

He drew a quick breath. "Give it no more thought." Without warning, he swung her into his arms. "I'll take you back."

"Thank you," she murmured.

"For carrying you? It would pain me to watch you suffer."

She shook her head. "For forgiving me."

"Ah, well. I've been a fool a time or two, myself."

"I suppose you think that a kind thing to say."

"More honest than kind."

She touched a hand to his shoulder. "I wish…" It was no use. She couldn't go on.

He glanced down at her, then away. "I have wishes, too, not that you want to hear them."

She could make no reply, for he spoke the truth.

He bypassed the front porch and set her down at the back door. "Promise you'll take more care with yourself." He touched her cheek with the back of his hand.

"I will try, Hael, but I seem given to mistakes."

"Hence my request." He stepped away from her. "Do you know anything about the Kindren who left tonight?"

"What? Kai wouldn't leave without me."

"Not him. I meant the Kindren you spoke with in the inn yard the morning you…left the inn. He stayed over last night. I helped him saddle his horse right before you came out. He seemed in a hurry to leave."

"Rand?" She stared at him, shaken to the core. "I didn't know he was here."

"You seem to know him well." Jealousy crept into his voice.

If only she did. "I wouldn't say that."

"Mara..." He touched her arm. "Should you ever have need of me, you have only to ask.."

CR

Mara's dreams peeled away, layer by layer. *Where am I?* She sat up in alarm. The reassuring shapes of the furniture in her chamber stood out in the slatted moonlight filtering through the window shutters. *Home.* Relief left her weak, and she sank back into her bed. She could almost let herself believe that everything that had happened since she'd left the inn had been nothing but a horrible nightmare.

If only she could stay here but that no longer seemed possible. Freaer wanted to kill her. What if he succeeded and also harmed those she loved? Tears slipped from the corners of her eyes and ran into her hair. She had to leave to guard their safety.

Softness feathered at the edges of her mind, the merest brush of another soul. It withdrew at once.

She peered into the shadows at the corners of the room, almost expecting to find someone there.

The unseen presence called to her, drawing her into a yearning embrace.

She shrank away, her heart pounding.

The presence did not press her.

Curiosity tugged at her. She reached out on her own...and found Rand waiting at the edge of her mind.

CR

Rand released his grip on Mara as her soul withdrew from his, the loss of her leaving him more lonely than before. He'd made his bed within the abandoned homefarm, in the part without a roof. Tonight, shadows held more terror for him than moonlight. He rolled onto his back and flung an arm across his brow. The moon rode a cold sky frothing with stars. A nightbird lamented, summoning an answering ache within him.

Life had taught him little of tenderness, except for that bestowed on him by his mother. Confusion had guided him to the inn, but a glimpse of Mara from the attic window had shown him what he should have known all along. He loved Mara beyond reason and could never bring himself to kill her, not to spare his mother, not even to save her from a harsher death. Now an errand of his own drove him back to Pilaer with the faithfulness of a lover. A mere scratch from his poisoned blade would end his father's wretched life, save Mara, and spare his mother.

10

JOURNEY

The wingabeast tilted beneath Mara as she clutched Kai's surcoat while wind whistled in her ear and tugged strands of hair from her plait. Her legs ached from a day spent in the saddle. They'd set out in early morning and rested little during the journey over snow-flanked passes that gave onto valleys where waterfalls fell in bright ribbons and flowers dotted new grasses.

With the sun hovering above the horizon, the gentler lands falling away behind, and rocky profiles pointing skyward, they must surely near Torindan, the mountain fortress of Rivenn and high hold of all Faeraven.

What would she find there? The thought of meeting the father she'd never known made her stomach twist.

Whether or not he rejected her, she'd welcome an end to her travels.

As if summoned by her thought, a stronghold appeared in the distance, jutting into the river they'd followed most of the way. Kai had called it Weild Aenor, Kindren for 'wild river.' She didn't need his sudden tension to tell her they approached Torindan. The high hold of Faeraven fanned wings of blushed stone backward against the surrounding cliffs. What would it be like to spend her days in the shadow of those peaks? If her father accepted her, she would find out.

What if he didn't want her? He'd thought her dead all this time and might find her appearance after so long inconvenient or even unwelcome. He could become so angry at Mam and Da for deceiving him that he'd forbid her to visit the Whitefeather Inn again. Her breath hitched at the thought.

She reined in her imagination. From what Kai had told her of Elcon, he wasn't cruel. At first sight, Kai had mistaken her for her mother. Would her father have the same reaction?

Having been raised an Elder, she knew enough of Aewen of Westerland to admire her bravery. What would it be like to forsake her homeland and take up the duties of a high queen in a nation not her own? She couldn't imagine it.

ભ

Two flags fluttered above the high hold, one embellished with the gilded rose of Rivenn. Kai's chest warmed at sight of the second flag, for its rampant golden gryphon announced Elcon, Shraen of Rivenn and Lof Shraen of Faeraven, in residence.

Torindan stood, and Elcon lived.

Flecht carried them over the narrow strip of thin soil with scant grass between the curtain walls. The outer wall stood tall at the gatehouse but as the ground rose, retained the soil of the motte beneath the keep and chapel, with the river swirling below. Kai frowned. The bastions built into the outer wall should shelter guardians of Rivenn keeping watch over the stronghold. Elcon had grown lax, indeed. Would he listen to Emmerich's warning?

Kai sent his wingabeast into a downward spiral to land at the place where the bridge leaped the moat to the barbican. His wingabeast's hooves rang first on stone then thudded on wood as he crossed the bridge. He reined in Flecht and caught his breath, recognizing one of the faces peering at him from above the gatehouse.

"Kai?" The joyous shout rang out. "Is that really you?"

"Aerlic." He forced the name past his clogged throat. The flame-haired archer had changed little.

"You're a sight I never thought to see again! Come inside." Aerlic withdrew from behind the battlements, then metal screeched while chains clanked as the portcullis lifted. Kai rode beneath the jagged iron teeth and along the short corridor lit by bars of light falling through arrow slits. Flecht's hooves rang on hollow wood as they crossed one of several trap doors. The portcullis lowered behind them but the wooden door that should have served a second barrier to entry remained open. At Torindan, convenience seemed to have replaced caution.

The second portcullis at the other end of the corridor clanked open. The bridge that spanned a channel of the moat to reach the gatehouse lay before him. He did not cross but dismounted as Aerlic hastened down the stairs from the barbican. They met in an embrace.

Aerlic stepped away, grinning. "We'd given you up for dead! Where have you been?

"In a place you'd never want to visit."

"I'm happy to find you alive and well"

Kai laughed."Not half as glad as I am. Tell me, where can I find Elcon?"

Aerlic stared at Mara. "Lof Raelein Aewen!"

"Syl Marinda is much like her mother."

Comprehension chased shock across Aerlic's face. "Forgive me, milady, but I thought a ghost walked among us. You are the very image of Lof Raelein Aewen."

KaiI should have expected this. He'd had a similar reaction the first time he'd seen Aewen's look-alike daughter. "Syl Marinda,meet Aerlic, first archer of Rivenn." He stepped in to diffuse the awkward situation.

"I am honored." Aerlic made an elaborate bow.

Mara smiled. "You speak with grace."

Aerlic gave her the charming smile he awarded to beautiful maidens. "And truth."

"Where may we find Elcon?" With pressing business at hand, Kai had little patience for courtly speeches, however well his companions might relish them.

Aerlic sobered at once. "He'll be in his chambers."

Kai lifted into the saddle. "Will I find him well?"

"The Lof Shraen is in health."

Kai sent Flecht across the small drawbridge over the murky moat and into the gatehouse. The smells of stagnant water and damp stone gave way to that of dry dust as they entered a dim passageway flanked by doors. It led to the small courtyard behind the gatehouse where light spilled through the archway into the outer bailey. The clopping of Flecht's hooves echoed along the stone walls. They had nearly reached the courtyard when a door cracked open.

A tall Kindren rushed out while the door slammed

against the wall behind him. "Do my eyes deceive me? Kai?" Craelin looked much the same, apart from some extra lines for his blue eyes to nest in and a scar on his throat that had not been there before.

"It's good to see you again." This time, Kai could do nothing to prevent the tremor in his voice.

"You, of course, are late for duty." The first guardian of Rivenn accompanied this chastisement with a smile replaced almost at once by a frown as he looked at Mara. "Lof Yuel! What magics summon Lof Raelein Aewen from the tomb?"

"This is Syl Marinda, Aewen's daughter and that of Elcon."

Craelin stared at her. "Are you certain?"

"I promise you, she is the daughter."

Craelin gestured into the small chamber from which he'd emerged. "Come inside and I'll give you something to drink. You must be thirsty from the journey."

Kai lifted Mara from the saddle and carried her inside to one of the benches at the chamber's rough trestle table.

"Will you take cider?" Craelin poured golden liquid from a crock into cups and presented one to Mara with a small flourish.

She thanked him with a smile and accepted his offering.

"You are injured, Lof Raena," Craelin gestured with his own cup toward her bandaged feet.

Mara's forehead had creased in apparent puzzlement, but Kai decided not to explain that Craelin had addressed her by the Kindren term for high princess. He quaffed his own cider with memory catching at him. On a day long ago in this very spot, he and Craelin had questioned the guardians of Rivenn, looking for traitors. They'd found each one faithful. He should have known that the wingabeast riders who had burned Elder homefarms in night raids had not come from among the guardians. Benisch, former Steward of Rivenn, had confessed to the crime after his arrest, stating that he and the servant, Chaeldra, had ridden with Freaer in the raids.

His thoughts propelled him to his feet. "Duty constrains me to find Elcon at once."

"Spoken like the Kai I remember. And so you shall, but I'd better warn Elcon to save him a shock. You could both be specters."

"I hadn't thought of that." Mara's gaze flew to Kai's, and he gave the first guardian of Rivenn a reassuring glance. "I carry a message informing Elcon of a threat against him."

"Who sends you?"

Kai hesitated. "Emmerich."

Craelin's eyes nested in lines "You speak of the DawnKing."

"How is it you acknowledge him when Elcon does not?"

"You've been away a long time, my friend."

Hope flickered within Kai. "What do you mean?"

Craelin spoke above the rim of his cup. "Elcon...reversed his opinion about Emmerich."

"When did this happen?"

Craelin drank the last of his cider and plunked the cup down on the scarred table. "After Lof Raelein Aewen's death. Torindan had survived one siege and begun to prepare for another when Elcon went off looking for Emmerich. I'll confess I thought them both mad, but then Emmerich saved us."

"He saved Torindan?" Mara had fallen silent with her head tilted as she listened. Craelin followed his gaze to her and went on in a softer tone. "It's hard to explain what happened. He brought about a darkness that cast the enemy into confusion. First they fought one another, then broke and ran."

"I must carry Emmerich's message to Elcon," Kai reminded Craelin.

"I will take you to him, but I must know what has kept you from your duty."

"Erdrich Ceid ensnared me." Kai spoke the words half-expecting to be met with amused disbelief. Only children believed the Ice Witch was real.

Craelin's eyes widened. "She exists?"

"After a manner of speaking." He watched the first guardian's expression as he grappled with the idea.

"How did you escape from her?" Craelin asked.

Kai cast about for an explanation and settled on the only one he understood. "Emmerich called my name, and I answered him."

ᎪᏝ

In his outer chamber, Elcon laid his head against a velvet-cushioned chairback and stared at the ornate ceiling where a gilded rose of Rivenn unfurled and golden gryphons spread their wings. Weariness pulled at his eyelids, and he let them shut by their own weight. A dream had woken him in the night, and afterwards he could find no comfort in sleep. He released his breath on a sigh and pushed to his feet. Sleeping in a chair would gain him nothing but a stiff neck.

"Elcon, will you eat?" Arillia bent over him, her forehead creased. "You've taken nothing today."

He always found it hard to eat after the dream, but he hated worrying Arillia. He inclined his head toward his servant, Anders, who hovered nearby. Anders went to do his bidding while Arillia sat on the stool beside his chair, and he stroked the golden hair cascading down her back. "You are plagued with a difficult husband, I fear."

"I am sure of it." She softened her words with a smile. "Did Aewen haunt your sleep again?"

She read him far too well to give her anything less than the truth. "She did." In his dreams, his dead wife ever searched for their lost babe.

"Will you never be free of her?" She pressed her lips together as if to hold back words, but then continued. "If I could give you children, could you let her go?"

He made no answer, for nothing he could say would ease her, especially since the questions she raised mirrored his own.

Arillia gazed at him with sadness. "Your silence speaks what you do not." She slipped from the room, leaving him alone in his misery.

Anders returned with maids bearing bread and cheese as well as roasted crobok and honey mead. Elcon's appetite had fled with Arillia, but he sat at the table in his meeting room and took enough nourishment to ease the frown lines on Anders's forehead.

He ought to have offered Arillia assurances of his love, but whatever he said seemed to upset her. Each time she whispered to him of a precious life within her, only a few moons later they would hang their heads in sorrow. No amount of infusions or special foods could change that Arillia's womb would not carry a babe to birth, and he couldn't help his reluctance to create more opportunities for grief. He wasn't proud of withdrawing just when Arillia needed him most, but it didn't help that each new death raised the specter of the child he had conceived with Aewen.

A knock came at his outer chamber door, and then a tap on the meeting room door. "Pray enter." He hadn't meant to sound irritated. The door swung open and Craelin strode into the room.

"Lof Shraen." The first guardian made his bow.

Elcon inclined his head in acknowledgment. "Craelin. Join me, if you wish." He bit into a roasted crobok leg and forced himself to chew.

"Thank you, but I come upon an urgent duty."

Elcon contemplated the first guardian. Taller than most, Craelin's height added to his authority. The fading scar at his neck attested to the arrow he'd taken at the siege of Torindan. They'd almost lost him on that occasion. Whatever brought him now must have put that gleam in his eye. "What matter brings you so late?"

"Lof Shraen…"

Elcon had never seen Craelin at a loss for words. "Yes?"

"This will come as a…surprise, but I must inform you…"

"Yes?"

"Kai has returned."

"Kai?" Elcon leaped to his feet. "Where is he?"

"He stands in your outer chamber."

Elcon strode to the door.

"Lof Shraen, wait..." Craelin's cry followed him from the chamber.

Elcon slid to a stop and gazed in helpless confusion, but not at Kai. How could this be? The wife he had thought dead gazed back at him with frightened eyes. "Aewen?"

"I meant to give you better warning, Lof Shraen." Craelin spoke from behind him. "This is not Aewen."

"Not Aewen?" Elcon repeated the words to make sense of them. But yes, something about her seemed not quite the same... "Who are you?"

The maiden's face paled, and she rocked on bandaged feet.

Kai touched her arm, and she leaned into his support. He spoke above her head. "Lof Shraen, this is Syl Marinda, your daughter."

11

JOURNEY'S END

Mara had hoped to feel a spark of kinship, but the Kindren across the chamber seemed no more than a stranger. With his burnished hair untouched by gray, he didn't look old enough to be her father, and his nobility lay beyond her ken. A yearning to go back to the inn took hold of her.

"I can hardly credit what you say." Her father spoke at last, his voice deepened by sorrow, an old pain on his face. "Quinn showed me my daughter's grave."

Kai tensed beside her. "He confessed to that."

Mara's stomach churned. She hadn't known Da as well as she'd thought..

Elcon frowned. "What do you mean?"

"Sad to say, but both the innkeeper and his wife deceived you." Kai shook his head. "They placed a stillborn child in the nurse's coffin and paid the mother to hold her tongue."

"Why would they do such a thing?"

Mara stirred. "Please—"

"To steal a child not theirs." Kai spoke the ugly truth. "I wouldn't have thought this possible of them."

She had to speak up for them. "They wanted to protect me."

Eyes the same green as her own narrowed. "Did they think me a danger to my own child?"

"They worried of war." Mam's excuse sounded feeble on Mara's lips.

Her father gazed at her with sorrowful eyes. "Will you defend them?"

"They have made that difficult."

Elcon strode to the fireplace and gripped the mantle for so long he might have forgotten her.

With her feet throbbing, she glanced at a nearby chair, tempted to seek its ease, but remained standing. She hadn't been invited to sit.

Her father turned at last, his gaze running over her. "Did they treat you well?"

"I worked hard, but we all did."

"They robbed us of the life we could have had together and made the Lof Raina of Faeraven into an inn servant." He paced before the cold hearth for a time before coming to stand before Mara.. "Why have you only now come to me?"

"They kept her identity from her." Kai's voice made Mara jump.

"I thought as much." Elcon's jaw tightened. "I've a mind to call them both to account."

"Lof Shraen, if I might intercede..." Kai's voice cut across Mara's protest. "Despite all their wrongs, they brought Syl Marinda up as a daughter, and she loves them."

Her father stared into the flames in the hearth. Whatever inner battle he fought, Mara did not see. "Very well." He turned back to them. "For my daughter's sake alone, I will not seek revenge."

She closed her eyes on a wave of relief. "Thank you."

Kai put a hand to Mara's back in silent support. "I have learned that leaving justice in Lof Yuel's hands works out better."

Elcon turned to him. "I have missed you, Kai. Where have you been all this time?"

"Trapped too long in a place I hope never to visit again. Emmerich freed me."

"I might have guessed he would find you. He wanders like the wind, venturing into places others fear."

Emmerich had saved her, too, but she didn't want her father to know about that episode.

He started toward her, and Kai pressed her elbow, urging her forward, and then released her and moved away. She held back, uncertain.

"My child." Her father extended a hand to her.

She went to him, and he gathered her in his arms. For a time, words were not needed.

He gazed upon her at arm's length. "You are beautiful, like your mother. I wish you could have known her." His voice broke as his emotions swept over her—guilt sorrow, regret, but also joy. She reached out from within to soothe him.

Surprise lit his face. "The shil shael has not passed you by, I see."

"Of what do you speak?" But she could guess what he meant.

"Lof Yuel has blessed most of the sons and daughters of Rivenn with the ability to touch one another's souls."

"It is a blessing? I thought it might come from evil..."

"As with the touch of a hand, the shil shael can be used for good or evil. Tell me what you have experienced that made you wonder that." Tension throbbed in her father's voice.

She clasped her arms about herself. "Someone or something torments my dreams."

"Freaer searches for her.," Kai shifted closer as if to protect her from unseen dangers.

"He is a son of Rivenn?" Mara asked.

"Yes, but an illegitimate one," her father answered.

"Another soul visited me." Mara told herself that naming Rand wasn't important. "It seemed...kinder."

"Who can it be?" Elcon looked past her to Kai. "I have no other children, Rivenn's other line has faded, and Freaer's son is said to rival his father for cruelty."

"What do they call him?" Mara prepared herself to learn the worst.

"Draegmor."

Overwhelmed with relief, she swayed on her feet. Why had she cared so much that her father not name Rand?

Without a word, her father guided her to a chair. With a grateful smile, she sank into its cushions and bent to rub her feet.

"Forgive me." Her father looked guilt-stricken. "I should have invited you to sit before this. What happened to your feet?"

Heat climbed into Mara's cheeks. "I walked too long in the snow."

"If Quinn and Heddwyn had anything to do with this—" Her father clenched his fists at his side but broke off before finishing his threat.

"Nay, the fault was all my own. I ventured too far off the path." She waited for Kai to elaborate, but thankfully he kept silent.

"We'll have Praectal Daelic look at it." Her father turned his head. "Anders! Bring food and drink. Oh, and send a maidservant to tend Syl Marinda. Craelin, come! We must celebrate."

She had forgotten the first guardian, waiting in the background with her father's servant. The first guardian now joined them, while the servant went off to do her father's bidding. In truth, Mara wanted only the solace of sleep but would not rob her father's joy by refusing.

"You'll want the chance to change." Her father suggested in a quiet voice.

Her face warmed. "Thank you, but I have no other garments than those I stand in." Kai had promised that all her needs would be supplied at Torindan, but mentioning that would be awkward.

"That's easily remedied." He assured her with a quick smile.

Her father summoned a golden-haired maid named Traelein who showed her to a beautiful chamber adorned with tapestries in luminous colors. Another servant followed with garments of velvet, silk, and wool. Mara washed the grime of travel from her skin and changed into a clean chemise that lay soft against her skin. She gritted her teeth while Traelein dealt with her tangles, but with her hair combed and cascading down her back, she felt better. Traelein helped her into a kirtle of green velvet and laced an elk-skin bodice dyed red. Mara studied her reflection in the mirror glass, startled by the transformation. Ah, but dressing a country maid in finery did not make her a princess.

CR

Arillia let the rough texture of the embroidered hangings at her window run through her fingers while she breathed in perfumes from the night-blooming flowers hovering like pale ghosts outside her window. In the early spring when warmth stirred nature to wakefulness, Elcon had stolen her heart with a kiss in this very garden. Here, too, he had declared his love and asked her to marry him. Between those two events lay a deep void of despair.

She'd chosen to forgive him for betraying his promise to court her, but sometimes unruly thoughts countered her will. The image of Aewen as a radiant bride on her new husband's arm could come in an instant to steal her peace of mind. It had been all she could do to muster a greeting when presented to Aewen. The new bride's startled expression had warned Arillia that she'd not entirely hidden her heartache. The guilty glances and words of apology Elcon had cast her way had only made matters worse.

Why think of this now?

She huffed a breath and turned from the window. Aewen lay in the tomb, and someday Elcon might let her remain there.

Her maid looked in at the door. "The Lof Shraen sends for you."

Arillia's spine stiffened. Sending for her as if nothing of consequence had happened between them marked Elcon as unfeeling. She tilted her chin. "Tell him I am indisposed."

"Yes, Lof Raelein." Lyneth withdrew.

Arillia perched on a velvet-cushioned bench beside the hearth. Marble unibeasts with horns entwined supported the mantle. A draft made her shiver. She would shut the window on the scents of the garden and bid Lyneth to light a fire against the chill.

ℭℜ

Elcon's servant, Anders, backed away from the door to allow Kai entry to the Lof Shraen's outer chamber. He'd meant to relay Emmerich's message yesterday but hadn't been able to bring himself to spoil such a joyous reunion. He would put it off no longer.

Elcon paced before the hearth. He wore the look of his father, Timraen, most strongly when problems weighted his mind. Whatever troubled him now, Kai misliked adding to his burdens. "Kai. I hope you are settling in well."

"Craelein had my chamber in the gatehouse prepared for me."

"You still have a cot here, as well, should duty keep you near."

That might happen sooner than Elcon imagined. "What of Weilton? Does he act as your guardian in my place?"

Elcon waved a careless hand. "I don't require close watching these days."

"According to Emmerich, that is about to change."

"Tell me what he said."

A knock roused them both, and Anders admitted Craelin, who made his bow and glanced at each of them in turn. "Do I interrupt?"

Elcon shook his head. "You should hear this, too. Go on, Kai."

"Emmerich instructed me to warn you that Freaer has rebuilt the stronghold of Pilaer and now gathers his forces to launch another attack against Torindan."

The fire behind Elcon flared in a draft, and he glanced into the flames absently. "After all this time...I had hoped.... Freaer seemed to have given up."

"You must not persuade yourself that will ever happen." Kai countered the idea with caution, not wanting to offend Elcon by overstepping but mindful of his duty to inform his Lof Shraen of impending danger.

"Well then, Craelin..." Elcon looked to the first guardian. "It seems I must call upon your keen mind for battle."

Craelin's eyes glinted. "We'll prepare for the worst."

"I'll rely on you." Elcon frowned. "Meanwhile, perhaps we can forget for a little longer that evil exists."

"Of course." Kai turned as Anders admitted Mara, escorted by her maid.

She crossed the chamber and curtsied before her father. "You called for me?"

Wearing garb fit for a lof raena and with velvet ribbons woven through her dark hair, she could have been Aewen in her youth. Kai glanced at Elcon. What might it cost him to look upon her?

Elcon smiled at Mara. "Don't look so alarmed, my daughter. I only want to feed you. Come." He included them all in his glance.

Servants piled food on the table in his meeting room. Craelin sat in his honored place beside the Lof Shraen and Elcon seated Mara on his other side. Kai took his customary chair beside Craelin.

Weilton put his head in at the door. "Kai! I'm thankful to see you again." The second guardian came into the chamber, his appearance much as Kai remembered, although laughter had cut lines more firmly about his mouth and crinkled the corners of his eyes.

Kai beamed at him. "I can say the same of you."

"Stop lurking about the doorway and come in!" Elcon demanded in mock severity.

Smiling, Weilton obeyed. Eathnor and Dorann followed him into the chamber. The two brothers could not be more different. Eathnor wore the green surcoat of a guardian of Rivenn with a gryphon embroidered in gold standing on its hindlegs, its forelegs curved into claws. By contrast, Dorann garbed himself in the leather jersey of a tracker. Eathnor's vibrancy shone from his light eyes, whereas Dorann remained silent.

Kai jumped to his feet and embraced each brother in turn.

Eathnor cocked his head. "Lose your way?"

Kai's smile slipped away. "That I did."

"Never mind," Eathnor said in a bracing tone. "You're home now."

Guaron entered at the door, and Kai greeted him with joy. He belonged here among his liege lord and friends, but he must return to his family in Whellein when Elcon allowed. The thought tugged at him. What changes would he find there?

Eathnor and Dorann made belated bows, and Elcon bestowed a tolerant smile on them before holding up his hand to speak. The chamber quieted. "Lof Raelein Arillia sends her regrets. She is unwell and cannot attend." Elcon made the announcement in even tones, but his ears reddened.

A polite murmur ran through the gathering. Kai wondered if the gossip following it would be as reserved.

"This night I introduce my daughter, Syl Marinda, Raena of Rivenn and Lof Raena of Faeraven, now restored to me."

A murmur ran through the crowd, and all eyes turned toward Mara. Mara sent a frightened look to her father, who gave her a reassuring smile. Watching the exchange sparked amusement in Kai and a little of the pride that, had he lived, might have belonged to Timraen for his son. Elcon had changed, becoming more at ease as Lof Shraen.

They feasted on elk, stuffed crobok, venison, and even a bruin's head roasted with an apple in its mouth. The fare included soup made from greenings, smoked trout, salad, and spring mushrooms awash in butter. Sweet puddings, cakes, and tarts in vast array concluded the repast. The table groaned under the weight of the offerings until the guests moaned alike and could eat no more. They talked long and merrily, but eventually made their goodnights.

Kai escorted Mara to her chambers with her maid lighting the way. At her door, Mara restrained him from leaving her with her hand on his arm. "You knew my mother, didn't you? Tell me what she was like." She spoke in a rush.

He ought to have expected the question but it surprised him nonetheless. "In her kindness, Aewen tended the poor and healed the sick. She could act on impulse, not always wisely, and moods took her at times, but she loved her husband, and I am certain she loved you." The torchlight heightened the shadows beneath Mara's eyes and revealed the glistening of unshed tears. "Thank you."

Kai never quite knew what to do when a maiden wept. He cleared his throat. "You are weary. I'll leave you to your rest."

The shadows beneath her eyes and strain in her face presented mute testimony to her exhaustion. She nodded. "Thank you for your care of me."

How like Aewen she looked–Aewen who shouldn't have had to die. Kai bowed to her. "By this I give my last service to your mother."

ɑ

Mara allowed Traelein to remove her fine kirtle and the velvet ribbons in her hair. Being undressed by a maid sat ill, but she hoped to honor her mother's memory and avoid bringing shame to her father by fitting in at Torindan.

Tonight her father had entertained her with lively stories from his youth. He'd only frowned once, after announcing that the Lof Raelein would not join them. Truth to tell, the news had relieved Mara's mind. After the long journey, meeting her father had been strain enough.

Standing barefoot in her chemise, she wrapped her arms about herself for warmth as Traelein's brush crackled through her hair. Afterwards, she climbed into a carved and canopied bed so large it dwarfed her. Her maid pulled the bed hangings closed and withdrew with the lanthorn. Thankful for the warmth of her coverings, Mara settled down to sleep.

Every ache returned anew, and it felt that the pitch and sway of a wingabeast's flight still tossed her about. She pictured again her father's shock at mistaking her for his dead wife and his anger after learning how Mam and Da had tricked him. Would he keep his word not to retaliate? Did Mam sleep right now or lie awake, thinking of her stolen daughter, now all but lost to her?

Mara tossed and turned. Her bed supplied the comfort needed for a good night's rest, but her small bed at the inn had suited her better. Would she ever go home again? Hot tears stung her eyes and spilled onto her cheeks. She brushed them away with an impatient hand. Her own anger had brought about her sorrow, and weeping could not cleanse her guilt for running away from the inn.

She drifted into restless sleep and woke with Rand's touch trembling like a promise at the threshold of her mind. What did he want with her? Unable to resist her curiosity, she opened herself to him, but then gasped. Dark emotions lashed her, too many to name, but chief among them burned anger. She thrust away from Rand, breaking the slender thread that bound her to him, and hid herself with Lof Yuel in the quiet place within. When her breathing calmed, she tried to go back to sleep, but worries plagued her. She had trusted Rand with her life, but what did she really know of him?

∞

Kai plucked one of the earlyflowers glowing pale in the moonlight beside the path and breathed in its sweetness. He should be in bed, not wandering the garden by night. His steps took him to the fountain, and he tilted his head to gaze upon Talan, cast in bronze, ever upon his wingabeast. He had remained in a similar state, frozen while time flowed past, never to return.

His mind returned to Shae with the faithfulness of a starving cur to a scrap of food. A memory of her combing her hair by the river, too shy to gaze upon him, stirred his heartache. Had an enemy flayed his flesh, he could not have felt more pain than the loss of her brought. He drank in a cooling draught of air and waited for his sorrow to ease. Would it never end?

The flower in his hand caught his eye, each curving petal delicate as a maiden's love. On impulse, he floated the blossom in the pool below the fountain. The fragile craft floated away on a hidden current and wobbled before vanishing beneath the water. Gone.

He closed his eyes. *Lof Yuel. I release her to you yet again.*

Kai. A sigh breathed across his cheek.

His eyes flew open. "Shae?"

Silver leaves draped from twisted branches along the empty pathways. No gentle maiden waited beside the pool. Only the splash of the fountain and the call of a nightbird met his straining ears. And yet...Shae had come to him. He knew it. But she had reached to him more feebly than before. Emmerich had said the worlds tilted out of balance. What did that mean for Shae, trapped between worlds?

He had to find out.

12

Irritation did not make a suitable sleeping companion, as Arillia discovered to her cost. The long night afforded her more than enough time to reflect and also ample time for regrets. Who had she become in her bitterness? She should not have blamed Elcon for dreams over which he had no control or for succumbing to melancholy in their wake. Neither should she consider his silence a mark of guilt, although it cut her to the quick.

If only her inner wounds did not fester and refuse to heal. In truth, she could never quite convince herself that her husband loved her. Elcon could not know, because she'd never told him, how she had suffered when he'd married Aewen. She'd wept night after night, muffling the sound of her grief in a pillow.

She'd felt herself a pale shadow beside Aewen, who had been beauty itself. Perhaps if she could have birthed a child to replace the one her husband had lost, he might have drawn closer to her rather than keeping so much to himself. In a burst of honesty, she admitted the truth.

Her jealousy had driven him away.

She escaped the discomfort of her thoughts near dawn but soon woke. She sat up with a groan. If only she could remain in sleep's embrace rather than seeking her husband's, but she must confess her wrongs to him and seek his forgiveness.

CR

"You sent for me?" Mara tried not to sound breathless, but she'd been sleeping late when her father's summons arrived.

"Come warm yourself." With a hand on her back, he guided her to a chair near the fire in his outer chamber. "Did you rest well?"

"Well enough." She should tell him about Rand visiting her through the soul touch, but not with Traelein, who had accompanied her to her father's chambers, stationed near the door beside Anders. Her father might be used to ignoring servants, but such a thing lay beyond her ability.

"Your feet are recovering, I see. Did Praectal Daelic tend you?"

"He did." Mara studied her hands, folded in her lap, to hide any guilt on her face. Neither Kai nor the physician her father had sent to care for her would approve of her walking the small distance to the Lof Shraen's chambers.

He tilted her face. "You resemble your mother, it cannot be denied, but also my own."

"You speak of High Queen Maeven." Mara had heard of the legendary ruler of the Kindren from stories told by travelers. The wandering people who lived in wagons had long fascinated Mara, and she'd crept away whenever she could to listen to their music and the stories they'd told.

He smiled. "You know of her. She would be glad of that."

"I could not fail to learn her legend while living at the inn."

He smiled, but with a hint of sadness. "I wish you could have met her."

A tap came at the door. Anders admitted a beauty garbed in gray with skin delicate as a petal and golden hair plaited. She turned clear blue eyes on Mara and gasped. With one delicate hand she clutched her throat. Her chest rose and fell as she heaved in air. "Elcon, what insanity is this?"

"Arillia, allow me to introduce my daughter, Syl Marinda." Her father claimed Mara with his words even as he eased away from her side.

This must be the same Arillia who could not attend last night's feast. Mara bit the inside of her lip, ill-prepared for this meeting.

Emotions warred on Arillia's face. "I thought her the mother."

Elcon frowned. "This is your step-daughter, Syl Marinda."

Not quite certain how to greet a step-mother who was also a high queen, Mara curtsied and cast about for something polite to say. "I hope you have recovered from whatever vapor troubled you last night."

Arillia stared at her as if she had spoken in another tongue before returning her gaze to her husband. "Surely you don't expect me to…"

"She's my daughter, Arillia."

"And I am your wife." Her step-mother's tone could not have been more precise.

A lump formed in Mara's throat as she waited for the rejection that would surely come.

Her father sighed. "What would you have me

do?"

Arillia lifted a shoulder. "Send her whence she came and, if you must, visit her there."

Heat crept up Mara's neck. She longed to go home to the inn, but not in disgrace.

Her father's jaw tensed. "Out of the question."

"Well, she can't stay here." Arillia countered her husband and king in a light voice that belied the wariness in her eyes.

"You take too much upon yourself." Her father ground out every word.

Mara winced, wishing to be elsewhere.

Arillia lifted a brow. "Am I to have no say on the running of my household?"

""Be reasonable, then. Would you have me put my own flesh and blood out with nowhere to go?"

"I suppose you would rather I take to the road."

"Arillia!" Her father spoke in shocked tones. "What's come over you?"

"Even lying in the tomb..." Arillia stopped to take several breaths with tears standing in her eyes. "...Aewen gives you what I cannot."

"Stop this!" He reached for her, but she twisted away and ran from the room.

Scowling, he began to pace.

"I'm sorry." Mara tried not to let the rejection hurt, but it did. She had only just escaped Brynn's dislike, only to fall prey to Arillia's. "I shouldn't have come."

"You've done nothing wrong," her father assured her.

"I gave no thought to what my sudden appearance at Torindan might bring."

"Nor should you have." He rubbed the back of his neck. "These matters lie between Arillia and me."

"Perhaps you should follow her," Mara suggested.

"Like a cur brought to heel? No thank you." He strode from the chamber.

Mara wrapped her arms about herself, chilled despite the fire's warmth. Remaining at Torindan would only stir more trouble. Tears sprang to her eyes, and she turned blindly to leave.

"Lof Raena." Her maid's gentle hand cupped her elbow.

"Take me to the chapel."

"Chapel?" Traelein's forehead creased.

"Surely Torindan has a place of prayer."

"Oh." Her maid's expression cleared. "You speak of the allerstaed. I will show you the way." Traelein led her along a corridor to a carved door standing open beneath an archway.

The beauty of Torindan's place of prayer made Mara catch her breath. Carved columns marched the length of the chamber on both sides with passages running behind them. The ceiling vaulted into shadow. Light filtered through rows of high clerestory windows set with stained glass to strew colors across the strongwood floor. At the far end of the nave, steps rose to a prayer rail at the edge of the dais that raised the altar.

Mara left her maid waiting inside the archway and, with steps echoing, crossed the allerstaed. She climbed to the prayer rail, where she knelt and bowed her head. A peaceful tide flowed over her, and she closed her eyes. Time spun away, and she no longer marked its passage...

Footsteps rang out, and she lifted her head.

Kai looked up at her from below the dais. "May I join you?"

She would rather be alone but simple courtesy prompted her response. "Please."

He climbed the steps and lowered to his knees beside her.

"Why did you come?" She regretted her question at once for it brought sadness into his face.

"I'm here to wrestle with Lof Yuel."

"I'm sorry," she hastened to say. "I shouldn't have asked something so personal."

"And you?"

Her face heated, but she could hardly withhold her answer after he'd given his. "To yield myself to him."

He turned eyes more gray than silver on her. "You have the greater task."

ଔ

Elcon leaned his forehead against his wife's door and groaned. Nothing he said or did seemed capable of convincing Arillia of his love, and now she refused to emerge from her locked chambers even when commanded. This difficulty with his wife had reached the point of humiliation. It fostered uncomfortable questions. Anders had overheard servant's gossip asking how a Lof Shraen who couldn't unite his own household could bring together a divided kingdom.

He strode to his chambers, careful not to slam the door lest his behavior incite more whisperings. In a huff as he entered, he did not at first see Arillia seated at the fireside in his outer chamber. She had changed into his least favorite gown of brown wool and wore her hair coiled on either side of her head beneath a golden net. She, of course, knew he preferred it down.

"How did you come here?" He had watched over her door most of the day, and she had failed to emerge.

She lifted her chin with a proud tilt to her head. "The Lof Shraen of Faeraven commands my presence and then asks why I give it."

"Do you mock me?" At first sight of her swollen eyes, he'd almost given in to sympathy for her, but now he hardened his heart.

"And if I did, would you punish me?" Her voice escalated in pitch and volume. "Have me whipped? Thrown in the dungeon? Deprived of food?"

"Pray calm yourself."

His words acted as a spark to tinder. Nostrils flared, she rose from her chair. "How dare you speak to me in that tone when you are the cause of my ills!"

"You bring these ills upon yourself," he bit out, past restraint.

The fire went out of her, and she collapsed into a huddle in the oversized chair. "I believed that myself. I even came to your chambers to beg your forgiveness until I saw how little you care about my feelings."

His patience snapped. "I fail to understand. You are well fed and clothed, hold a position of envy, and have a husband who would lay his life down for you. And yet, you believe yourself disadvantaged. Your behavior shames us both."

"I won't inflict myself on you further." She stood up with tears shining in her eyes. "I leave tomorrow for my father's hold in Chaeradon."

"I forbid you to go."

"I...will obey." She lowered her head in defeat, which was not what he'd expected her to do. He restrained the ridiculous urge to kiss away the tears bathing her cheeks. She would not welcome his touch. Besides, after the way she had spoken to him, he shouldn't yield to tender feelings too soon. He tried again to understand. "Tell me what troubles you."

"Can you not see the wretched thing you ask me to do? How can I accept the child Aewen gave you when I have borne you none?"

"Take heart, Arillia. Lof Yuel may have brought her to us for your sake as well as mine. This fixation on Aewen poisons your mind. You must release yourself from it." That had been the wrong thing to say, he could tell by the speed with which she looked up.

"Will you ask me to do something you cannot?"

He hated the anguish in her voice. "Mara is my daughter. Can you not accept her for my sake?"

She sighed and dashed her tears away. "As you wish. I will bear her for your sake."

"Thank you." He caught her hand and kissed it. "I hope you will find her less of a burden in time."

Pulling free, she stood with quiet dignity. "You have what you want of me, *Lof Shraen*. Am I now dismissed?"

He bit back his sharp reply. She had yielded, at least.

13

REJECTION

A marsh bird sobbed from the reaches of Weithen Faen, the lonely lament resonating within Rand. The tide lapped the edges of the road at his feet as if seeking to consume it. In the bruised sky above Pilaer, clouds filtered the dying light while shadows swept across the faen. The beauty of his surroundings held its dangers, for it could lull the unwary into taking a careless step. Beneath the water's silken surface, quickmud waited, a small peril compared to others he could face. Worse among them were specters ready to drive him mad with his own regrets.

If only he had understood about his father sooner, his mother might not now suffer. He should have rescued her instead of trying to placate her tormenter. And he should never have plotted to harm Mara. At the thought of her, a sweet longing pierced him, nearly bringing him to his knees. He would embrace the love that caused this pain, for it would help deliver him from the evil that throbbed within the black heart of Pilaer.

The road that cut across the faen brought him to the stronghold as shadows lengthened into night. Voices rang and boots thumped from behind the wall—the guardians of Pilaer tromping toward the great hall for the evening repast.

Rand waited until the voices echoed within the

hall before skirting the outer wall with careful steps. He stole past the gatehouse toward the moonlit postern gate at the rear of the inner bailey. He would bide his time until the chatter within the hall gave way to raucous laughter. Then the corridors of Pilaer would be empty.

He'd barely rested on his journey, either in body or soul, for shielding his mind from his father's touch required constant vigilance. With exhaustion tugging at him, he settled against the wall and tipped his head back. The moon shone above the horizon and stars burned from the sky, so bright he shut his eyelids. A fresh breeze caressed his face like a mother's hand, removing the stench of sour mud that emanated from the faen at low tide. Crickets chirruped and marshfrogs thrummed...

A mosquito droned in his ear. Jerking awake, he batted the parasite away. The moon sailed high, cast adrift in a silent sea. Night creatures called from the faen, but otherwise, silence reigned.

He'd waited too long. The one he had come to kill would already slumber in the safety of his chambers. He'd have to wait until the next night to carry out his plan. Meanwhile, he needed somewhere to hide, and the best place for that lay within Pilaer itself.

The wind off the faen buffeted his face as he groped along the wall. A small stone, still warm from the day's heat, gave beneath his hand. He pried it out and reached into the cubbyhole, groping for the hidden lever that opened the postern gate. He'd found it in his early days and had afterwards returned from exploring Weithen Faen by this means. His fingers closed on the lever, and he gave it a pull. It held fast.

He used more strength with the same results. The

lever must have rusted in place. Gritting his teeth, he made a last effort.

Had it yielded?

He pushed again, putting his shoulder into the task. The lever screeched as it echoed through the faen, loud in the night. An owl burst into the air from the arch above the gate and passed overhead in a flurry. Heart pounding, he watched the bird cross the faen on wings silvered by moonlight. Beyond the gaping postern gate, a cobbled path led to the ruined allerstaed. He longed for its refuge but crouched in shadow at the base of the wall, straining to hear. After the ruckus the owl had set up, the watchguard might come to investigate.

This night must not end in his captivity. He knew his surroundings well but scanned them anyway, planning an escape route. On three sides of Pilaer, tidal flats stretched into blackness. Mud soft enough to swallow him whole offered no way out if he went that direction. He pressed against the wall, tensed to flee.

Only the wind stirred. The guard must slumber. He sidled through the opening, pulling the gate shut behind him. The cobblestone path passed beneath his feet, then he climbed the crumbling steps to Pilaer's place of prayer. The grime of ages obscured the few panes still guarding window openings set high in the walls. From those devoid of glass, owls watched him with luminous eyes.

The strongwood door groaned from long disuse as he slipped into the dark building. He could wait out the daylight in this forgotten sanctuary. He'd hidden from Draeg's cruelty within these walls, vanishing for days at a time. His mother had known where to find him. When not blinded by her own miseries, she'd brought him food and water. Sooner or later, she'd coaxed him to take up the raveled threads of his life at Pilaer again.

Sorrow at what she must now endure twisted like a knife in his gut. He must save her, even if it meant losing his own life.

CR

"Why do I find you in bed, Lof Raena?" Traelein's voice penetrated to Mara beneath the counterpane. "Kai waits to escort you to the great hall."

Mara sat up in bed and held her pillow before her like a shield. "Tell him I am ill and do not wish to take food. And please, call me Mara." She could not get used to being called a princess.

Traelein pressed her lips together in obvious disapproval but went away. She'd left the door ajar, but Mara couldn't pick out words from the murmuring in her outer chamber.

Traelein returned with a frown marring her brow. "Kai asks if you are certain. He says that this night the Lof Shraen plans to present you to the Lof Raelein in the proper manner."

In other words, her father wished to pretend his wife didn't detest the sight of her. "I am definitely unwell." She spoke the truth, after a manner of speaking. Her stomach really did churn.

Traelein's eyes glinted. She opened her mouth to speak but shut it again.

"Do you have something to say?" Mara couldn't resist the question, although uncertain she wanted an answer.

Traelein shook her head. "I should keep my opinions to myself..."

"As you wish—"

"...but I don't like seeing you in bed all day when you do not seem sick."

"Some ailments remain hidden." Mara clutched her pillow more tightly as sobs wrenched from her.

"Lof Raena!" Traelein stepped toward her. "I did not mean to make you cry."

Mara drew a shuddering breath. "It's that I ache to go home."

"You have only just arrived. Give yourself time, and I'm sure you will come to think of Torindan as home."

"How can that happen when my step-mother rejects me?"

Traelein's brow puckered again. "Lof Raelein Arillia is not by nature unkind. She also needs time."

Fitting in at Torindan had become impossible, but Mara felt too weary to argue the point.

CR

Rand's boots made little sound on the cobbled path. The keep's western side door opened beneath his hand. He peered inside. Most of the torches had burned out, casting the corridor into darkness pushed back here and there by the fitful light from those still guttering. He latched the door with the merest click, although the bawdy shouts and laughter from the hall would cover any sound he made. Carnal or blood lust, possibly both, would find fulfillment this night among the warriors of Pilaer. His mother's influence had saved him from this much. He didn't need to imagine the night's entertainment, having been subjected to it during his father's attempts to make him a real warrior. He'd hidden his revulsion until his father and Draeg sank deeply into their cups, and then escaped into the fresh air.

Avoiding the light, he slipped from shadow to shadow. Chill air settled like a fog in his lungs. Grey shapes formed in his side vision. Rather than running at him as they always had done, the wraiths of Pilaer coursed alongside him, mouths open on silent howls. Perhaps the darkness of his purpose summoned them. He'd known since his early days that the wraiths fed on hatred and fear, jealousy and lust, and on every other black emotion ravenous to consume him. Avoiding the wraiths had turned him away from impurity. He'd called upon Lof Yuel to shield his mind, a tactic that had served him often and well. Using it now would end his dark errand, but at a cost he was unwilling to pay.

Frear's voice echoed down the corridor, singing a ballad Rand knew.

"Iewald fought and won the day
By wit, by speed, by might,
But death came, perfumed and gay,
In beauty leading him astray,
And Pilaer lost the night."

Why did "Iewald's Betrayal," which told how treachery born of lust had destroyed a friendship and a kingdom, have to be his song? Rand had always thought his father's voice beautiful, even when he slurred his words, as tonight. The old yearning came rushing in a flood that threatened to drown him. His throat swelled, and he swallowed the taste of regret.

The wraiths, having grown in number, rushed in and plucked at him. Evading them had never been harder. He jerked away from one then another, but finally summoned the strength of mind to look beyond them. He had discovered long ago that there was room to hide in the alcove behind the statue of Freaer. It had been easier in his early days, but he could still wedge himself into the space. Mother had told him that a statue of Kunrat, whose sacrifice had imprisoned the Contender within the Well of Light, had stood here until his father melted it and used the gold to cast an image of himself. Across the corridor in a twin alcove, the likeness of Rivenn, first ruler of the Kindren, raised his scepter as if in disapproval.

"What then of mortal might?
What then of faithful art?
Meriwen whispered of delight
And Iewald fell without a fight,
Overcome by his own heart.'

His father came into view in the torchlight, staggering a little beside Urwan, the garn assigned to protect him. Rand's breath caught. *Only an instant more...*

He forced himself to wait until the pair drew even with him.

Now!

He shoved the statue in front of him.

"Lof Shraen!" Urwan's warning rang out as he stepped in front of his master.

The statue teetered on the brink of toppling but rocked back into its base with a thud. The wraiths howled.

Rand braced against the wall and pushed with his feet.

The statue crashed, and the floor vibrated as cracks radiated through the marble. A golden arm rolled away.

His father peered from behind his protector. The garn unsheathed a sword that nearly matched Rand in height and slashed the air.Rand sidestepped.

Urwan advanced, drove him to the wall, and thrust again. Rand flung himself sideways, touched by sparks as the sword pingedthe stone wall. He backed, more from instinct than plan.

The garn followed.

Outpaced, Rand stopped retreating and stood ready.

Shifting to the right, Urwan brought his sword around.

Rand dove to the floor and rolled into his opponent's legs.

Going down with a roar, the garn crashed into the broken statue.

Rand scrambled to his feet while the garn moaned and clutched his back. The injury probably wouldn't stop him for long, but it bought a little time. Jerking the dagger from his boot, he started toward his father, who had not moved. Rand could slash his throat in an instant.

The tension around his father's mouth belied his casual posture. He flicked a glance from Rand's face to his dagger. "You...surprise me."

The stench of spirits wafted to Rand, and he fought the urge to vomit. "How so?"

The corners of Freaer's mouth tilted. "You remind me that you are my son."

Bitterness welled into the back of Rand's throat. "Don't call me that!" He spat the words. "I'm nothing like you."

His side vision alerted him. Urwan already pushed to his feet. Rand must strike or lose the chance. He leveled his dagger, but it shook in his hand.

His father smirked. "You never were a warrior."

A wave of sickness thundered over Rand. If anyone deserved to die, his father did. Why couldn't he kill him?

Urwan thrust his ugly face into Rand's, gagging him with the foulness of his breath. The garn's claws dug into Rand's knife hand and twisted. He screamed in pain, and the dagger clattered to the floor.

Soft laughter reached him as he cradled his bloodied hand. "You are useless, like your mother."

The garn gripped Rand's neck and squeezed.

Blackness edged his vision, and he wondered with strange detachment if his neck would break before he suffocated. He closed his eyes so he didn't have to die with a monstrous face filling his vision.

"Don't kill him." Freaer voice sounded bored. "Only remove him from my sight."

The pressure on Rand's throat eased, and he gasped in air. His tormenter pressed his back, thrusting him off balance. Rand slammed into the wall, scraping against rough stone, and then Urwan was dragging him down the corridor.

His father had spared his life, but Rand didn't delude himself it had been out of kindness.

14

IMPRISONED

Mara startled awake and fought to breathe. The feeling of suffocation eased almost at once, but something dark had happened. She knew it. For the rest of the night she wove in and out of restless dreams. Traelein woke her with a summons. She dragged from bed with aching eyes and submitted to her maid's care.

Her father met her at his door, concern plain on his face. "Are you feeling better this morning?"

Her face heated, and she couldn't quite look at him. "I am weary this morn but otherwise well, thank you."

"I'm glad to hear it." He stepped back, allowing her into his chamber. "The day has yet to warm. Will you take a chair by the fire?"

Her feet sank into the woven mat before the hearth. "Thank you, but I'd rather stand." Sometime during the long, wretched night she'd made a decision. She faced her father with her shoulders braced. "I have something to say."

"Oh?"

His kind tone made what she had to say harder. Mara steadied herself. "I want to go home."

His brows shot upward. "*This* is your home."

"I beg of you—"

"Syl Marinda—" He pushed a hand through his

hair, leaving it ruffled.

"Stop calling me that!" Regretting her outburst, she went on more quietly. "My name is Mara."

"I prefer your mother's choice of name for you rather than that of thieves."

She had no answer for that, but she couldn't have spoken past the lump closing her throat.

"You ask the impossible." He took her hands. "Try to understand."

"Why?"

"You are my only child and heir. I refuse to put you at risk"

She pulled away. "But what of the Lof Raelein and her children?" Heat surged up her neck. It had been indelicate to bring up childbirth, even in a future sense.

"She...cannot bear children."

Her cheeks flamed. "My presence can't make it any easier for her."

"You must stop thinking of yourself as a burden."

How well he read her. "I need to hear those words from her."

"Arillia would have acknowledged you last night."

And she had sent her excuses. "Today I will come to the hall."

"Thank you."

"And yet I wish...If only I could see Mam again."

"It would not be safe."

"Ever?" Her lower lip trembled as tears fell to her cheeks.

"My daughter—" He tracked a tear with his thumb. "Never doubt that this is where you belong. Your place is with me, and the Kindren need you. As a trueborn daughter of Rivenn, you will one day rule

Faeraven."

ꞔ

Kai gripped the prayer rail. He determined to wait upon Lof Yuel each day until he received an answer to the question raging within him. Why did Shae remain trapped between worlds? She had sacrificed enough. If only he could take her place, he would gladly free her. He'd once knelt with her and Elcon in this very place to pray for the life of Lof Raelein Maeven, the mother who'd revealed herself to Shae just before dying. As strong-minded as her mother, Shae had sorely tried his patience. At the memory, a smile played at his lips but faded with the longing to hold her again. Since she had gone through the gateway of Gilead Riann to the corridor between worlds, his life remained suspended with hers.

"Why?" The plea wrenched from his soul and echoed through the Place of Prayer to fade into silence. He rose to his feet.

On the morrow, he would ask again.

ꞔ

The door to Arillia's chamber swung open the first time Elcon knocked, a positive sign. His wife's maid bowed as he entered. "The Lof Raelein is unable to receive you, Lof Shraen."

Irritation seethed through him, and he cast a glance at the inner chamber door, firmly shut against him. "Very well." He spoke with irritation. "Pray tell her that, should she remember she has a husband, she must seek him."

He stomped down the corridor and shut his chamber door behind him with a satisfying bang that he at once regretted. After his marriage to Aewen foisted a Lof Raelein of Elder blood on the Kindren, he'd worked hard to regain their respect. He must not appear weak in leading his own household, especially after the warning Emmerich had sent through Kai. With Freaer challenging his rulership, he could not risk losing the loyalty of any more of his people.

A knock sounded, and Anders opened the outer door to Kai, seemingly summoned by his thoughts. Elcon strode across the chamber to greet him. "Come into my meeting chamber. I want to know more about what Emmerich said."

Kai took his accustomed place at the strongwood table while Anders closed the door. "I gave you the gist of it. Freaer will soon strike Torindan from the stronghold of Pilaer."

Elcon gripped the armrests of his chair. "It's hard to consider war after being so long at peace. I haven't sent you home to Whellein as you deserve, but you will return there, I promise, once we win peace."

Kai said nothing but gazed past him to a tapestry depicting two figures locked in mortal combat as they fell together into the Well of Light.

Elcon studied the depiction of his ancestor's heroic deed. "If only Kunrat's sacrifice had been enough to bind Freaer within Lohen Keil forever, we would not now face war."

"I can't bear going home without Shae, anyway."

Quick sympathy chased away Elcon's lingering resentment over Kai's return from Lohen Keil without his sister. "I miss her, too." He cleared his throat. "Tell me, where is Emmerich now?"

"I'm not certain."

Kai's response came as no surprise. Elcon nodded. "He keeps his own counsel."

"Craelin tells me he saved Torindan when Freaer besieged it."

"We have need of a miracle again."

☙

Rand strained to see in the dimness. From the scuffling, the rats had returned. He could snatch scraps of sleep while propped in a sitting position until the rats moved in again. He kicked at the rodents, groaning when the movement jarred his injured shoulder. Hunger crawled in his belly. He'd received no food since being lowered into the dungeon by ropes. How many days had passed since then, he had no idea. If his father failed to remember him, he would die in this wretched place.

His mother was not here, or at least he did not hear a woman's voice among those haunting the dungeon. He hoped his father had released her but suspected she had been imprisoned elsewhere, perhaps in one of the tower cells.

Cold seeped into his bones, making him shiver and aggravating the wounds Urwan had inflicted on him. To ease the pain in his body, he sent his thoughts winging past the walls of stone confining him. In his mind's eye, he walked shaded paths in a wilderness where trees lifted their arms in praise to Lof Yuel, bright birds flitted, and streams ran clear…

Rustling sounds wrenched him from sleep. He jerked awake, already kicking, and drove the tiny fiends away. This time the rodents didn't retreat as far, but remained barely out of range as they watched him.

An image of Mara came to soothe him but also awakened his yearning to live. Did she ever think of him?

He frowned. She might, but with loathing. Memories of her arose before him. He watched her ride through the storm to him, lie down to sleep in meadow grass not far from where he lay, and comb her hair by morning. He smiled. Her lips had softened under his when he'd kissed her at the waterfall, signaling her surrender to passion. He drifted in a tide of longing...

The scritch of tiny claws on stone warned him. He'd fallen sideways, and one of his tormenters snuffled in his hair. The rodent squealed as it hit the wall. Others crept toward him. He booted the vermin more violently than before.

The rats moved away but returned to ring him, staring with glowing eyes. Rand glared back at them, determined to remain awake. "Lof Yuel, help me." He breathed the prayer.

A flame flickered from above as a lanthorn swinging on a rope lowered. The circle of light spread down the walls, and the rats scampered off. Rand raised a hand to shield his eyes and lurched to his feet. He braced against the wall to steady himself in the cramped cell. A rope with a loop at one end fell before him, looking for all the world like a hangman's noose.

"If you still live, come up!" Urwan's gravelly voice called from above. "The Lof Shraen summons you."

Rand wasn't sure he didn't prefer the company of rats to another encounter with the garn, but he caught the rope and put his foot in the loop. It spun him around as he rose, and it was all he could do to hang on. Heat from the lanthorn touched him in passing. The rope carried him a long way up. Rough hands grabbed at him and heaved him over the parapet surrounding the dungeon. He would have lain there like a stunned fish, gasping and blinking in the light of day, but for the booted foot that slammed into his side. "Rise!"

He struggled to his feet, just making out the dark shape that must be Urwan. A hand struck his back, and he pitched forward but caught himself with his hands. The garn hauled him to his feet and hurtled him forward. Rand stumbled onward with a growing sense of dread. Being remembered by his father might be worse than being forgotten.

The golden likeness of Freaer stood in the alcove, exactly as if nothing had happened. No cracks marred the floor, but some of the marble tiles shone more than others. His father would have had replacements quarried at once.

Rand's knife had vanished from the floor where it fell. Had Urwan snatched it up? Or maybe his father had taken it. Should he reveal that the blade held the poison of a grillon? If he did, they might use it on him for sport. While his death seemed inevitable, he'd rather not help it along.

Urwan renewed his shoving, as if to prove he wasn't shirking his duty.

Rand's father, looked up from a platter of crobok legs at a small table.

A chill walked down Rand's spine. Had he been rash enough to hold any lingering hope for mercy, the calculated fury on the face before him would have dispelled it.

His father jumped to his feet. "My son."

Rand had long yearned for this very acknowledgment on his father's lips, but revulsion shuddered through him rather than the joy he'd imagined. He waited in silent resignation for the pronouncement of his doom.

His father circled him. "You interest me. I never thought you'd find the courage to attempt taking my life. Although you were foolish enough to spare it, that may not indicate weakness, but rather lack of experience. I left you too long with your mother, neglecting your training. Well, no longer. You deserve a chance at redemption."

Rand kept his mouth shut. Announcing that he'd be unable to fulfill whatever ghastly assignment his father had in mind could end his life on the spot.

"Urwan will take you to the prison tower, where you will remain during your training."

"Training?"

His father smiled. "I've decided to let Draegmor make a warrior out of you."

15

OUT OF BALANCE

Arillia lifted her head from the pillow as her maid entered carrying an earthen jar. With her copper braid falling across one shoulder and her blue eyes tilted at the corners, Lyneth looked young and fresh. Arillia turned her face to the wall.

"Don't take on so, Lof Raelein," Lyneth said in a gentle voice.

Arillia balled her hands into fists. "I should never have married Elcon."

"Hasty words bring swift regrets."

She fell silent, chastened by her maid.

Liquid splashed. Lyneth wrung out a cloth above a blue wash bowl decorated with white unibeasts "Let me bathe your eyes, milady." She coaxed. "I've made an infusion of yarrow and mullein."

"Very well." Arillia surrendered to her care, sighing when Lyneth placed the rag's coolness against her aching eyelids. If only all her hurts could be as readily soothed. Last night she had braced herself to acknowledge Aewen's child, only to be ignored. The vixen's rejection had come as a shock but also a relief. She could hope to be spared the ordeal again tonight, but sooner or later she'd have to accept the child, may Lof Yuel forgive her the lie. Elcon wanted a dutiful wife, and she must give him one.

Prompted by the maid, she chose a kirtle of plum

velvet, one of Elcon's favorites, and girded her waist with golden links. Lyneth wound her hair into a braided coronet. Arillia frowned at the mirror glass, for it revealed that the jewels in her hair shone brighter than her eyes. She entered the great hall with her stomach in knots. Her husband's gaze clung to hers in a silent plea that made her breathing lurch. Ignoring her desire to be in his arms, she crossed the hall to stand before him with dignity.

Elcon inclined his head to her with a wry smile but also a look of pain. Did he suffer as she did? Satisfaction tingled through her at the thought.

And yet...

She did not really wish to hurt him. He'd denied himself for her sake, ignoring his desire for children and the need of Faeraven for an heir. His daughter turning up alive might be Lof Yuel's provision to them both. Elcon thought so, at least, and she would not stand in his way.

She could summon no answering smile but rested a hand on his arm.

He searched her eyes, his sadness chiding her, and covered her hand with his own. "Come."

He led her up the steps to the dais at the far end of the chamber and seated her in the carved and gilded chair beside his own. The aroma of steaming yellowroot, sausage, and onion soup scented the air as servants carried in trenchers and platters laden with food, the first of many courses. Bread made from flour sifted thrice to remove impurities sat beside a bowl of fresh-churned butter, while smoked perckens with their heads and fins intact emitted a heady aroma. With no appetite, she'd dreaded the thought of eating but now looked forward to the task. She picked up the horn cup before her. It held a pale amber liquid that, when sipped, delivered the mellow sweetness of cider.

Below the dais, guardians of Rivenn lined up at boards on trestles. Flames leaped in three cavernous fireplaces in the outer wall. Musicians struck up a lively melody in the minstrels' galley elevated at the other end of the great hall.

Kai escorted Aewen's daughter through the open doors beneath the main archway. The emerald velvet she wore highlighted her dark beauty, so like her mother's. Cider caught at the back of Arillia's throat, and she swallowed to avoid choking. The maiden carried herself with all the nobility of a daughter of Rivenn, she had to admit.

Kai guided the maiden on his arm to stand below the dais. She curtseyed and her glance touched Arillia's, light as a butterfly, before flitting away.

Elcon rose, and those seated at the tables below the dais stood as well.. "Pray welcome Syl Marinda, Raena of Rivenn, and Lof Raena of Faeraven, the daughter now restored to me." He made the announcement to everyone gathered, but Arillia knew he directed the words to her. The maiden gazing up at her had eyes the green of seawater, like her father's. Arillia's heart pounded at the discovery. Aewen's eyes had been blue.

"Lof Raena Syl Marinda, you may greet Lof Raelein Arillia." Elcon gave them a formal introduction.

With Kai beside her, Elcon's daughter climbed the steps. Fear flickered across her face, and sudden sympathy washed through Arillia in a flood that soothed the dryness of her heart. She had no need of Elcon's urging, but she extended her hand to his daughter.

A look of surprise lit the maiden's face. Hesitantly, she placed a trembling hand in Arillia's. "I'm happy to meet you, Lof Raelein."

Arillia barely caught her whisper, so quietly did she speak. What had this child endured to roughen her hands with calluses? Arillia's conscience smote her. Buried in her own misery, she had spared little thought for anyone else. She smiled and a bitter root deep within withered and died. "Sit here, beside me."

"You honor me." The child had her father's smile, too, and something of his charm.

Arillia's next sip of cider went down more easily.

ॐ

Early light fell across Kai through the high windows in the allerstaed. He bowed his head but could not compose himself for prayer. One memory never left him, that of Shae gazing at him across the chasm of Lohen Keil before walking through the gate of Gilead Riann while, singing her own death song. His throat swelled now, as it had then, with pride and sorrow.

"She once asked me to release her." He rose, his words to Lof Yuel ringing through the silent chamber. "I could not do it then, but it is the only way to gain peace." He pulled in an aching breath. "I release her to you."

A breeze lifted his hair and breathed through his soul. Weeping sounded at the edge of hearing.

"Who's there?" He spun about.

No one lurked behind him. He turned back

toward the prayer rail.

Shae stood before him, glimmering like a wraith, more beautiful than ever. "Kai!" While whispering his name, she vanished.

He reached for her anyway, but his hands passed through thin air. Why had she been crying? He'd had no time to find out. Why had she come to him only to disappear? It made no sense.

Struck anew by his powerlessness to help her, he sank to his knees.

გ

Rand slid across the grass, the taste of blood in his mouth.

Urwan, watching from the path, barked with laughter.

Draeg dug his toe into Rand's side. "Stand and fight!" A string of rude names followed, but Rand had heard them all before. Nothing much had changed except that Draeg now pummeled him by right. "I said, rise, *Misbegotten!*" Draeg kicked him for emphasis, but Rand knew better than to obey. The agility with which he normally defended himself required strength he couldn't summon, not after his ordeal in the dungeon.

Draeg stepped back. "Raise him!"

Urwan jerked Rand to his feet, holding him while Draeg let fly. A fist in the stomach doubled him over. Gritting his teeth, he twisted free before the next blow could land. His legs shook so badly they barely held him. Draeg caught him and drew back a fist. Rand mustered the strength to sidestep. Draeg's surprised face touched off an urge to laugh within Rand. He restrained himself however, knowing he'd pay for the privilege.

Draeg came after him with a roar.

Rand's legs forsook him altogether. He went to his knees, holding up an arm in a vain effort to shield himself. Draeg cuffed the side of his head, and he fell with ears ringing as Draeg pummeled him.

And then, mercifully, the blows stopped.

Rand dragged his eyes open to find Urwan hauling Draeg backward. "Your father wants him alive," he snarled.

"Pity." Draeg flexed his hands. "It would be entertaining to kill him."

"You said you'd show Melric the wrong way to ride a welke," Urwan reminded him.

Draeg barked with laughter. "Is that what's on your mind? Well, yes. There's nothing I like more than teaching a fledgling warrior to ride." He hocked spittle Rand's direction. "Much as I've enjoyed this part of your training, Misbegotten, tomorrow we move on to finer skills. You must learn to take a life without regret." He flashed a wolfish grin and strode off.

Urwan hauled Rand upright by his jerken and propelled him to the tower. The door of the tiny chamber that had become Rand's prison slammed shut behind the garn, and the iron bar that locked him in clanged into its rests. Rand leaned against the scarred strongwood door, aching in every muscle. He ran his thick tongue over his cracked lips, yearning for water with no choice but to wait until and if Urwan brought some.

But he had more to occupy him than the sufferings of his body. Enduring beatings in the name of 'training' paled in comparison to the ordeal he would face on the morrow.

CR

At another time Kai might have savored the sight of dawn light gilding the strongwood trees in the inner garden while early flowers bent their heads under the weight of dew. His mind far from the beauty of nature, he strode the garden paths with purposeful steps.

Elcon sat at the edge of the pool with water falling from the fountain in rainbows behind him. He looked up at Kai's approach.

"Lof Shraen." Kai made his bow. "I saw you from my window."

"Come and sit beside me." Elcon gestured toward the stone ledge of the wall retaining the pool.

Kai perched beside Elcon. "I would ask something of you, Lof Shraen."

"I thought you had an intent expression on your face."

"Let me go in search of Emmerich," Kai burst out.

"A messenger from Graelinn has reported activity on the road to Pilaer. Freaer may move on Torindan any day. You could come across his armies."

"I'm willing to take that risk."

Elcon shook his head. "Don't ask me to face losing you again."

"But I fear for Shae."

Elcon gaze became piercing. "Tell me why."

"I know nothing for certain." As he spoke, Kai spread his hands in a helpless gesture.

"What do you suspect?"

"She may have little time left." His voice sounded

raw. "She came to me in the allerstaed, weeping, but vanished quickly."

"Could it have been…her specter?"

Kai had wondered the same thing, but he trusted his instincts. "Shae lives, I'm certain. She's come to me more than once through the soft places between the worlds."

"Please explain," Elcon prompted him. "Why can't my sister return to Elderland as she left it, through the gate of Gilead Riann?"

Kai pulled in a breath as she passed into the corridor between worlds again in his memory. "Once she went through the gateway, it vanished. I believe she is in peril. Emmerich told me the worlds are out of balance."

"That's an unsettling notion." Elcon dipped a hand in the water, letting it slip through his fingers, then tilted his head toward Kai. "I'm sorry, but I can't let you go."

Kai made a ragged sound in his throat and thrust to his feet.

"Sit down again and let me explain," Elcon said in a patient voice.

Kai had never regretted serving Elcon until now, but he obeyed. "There's Mara to think of, too," Elcon went on. "If Torindan falls, she'll need your escort to Westerland."

"To Westerland? Euryon may not receive her."

"She is his granddaughter, despite all. Perhaps he will accept her for Aewen's sake if not mine. But if he fails in that, take her to the inn at the White Feather. Despite their sins, the innkeeper and his wife would care for her."

Kai could scarce fathom what he had heard.

"Don't you fear they would hide her from you again?"

Elcon gazed up at Talan, riding his wingabeast at the fountain's center. "I'll not abandon my people, even if that means defending Torindan to the death."

"Sacrificing yourself will save no one."

Elcon sighed. "I have no desire to make a martyr of myself, but if I am ever to win the loyalty to unite Faeraven under one ruler again, it will be because I prove myself worthy of their trust."

"You are aware that a dead ruler cannot lead." Kai left it at that, for he knew that particular jut of Elcon's chin too well.

Elcon's lips quirked upward at the corners in a slight smile. "That has occurred to me."

16

WARRIOR IN TRAINING

Mara lingered at her inner chamber window as sunrise blossomed in the sky, purging the deadness of night. In the inner garden, strongwoods bent their heads toward grasses threaded with early flowers. She cracked the window and breathed her fill of the scented air but could not free herself of a sense of dread.

A tap came at her door, followed by the sound of it opening.

Mara turned to find her maid in the doorway. "Traelein, have you ever felt something fearsome was about to happen?"

Her maid arched golden eyebrows. "I'm not sure what you mean."

"It's hard to explain." Mara sought for words. "It's almost as if at the very edge of thought, a venomous snake lies in wait, ready to strike."

"Do not speak so, Lof Raena!" Traelein warned in hushed tones. She stepped into the chamber and closed the door behind her. "You may bring this curse upon us."

"If only my silence would stop this." All at once cold, Mara crossed her arms to warm herself. "I fear nothing will."

Traelein's gaze ran over her. "How come you to know these things?"

Mara shrugged. "T'was but a feeling." One she might better have kept to herself, it seemed.

Traelein shook her head. "The world breeds evil enough, may Lof Yuel save us, without looking for more."

With her maid so distraught, Mara said no more, resolving to carry her burdens alone.

CR

Rand fought to keep his gorge down.

Draeg brandished a headless dove, its wings still fluttering, while the crowd encircling them in Pilaer's outer bailey roared. Draeg tossed the dead bird on a pile of small corpses with muscles still twitching. He pulled a rabbit from a cage by its scruff and held the coney high as it kicked. The crowd had pressed forward more urgently with each new death, and now required three guards to hold them back.

If Rand had entertained any lingering doubts about his inability to become a warrior, his revulsion now laid them to rest. Appalling as this day might be however, Rand could not wish it gone. Today he had only to watch the carnage. Tomorrow he must perform the same atrocities as Draeg or perish at the hands of the mob. From the look of these ruffians, he would suffer if given over to them. The rabbit's scream snapped his attention back to Draeg.

This time he did vomit.

CR

Uneasiness clawed at Elcon, although it had been a long time since he'd battled a welke rider on the gatehouse stairs. Dorann, who had saved his life then, climbed beside him now. During the time of peace that followed, the siege of Torindan had become nothing more than a distant nightmare, one now ready to return. With sorrow weighting his steps, he passed through the light falling across the stairs, and then back into shadow. How many of his people would die this time?

He must seek Emmerich's help at once.

The tracker's boots echoed on the stone stairs along with his own. He'd found Dorann's penchant for silence comforting, for it allowed him to think his own thoughts uninterrupted. A memory of the steward Benisch intruded, and Elcon pushed it away in annoyance. He'd rather forget the distant cousin who had attempted to murder Aewen. Benisch rotted in the dungeons of Torindan and would one day expire there.

They emerged onto the ramparts into sunlight at odds with Elcon's mood.

"Lof Shraen!" Craelin called as he strode toward them.

Elcon smiled in greeting. "The watchguard told me I might find you here."

Craelin bowed to him. "Had you sent for me, I'd have come to you."

Elcon waved a hand. "I didn't want to wait."

Craelin squinted at him. "Does something press your mind?"

Indeed something did. He'd lain awake most of the night thinking of Shae. He'd refused Kai's request to seek out Emmerich, but that didn't mean he meant to do nothing for his sister. "I've decided to send

Dorann in search of Emmerich, but he'll need guardians to protect him."

"With all respect, Lof Shraen, I'm best alone," Dorann said before Craelin could reply,

Elcon swerved a glance sideways to the tracker. "Are you certain?"

Dorann nodded. "If it's all the same to you, keeping others alive in the woods would distract me." He spoke with confidence rather than pride.

"He's right, more's the pity," Craelin confirmed. "Besides, a guardian cannot hope to keep pace with a tracker in the woods."

Elcon still hesitated, loath to send even a tracker unescorted on such an urgent mission. "All right. Go by yourself, but return within ten days or you'll have company."

Dorann gave the hint of a smile.

Craelin laughed. "Don't look so smug. We can find you, if need be."

"I'll do my best to come back sooner," Dorann promised.

Elcon grasped his shoulder. "May Lof Yuel guide and keep you."

"Go on with you, then." Craelin gestured with his head. "Kai can tell you where he last saw Emmerich." He squinted after Dorann. "You've made a good choice in that one, Lof Shraen."

"I've no doubt. I should have sent him when Kai first gave warning."

Craelin's brow furrowed. "I outght to have advised you to do so."

"Can we expect any hope from Torindan's allies?"

"Messengers ride to them. I am certain the loyal shraens will respond to our call."

"And we will find out who those may be. Let me know of any word." Elcon braved the stairway, alone save for the uneasy memories that enveloped him. It always came down to asking for help. No matter how strong the defenses they built, Torindan could not stand alone. Surviving another onslaught from Freaer's armies meant calling upon all the ravens that stood by the alliance of Faeraven. He could admit the truth. That number had shrunk under his rulership. Foisting a Lof Raelein of Elder blood on the divided Kindren ravens had been a grievous error costing many lives, including Aewyn's. Had he given his people time to absorb such a drastic change, they might have come to accept Aewen, despite his breaking faith with Arillia to marry her.

Such realizations had come to him only in hindsight, but once they did, the weight of guilt would have destroyed him had not Emmerich urged him to embrace both Lof Yuel's forgiveness and Arillia's love. But the past still marked him, and with Freaer mounting a new challenge, he and his people would again face the consequences of his rash actions.

ଔ

Rand blinked in the harsh sunlight behind Draeg, who led him into the outer bailey where the sacrifice waited. Guards held back the crowd, preventing the victim from being torn apart. The figure languishing in the sun had been lashed to a pole carved to resemble a welke with its head back and wings spread. The weapon weighting Rand's hand resembled a welke claw and had steel talons honed to a fine edge. His unhappy task was to bloody the victim in order to draw the wretched raptor birds from the sky. As the birds of prey descended, all watchers would retreat to a distance but remain near enough to revel in the victim's shrieking. Rand fought the urge to bolt. The mob would turn on him, and Draeg would still murder the victim. .

He approached the sacrifice with a feeling of unreality and halted with his heart pounding in his throat.

He hadn't expected this.

The pale form sagging against the pole belonged to a female. She'd bowed her head, probably as a protection against the rotting fruit scattered at her feet. Lank hair that had not seen a comb in many a day tangled to her waist. As he neared, she lifted her head. A fist of pain slammed into his stomach. He fought to breathe. The padded end of the claw of death pressed into his hands, so tightly did he grip it.

Mother.

Draeg turned an excited face toward him. "This honor belongs to you, *Misbegotten.*"

Rand stared at Draeg, unable to form words.

A look of cruelty replaced his half-brother's smile. "Come now. The crowd awaits."

"Rand." His mother rasped. She struggled to continue. "You...must do this."

"*No!*"

"Listen to me!" He had never seen her eyes so frightened. "Why should we both perish? Save yourself for my sake, my son."

A whimper escaped him. He would rather die than harm her. How could she expect this of him?

"Fresh kill!" The chanting of the crowd grew

louder the longer he delayed. It seemed he must appease it.

"Do it *now!*" Draeg yelled.

Sobbing, Rand reared back to strike the first blow, the claws weighting his hands. Let them do their work quickly. He brought his arm down, and the claws found their mark. Draeg screamed and went on screaming. He fell to his knees, gripping the shredded side of his face.

The crowd broke past the guards. Someone took hold of Rand, as welkes screeched from the sky, and his mother's shrieking joined Draeg's.

Rand started up in bed, sweat running from him in rivulets.

Another nightmare.

Tears slid from the corners of his eyes, and he wandered a maze of pain.

At some point a soul fluttered against his, soft as a butterfly, Mara reaching to him with the shil shael.

He closed his eyes and reached for her, finding sanity.

She swirled around him, shedding peace, but slipped away too soon. He ached for her to return.

Sickness rushed over him as dawn's rays penetrated the barred windows. Urwan would come for him soon.

17

DREADED DECISION

Mara left her maid in the corridor and peeked into the presence chamber, expecting to find it empty, but her father sat on the larger of the two carved and canopied thrones. Arches framed the throne dais, and above them hung heroic scenes, rendered in paint on canvas with unerring skill. A central chandelier dripping prisms remained unlit while the High King of Faeraven mauled his thoughts in the dimness. From his scowl, they took him down unpleasant paths.

She started backward, hoping to leave him undisturbed.

He lifted his head. "Syl Marinda, what brings you here? Come forward."

She obeyed with slow steps as he leaned against the throne's velvet back.

Traelein, ever tactful, did not follow.

"Father." A hollow echo repeated the word throughout the large chamber. "I'm loath to disturb you."

"Don't worry about that. Your presence comes as welcome." His smile held tenderness but also a touch of sadness. "You stood in the archway from the allerstaed."

"I have come from there. I felt the need to pray."

He sat forward. "Your prayers leave you restless."

"Why should you think that?" A defensive note

slipped into her voice.

He gave her a gentle smile. "The frown on your face betrays you."

"It is only that I slept ill." She told him the truth, but only part of it, and now couldn't meet his eyes. The painting of a sea serpent twining its tail about a sailing ship in one of the heroic scenes caught her attention. She felt as fragile as that vessel, just now. How much could she reveal without being thought strange? Perhaps speaking of evil drew it to her, as Traelein believed. After Mara had repudiated the idea last night, a darksome presence had chased her in nightmares.

She'd woken in darkness, and her thoughts had turned to Rand. He had all at once seemed near. The awareness of him had transported her through time and space to touch his soul. An invisible cord bound her to the Kindren tracker, a tie natural as breathing. She had not recognized it as an enchantment until this morning but had immediately sought the allerstaed to beg deliverance from the High One.

"It's plain that something preys upon your mind."

Her father's voice brought her back to him. She shook her head. "T'is not a matter that can be helped."

"I suppose you yearn for the inn." He gusted a sigh. "You must adjust to Torindan."

"Why must I?" At the look of pain that crossed his face, she longed to take the words back, especially since the answer she suspected terrified her almost as much as the monster in her dream.

"Syl Marinda." He tilted his head as if testing the sound. "Your mother named you snow maiden. Do you know the story of your birth?"

"Kai hinted at it on the journey from Norwood."

She moved closer, drawn by curiosity. "Will you tell it to me?"

"I am told Aewen named you that because your life had its beginning on a snow bank along the wayside." His fingertips pressed his temples. "I'm not proud that my lack of faith in Lof Yuel caused my child to be born alongside the road. Kai took you and your mother to the inn at the White Feather. There she died, while you lived."

Tears pricked her eyes. "My poor mother! Why did she travel so near her time?" Her face warmed at discussing such a delicate subject.

"The fault is mine." He flung himself from the throne to pace. "I tried too hard to protect her. With Torindan under siege, I sent her away, thinking to keep her safe. Had I allowed her to remain with me as she'd wished, she would still live." He stopped before her. "Can you forgive me for taking your mother from you?"

Sympathy washed through her in a warm tide. "You couldn't know she would die. How can I hold anything against you?"

He blinked and looked away, but not before she caught the sheen of tears in his eyes. "Thank you."

"Father?" She waited for him to recover his composure. "Tell me of my mother."

He smiled, but his eyes held sorrow. "You have only to glance in the mirror glass to see her. You are much the same, except for the color of your eyes. Hers were the blue of a summer sky."

"Am I like her?"

"In many ways. She loved simple things, caring nothing for wealth. You are like her in this."

"You see me more clearly than I knew."

"I see you." He smiled and caressed her hair with the lightest of touches. "Your mother cared for the poor and helped the priests give alms. She dedicated her life to doing good."

Mara blinked away tears. "I'm sure I would have loved her."

"As she did you."

"Thank you for saying that."

"It's the truth. Now that you are restored to me, perhaps Aewen can rest in peace."

"Surely my mother does not...walk."

"Only in my memory." He covered her hand. "I will honor you as I failed to honor her. My mind is made up to acknowledge you as my heir."

The breath caught in her throat. "How can you think I want such a promise? You said yourself I am happiest leading a simple life."

He frowned. "You must set aside your wishes and ascend to the high throne of Faeraven for the good of all."

She stared at him. "But you occupy the high throne."

"At present, but that will change, and possibly sooner than later." He went back to pacing. "Time runs out even now. Yesterday a messenger brought the news from Enric of Graelinn that Freaer marches with his armies."

Could that have been the evil she'd sensed? "Who is this Freaer? I like nothing I hear of him."

He glanced at her. "Do you know about the Contender?"

"Not well."

"Ancient prophecy speaks of one who would smite the Kindren with fell powers. Only by sacrifice could this Contender be bound within the viadril burning within Lohen Keil."

"Please! I don't understand what you are talking about."

"I've forgotten you don't know our place names. Lohen Keil is the Well of Light at the rotting heart of Mount Despair. I can tell by your expression you've heard of it."

"Who has not heard of the place where the welkes roost in the east? But I've never heard of a Well of Light or a vi—vi...."

"The flames of virtue rise from a holy fire set by Lof Yuel to cleanse impurity and imprison evil. Our ancestor, Kunrat, gave his life to trap the Contendor within its flames. Peace followed but did not last, for the virtue of the House of Rivenn waned, causing the flames to burn less brightly. The Contender broke free and remained hidden while striving to divide Elderland. He revealed himself at my coronation in an upheaval that nearly cost my life." He shook his head. "I ought to have hunted him down then rather than letting him regain power."

"Can anything be done to stop him?" Mara asked in alarm. "Shae of Whellein sang her own death song at Lohen Keil. She gave another kind of sacrifice that allowed the DawnKing to enter Elderland."

Even as far away as Norwood, Mara had heard of the DawnSinger and of the miracles wrought by her song. She frowned. "But then, why hasn't this DawnKing saved Torindan?"

"Ah, but I have not found it a simple matter to let him."

Mara blinked. "Is he guided by your permission?"

"No, but Emmerich does not intrude."

"*Emmerich*, did you say?"

"Yes, Emmerich. I gather you have met."

"I've never known anyone like him." Mara searched for words. "He startled me at first, but then I hated to part from him, afraid I'd never see him again."

"Oh, Emmerich may be found, but he comes and goes like a wind. I've sent a messenger to seek him. We can hope I haven't left it until too late."

Long after Mara took leave of her father, his words stayed with her. After returning to her chambers, she questioned her maid. "Did you hear what my father said?"

Traelein sniffed. "Milady, I couldn't help but hear."

"Don't worry. I'm not accusing you of eavesdropping." Mara perched on a bench beside the cold hearth. "But, what am I to do? My father making me his heir could be as much a mistake as his marrying my mother. Shouldn't I spare him the shame of naming a half-blood his heir?"

"With all respect, it isn't proper for a maid to advise a Lof Raena on such a matter."

Mara stared at her, dumbstruck. Whatever else Traelein did, she always seemed to be giving her advice. "You will recall that I was first a kitchen maid."

"To be brought from so low a position to one so high—I can't imagine it."

"Have you wondered how you might feel in my place?"

"Lof Raena—"

"Would you not be frightened and lonely?"

"I would be terrified."

"Then you do understand. Tell me, if I needed to leave Torindan, would you help me find a way?"

Traelein stepped backward. "My duty lies with the Lof Shraen."

"And what if that duty called for you to save him grief?"

Traelein bowed her head. "In that case, I would perform it."

ଓଃ

Rand raised his bloody arms in a victor's stance, although he had never felt more defeated. The applause did not reach the same level of enthusiasm as the day before. Having dispatched each small animal with a minimum of suffering and gore, he'd disappointed the crowd and brought a scowl to Draeg's face.

He didn't care.

As he lowered his hands, the mob rushed in and snatched the dead animals at his feet for their cooking pots. His shoulders sagged, and he started toward his prison tower ahead of his guard.

A shove to his back sent him sprawling. He caught himself with his hands, wincing as pain flared in his wrists. He'd prevented himself from crying out, a thing that would prompt cruelty from his half-brother.

Draeg stood over him, nostril's flaring. "Rise!"

He pushed to his feet. Draeg's spittle struck his eyes. "You'll never be a true warrior. Listen to the crowd calling for your blood. I have half a mind to give it to them."

Rand waited in hopeless resignation for his half-brother's decision.

"Father wants you kept alive, or I would." Draeg

shouted to the guards, who advanced with clubs swinging. Blows thudded, and someone screamed. A fight broke out as the mob turned its bloodlust on itself.

Urwan thrust Rand in the direction of the path. He lurched off ahead of the garn while Draeg kept pace.

A final push propelled him into his prison cell. He fetched against the wall and shrank against it like an animal at bay.

Draeg stood in the doorway, a sneer on his face. "Tomorrow you'll bear witness to the execution of a Kindren. After that, you'll wield the claws of death yourself."

Rand did his best to keep his expression neutral, but Draeg gave a soft laugh. "Sleep well, *Misbegotten*." He nodded to Urwan and moved off.

The door slammed shut, and the crossbar scraped into place.

Rand stared at his blood-stained hands with helpless sorrow. With no water to wash them, he could only scrub at them with a strip torn from the rag that passed for bedding. They were raw and stinging before he forced himself to stop. Tears prickled behind his eyes, but he couldn't release them. Beyond the barred window, the aching beauty of Weithan Faen mocked him. He would never explore it again.

The dreary chamber's stone walls bowed away from the window to meet at either end of a wood-and-iron partition with a battered door at its center. Light from the window fell without relief into the chamber, painting stripes across the bed suspended by ropes. The stained tick stuffed with straw that topped the narrow frame offered little comfort but at least elevated him off the filthy floor. A broken stand held a cracked water pitcher that his guard might or might not refill. The tower room laid claim to no other furnishings

He lowered himself onto the cot and closed his eyes to shut out the cobweb-infested ceiling. The aches in his body reproached him, but he needed no reminder of the use he'd put it to. He could still see the wild eyes of the frightened creatures and hear their bones cracking beneath his hands. Strange that after the first couple of deaths, killing became easier.

The thought brought a shudder. He had already lost the scant freedom he'd cherished. Must he also lose his soul?

No! The tick's straw crunched beneath his thrashing head. He should never have killed to entertain the blood lust of others, not even animals marked for the cooking pot. Cooperating had only postponed his fate. He'd never pass the next trial.

That's what he'd told himself yesterday.

℣

Arillia twisted around, ignoring the pain as her hair jerked out of her maid's hands, half-plaited. "Tell me you do not speak the truth!"

Lyneth sent her a startled glance, then bowed her head. "Forgive me, Lof Raelein. I should not have repeated servant's gossip."

"Who told you of Freaer's approach?"

"I beg of you, don't ask me to betray a friend."

Arillia drew a sharp breath but kept her patience. "I promise that whoever you name will not suffer for it. Now tell me."

"Traelein gave me the news. She had it from her mistress. Don't blame her, Lof Raelein. She was too upset to keep such terrible news to herself."

"I can well imagine. Do you know how the Lof Raena knew this?"

"She carried the word from her father."

Arillia hid her reaction behind a mask of composure. "Finish plaiting my hair so that I may join my husband in the hall." She turned her back to her maid.

"Yes, Lof Raelein." Lyneth's surprise was evident from her tone, but she made no comment as she took up the task with gentle fingers.

Arillia allowed no other to braid her hair. Tears gathered in her eyes now that had nothing to do with the tenderness of her scalp. It would seem that Elcon now ignored his wife and confided in his daughter–one more sign of how distant her husband had become. Although he treated her with kindness when they met in public, he'd stopped coming to her chambers. She bit her lip. She'd driven him away, but why had he gone?

19

GUILT AND FORGIVENESS

Mara stared down at the trencher of elk stew with greenings before her, one of her favorite dishes. Its aroma had at first made her mouth water but now turned her stomach. Arillia sat at the table beside her, but with her shoulder turned. Her step-mother had begun to welcome her. Why had her affections changed?

After talking with her father in the presence chamber, Mara had made every effort to fit in at Torindan and with the Lof Raelein. Obviously, she had failed.

What was the use? No matter what she did it could never be enough. She was no lof raena, whatever the Kindren called her. How could she ever hope to become one? She'd been raised to serve, not lead. Her father would simply have to understand why she couldn't accept the scepter of Faeraven.

She stopped pretending to eat altogether.

Arillia kept her father busy talking, but once or twice his glance paused on Mara. She knew enough about the soul touch by now to recognize her father's gentle nudge. Kai, the only other Kindren who semed to really notice her, sat frowning. A pang of sympathy went through her. Whatever his troubles, she wished them more fleeting than her own.

During a lull in the music from the minstrel's

gallery, she murmured her excuses and started toward the dais steps.

"Syl Marinda!" her father called.

Having only just reached the end of the table, she could hardly pretend to be out of earshot. She turned around. "Yes?"

"Stay a little longer, my daughter, and I think you'll be pleased." His hand pressed her step-mother's shoulder. "Wouldn't you agree, Arillia?"

Her step-mother lifted one shoulder in a shrug. "Stay...if you will."

Trapped by the hope written on her father's face, Mara set aside the urge to escape. She returned to her chair, resigned to endure a long evening.

Servants carried away the last remnants of the repast and removed the trestle tables below the dais. In the gallery, one of the minstrels stood forth to sing a lively ballad. Excitement pulsed in the very air, and the crowd lining the edges of the chamber watched the central archway with increasing interest.

Acrobats garbed in bright jerkins and tight leggings ran in on slippered feet. They performed one feat after another. Mara watched in bemusement, never having seen the like. The acrobats piled on top of one another to form a living tower. She held her breath lest any fall. The tower broke apart as they all went tumbling. She gasped with everyone else. The acrobats sprang to their feet and raised joined hands. Laughing, the crowd applauded and called for more. Mara felt her father's gaze on her and returned his smile, grateful that he'd kept her from missing this performance.

Arillia continued to ignore her presence.

Anxious to retreat to her chambers, Mara went

down the side steps leading from the dais and slipped into the crowd.

A group of traveling minstrels marched in to a brisk melody. These minstrels did not play as well as Torindan's minstrels but dressed with more color and brought dancers with veils twirling.

The crowd pressed forward, cutting off Mara's escape route. "Who, pray, is that?" A serving maid was staring at a brawny minstrel beating a timpani.

"What do you want with a son of Ellendia?" A Kindren clad in the green and gold of a guardian of Rivenn asked from beside her.

"He's handsome enough to turn any maiden's heart." The serving maid retorted. "But I've no taste for a half-blood." She turned away with a final, lingering look at the minstrel.

The son of Ellendia had long eyes like a Kindren but the darker hair and sturdier build of an Elder. Mara's own eyes were round enough to be mistaken for those of an Elder, one reason she'd blended in among them. Unlike her, this minstrel could never hide his mixed blood.

Mara stared at the son of Ellendia in fascination, having long ago heard the story of the Elder huntress who fell in love with a Kindren. Ellendia and her Kindren husband Maeric settled in the wilderness of Dyloc Syldra, but not before strife caused by their union divided one of the Kindren kingdoms.

How could her father believe his people would welcome a half-blood Lof Raelein?

CR

"Why have you brought me here?" Arillia's voice quavered. In times past she wouldn't have had to ask her husband why he desired her company. The thought weighted her footsteps as she followed Elcon into his outer chamber. He banged the door shut behind them, the angry sound making her jump. Anders would normally have opened and closed the door, but Elcon must have dismissed him. Arillia folded her arms and waited for her husband's answer.

"Have you really no idea why I would want a word with you?" His nostrils flared as he spoke.

She tossed her head, not caring if her attitude roused further anger in him. "Why should I know anything? I am kept in the dark by my husband." *There.* She had named her grievance. His brow puckered, and satisfaction washed through her. She had drawn first blood in tonight's battle of wills. If, as she suspected, he meant to reproach her for slighting his daughter, she would make certain he knew how he had wronged his wife.

"Arillia, I'm not sure what you mean, but if you have a complaint, pray give it."

"Well, then." She squared her shoulders. "A wife should not have to learn from servants matters her husband confides to his daughter."

His eyes widened. "Have you taken to gossiping with servants now?"

"Don't chide me for a chance discovery."

"And am I to understand you are jealous of Syl Marinda?"

"No!" She waited until her breathing quieted. "Well, perhaps a little."

He turned away, shaking his head. "What is it that you want from me?"

"You no longer seek my chambers or send for me to come to yours." Her face flamed with heat.

He swung back to her in sudden passion, his eyes stormy. "Will you reproach me for that? I grew tired of cooling my heels outside your door."

She shook her head as if the gesture might clear her confusion. Elcon had wronged her, but why did his words make so much sense? She pulled in a painful breath. "What have I done?"

"You have treated your husband like a stranger—no, as worse than a stranger—like an enemy, and now blame his withdrawal on a lack of caring. Can you understand how frustrated that makes me? No matter what I do, I can't make you believe I love you."

She'd never considered that doubting her husband's love could imprison him, but the agony on Elcon's face testified to the truth. He'd said all this before, but somehow she hadn't really heard him until now. "I'm sorry, Elcon, for being the wretched creature you describe." Irony laced her words. He deserved a better apology, but she couldn't muster one. "Still, you should have told me of Torindan's peril before I heard it from servants."

"But I've worked hard to keep the news from you."

Stepping closer, she laid her hand on his arm. "Dearest husband. keeping me in ignorance only makes the truth, when it comes, strike harder."

He covered her hand with his. "I wanted to spare you."

Tendrils of sorrow twined about her, making breathing difficult. "Then you must protect me from heartache by remaining alive."

"Dear, Arillia." The corners of his lips tilted in a

gentle smile. "I will obey your wish if I can. But whether or not I live, I must ensure your safety."

She pulled her hand out of his grasp. "You mean to send me away."

"Only if Torindan seems ready to fall. I've arranged for you and Syl Marinda to escape by the tunnel within the allerstaed."

She had no need to ask if he meant to go with her. The set of his jaw gave her answer enough. "I would rather remain near you."

"That would not be wise. You could be trapped and unable to flee with none to save you. And if Freaer found you...well, I won't let that happen."

She clutched her throat. "Let us hope it will not come to such measures."

He pushed a hand through his hair, a haggard look on his face. "I don't want to send you away at all. That is how I lost Aewen. Torindan survived the battle I tried to protect her from, which became the final irony."

"I have heard this story from you many times, Elcon. If only I could expunge it from your mind, I would."

"My heart is given over to you, Arillia, but memories haunt my thoughts."

"I am selfish enough to want all of you."

"Perhaps, if I confess the shame I bear, I can be free of it."

"What shame?"

"I sent Aewen away to save her, it's true, but also to have her gone." He heaved a breath. "I'm not proud of this, Arillia, but I wanted to return Aewen to her parents to appease the Kindren who stood against her. Forcing a Lof Raelein of Elder blood on my people with no time to accept her was a mistake I'll forever regret."

Compassion tightened her chest. Had she thought more of her husband and less of herself, might he have unburdened himself before this? She pushed the suspicion away. If she let her own guilt overcome her, she'd be useless to help her husband with his. She enfolded him in her arms until his sobs stopped, then drew back a little. "Thank you for telling me, Elcon."

He touched her cheek. "Do you think me horrible?"

"I remember that time of turmoil. You ascended to the high throne so young. It's not surprising that you made mistakes." The realization fostered in Arillia a little more forgiveness for the way Elcon had jilted her. She'd accepted his apology long ago, but her wounds healed slowly. "A husband should not forsake his wife."

"That is not what you did, I am positive."

Elcon's eyes brimmed with sorrow. "She begged to remain with me."

She shook her head. "You had the babe to consider, too."

"And look how events turned out for her."

"Enough." She put a finger to his lips. "Your decision might as easily have saved them both."

"Thank you." He looked at her in a way that reminded her of the Elcon who had captured her heart in his youth. His gaze traveled over her face and settled hungrily on her mouth. He lowered his head, and she tilted her face to accept his kiss. His lips caressed hers in a gentle embrace. He cradled her against him, and for a time she heard only the beat of his heart. The warmth of his gaze touched her, sparking an answering heat within her. She parted her lips in invitation. Crushing her to him in swift abandon, he explored her mouth with his own. She melted into him, lost in waves of desire.

They broke apart, panting, and Arillia touched her blazing cheeks.

"As I recall, wife, you wanted proof of my love." Elcon caught one of her hands and nibbled her fingertips, his eyes gleaming with mischief. "I am only too happy to give it."

She opened her mouth to reply, but his kiss swallowed her words, and as he swung her into his arms, she forgot them entirely.

ᙅᙡ

Rand had never witnessed so brutal a murder. He swayed on his feet while Draeg pranced before his kill and the mob roared approval. The carved welke extended its wings with its head back as if crowing in victory. Lashed to the sacrificial pole, the victim thrashed in the final throws of death.

Rand ran a hand over his sweating brow. The events of the day clung to his mind in such vivid detail he might never shake free of their horror. He'd not thought his half-brother a monster until now.

Draeg let out a war cry, an uncanny ululation that, when taken up by the mob, raised the hair on the back of Rand's neck. The crowd surged forward. A guard went down, screaming, while the others broke and ran. The mob lifted Draeg, cheering as he waved the bloodied claws of death. They picked up Rand, too, and passed him from hand to hand. From this vantage point, he could see far too well, for the crowd descended on the body with knives. The victim's flesh would fill pots and roast on spits tonight.

Rand retched, a painful event since he had no food and little water in his stomach. A sensation of unreality crept over him, but he pulled his mind back. Now, more than ever, he needed his wits about him. Tomorrow, he would choose between life and death.

20

NIGHTMARE

Mara woke. Sweat bathed her brow. Her breaths rasped, loud in the night. Fear twined about her like a sea dragon's tail around a sailing ship. The bad dream had been so real it gripped her yet. She summoned the courage to sit up. Clasping her knees, she huddled in the darkness.

A tap came at the door. "Lof Raena?" Traelein sounded comforting and normal.

"Come in!" Mara's pulled aside the bed hangings with a shaking hand.

Traelein burst into the chamber wearing a linen shift, her hair bound in long plaits on either side of her head,. Her face swam strangely in and out of the flickering light of the candle she held. "You cried out, Lof Raena. Are you unwell?"

Mara hugged her knees. "'Twas a nightmare."

Taelein shrank back. "It's the evil you summoned, seeking you out."

She should never have confided in her maid. "The exertion of last's night entertainment brought it on, more likely. The traveling bards made me think of distant shores and the sea."

"Did you visit such places in your sleep?"

"I did." Mara offered no details that might foster superstitions in her servant's active imagination. How strange to dream of riding a ship upon the waves when she'd only ever glimpsed the sea from a wingabeast's back. Of course, the painting of the dragon and the ship in the presence chamber had played into her nightmare.

Traelein gave a delicate shudder. "Did you chance upon sea dragons or finfolk?"

"I've not heard of finfolk before." Mara avoided a direct answer.

"May you never be taken by a finman and carried away to the hidden isles, Lof Raena." Traelein glanced about, as if finfolk might lurk in the shadows. "I'll watch over you."

"Thank you, but you may return to your bed."

"I'll be glad of its comfort, although slumber will not return this night." With this dark pronouncement, Traelein withdrew.

Mara lay down again, but slumber remained as hidden from her as the finfolk's isles.

The possibility of being carried off by a finman did not frighten her more than the dangers of the coming siege. Would Freaer's armies hurt Rand if they discovered him on the road? Propelled by the disquieting thought, she reached for him with her mind. Such thick shadows covered his soul that she almost didn't find him.

She gasped. The stench of death clung to him. Fighting the urge to pull away, she encircled him instead. She could not endure long and let go with tears gathering.

He barely seemed alive.

○శ

Mara's touch drove away the smothering darkness and stirred memories for Rand–the morning sun breaking over the faen, his mother's rare laughter, the curve of Mara's cheek. When her touch faded, the night seemed blacker than before but new life stirred within him.

The sliver of sky at the window lightened. He found little joy in the sight, for it marked the beginning of the day he would die.

The crossbar grated, and the door scraped open. Urwan waited in the entrance, a silent angel of doom. Rand walked before him to the outer bailey. The whistle of a whip sliced the air behind him and lashed his ankle, searing his skin. The thong tugged backward, and he fell on the stone path.

"Not that way, *Misbegotten*! Father summons you."

Rand rolled over to face his tormenter. Draeg, in a blood red surcoat emblazoned with a rampant golden dragon, gathered the whip he had used.

Behind him, Urwan spread his thick lips in a malicious smile.

Hiding his surprise, Rand skirted around Draeg. The hair on the back of his neck bristled, but his half-brother let him go by unmolested. Rand turned his steps toward his father's chambers. He didn't look back, but from the sound of footsteps behind him, both Draeg and his guard followed.

The golden statues of Freaer and Rivenn contemplated one another across the corridor outside his father's chambers. Urwan rapped at the carved and gilded door.

A warrior dressed like Draeg in assassin's red, opened it to reveal his father, garbed in robes of scarlet and ermine, lounging in his high-backed throne.

The warrior stepped aside while Draeg swept into the chamber. Urwan shoved Rand after his half-brother.

Draeg bowed to his father, but Rand held back.

"Bow to your Lof Shraen!" Draeg's voice and the whip snapped out at the same time.

Rand fell to his knees, strangling as the leather thong cut off his wind. Blackness pressed in on him, but it loosened, and he clawed free.

Draeg marked him with a glittering glance, and then gave his attention to his father. "I have delivered the prisoner at your bidding, Lof Shraen."

A cold gaze flicked over Rand. "Rise."

Gagging and grasping his throat, he stumbled to his feet.

His father pushed out of his chair and circled him.

Rand glared at him.

His father laughed. "There's a dangerous light in his eyes not present before. I'd not turn my back on him now. I'm pleased, Draegmor. Here stands a fledgling warrior in place of the coward I gave you. I'll warrant you've trained him without mercy." His voice held a wry note.

Draeg smirked. "I'm always glad to do my duty."

"I have no doubt of that. On this final day of Rand's warrior training, I've decided to grant him a special contest."

Rand hid his surprise and dismay. Draeg twitched but did not otherwise betray any emotion. A special contest, being a fight to the death with a heavier opponent, would ensure Rand became a member of the assassins with a rank equal to his half-brother's—if he survived. It was all he had once wanted, but now he swallowed a sour taste at the prospect.

His father smiled. "You will fight to the death against Urwan."

ೞ

Arillia's sigh stirred the hair at her husband's temple as he slept beside her in his bed.

His eyelids twitched.

She smiled and pressed a kiss to the corner of his mouth.

He turned and pulled her into his warmth.

She went willingly, rejoicing in his love. If only he didn't have to leave her to discuss Torindan's defenses with Craelin and Weilton. The intrusion of war chilled her, and she returned to her chambers for a warm bath. Afterwards, dressed in scarlet wool, she summoned Elcon's daughter.

Lyneth opened the door when Mara and her maid arrived. The wary look on her step-daughter's face pierced Arillia to the heart. Without doubt, she had placed it there.

"Lof Raelein." Mara curtsied. "You summoned me?"

Arillia gestured to the chairs grouped around the marble hearth "Pray, sit down."

Mara cast an anxious glance at her before settling into one of the chairs.

"You may leave us." Arillia dismissed the two maids and seated herself across from her step-daughter. "I treated you ill last night. Can you forgive me?"

Mara's eyes, so like her father's, widened. "I—yes, of course."

"Thank you." Arillia released her breath.

"Lof Raelein…" Mara bit her lip. "My coming to Torindan hasn't been easy for you."

"I'll admit that your resemblance to your mother came as a shock."

"Your reaction was only natural."

Arillia examined her hands, folded in her lap, but then looked into Mara's eyes, green like her father's. "I hope we can begin anew."

Mara smiled. "I'd like that, Lof Raelein."

"Call me Arillia."

CR

Rand's mouth went dry. Blood pounded in his ears. Sweat beaded his forehead. He'd kept company with the idea of his own death for a long time, but as a thing walking beside him, not staring him in the face as now. Urwan, twice his size and half again as tall, strutted with scarce-constrained eagerness across the outer bailey. Guards at the edges of the roped-off area held back the jockeying crowd, the better to watch the carnage to come.

Rand's father occupied an elaborately carved chair elevated on a dais beside the fighting area. His hair shone in the sun, giving him an angelic appearance. Beside him, Draeg leaned forward as if eager for the fight to begin. A fleeting sadness touched Rand for this brother who had never been a brother. He'd once idolized Dreag and longed for his approval, but that sentiment stirred him no more. Now their only ties were forged by hate.

Clad in heavy armor, Urwan raised a giant shield

and massive sword. His roar prickled the skin on Rand's arms.

The crowd raised an answering howl.

Rand lifted his own shield and the slender sword that, although made of steel, would prove a paltry weapon against the garn. Beneath a surcoat in the blue and gold of the garrison, he wore chain mail that would not stand up against Urwan's blade. Narrowing his eyes, he sized up his opponent. He'd never match a garn for brawn, but the agility his brother had unknowingly taught him while growing up might serve him now.

He probably wouldn't escape this contest with his life. However, if he could win today, he would do it for Mara, who had comforted him in the darkness of his soul, and for his mother, who shouldn't have to die. He no longer cared to become a guardian of Pilaer or fight his father's battles. How ironic that his father's approval mattered less than nothing to him anymore. A surge of panic stole Rand's breath. He resisted its pull. Draeg's attacks had taught him nothing if not clarity under stress.

Urwan sounded off again, playing to the crowd.

Gritting his teeth, Rand charged.

Urwan raised his sword and swerved to face Rand on his right side.

Rand dashed in to jab Urwan's hand where it gripped the shield boss. Metal pinged as his sword tip met Urwan's hand guard.

Urwan bellowed and his shield struck the ground. The impact must have bruised his hand. His face went red.

Rand leaped away in time to avoid being sliced in two.

Before Urwan could recover his balance, Rand rolled toward him and hooked his feet.

Urwan went down with his armor clanking.

Rand caught up Urwan's shield and tossed it outside the fighting area. A squabble broke out over the fallen shield. The crowd cheered and hissed at the combatants. Rand snapped his attention back to his opponent.

Urwan was regaining his feet. He glared at Rand, his face contorted with rage not unlike Draeg's when bested. The garn unleashed a battle cry that the crowd took up.

Rand held himself steady.

Urwan charged.

At the last possible instant, Rand sprang to the right.

The garn followed.

Darting left, Rand struck at his opponent's unguarded side, but he had no time to aim the blow. It fell short. Already the garn faced him. Their swords clashed, sparking.

Rand bit back a cry as his shoulder took the impact. He'd never last against such strength, but he couldn't seem to break away. Urwan drove him backwards. The rope pressed into his back. The mob crowed. Harnds reached for him across the roped aisle. Fear leant Rand a burst of energy, and he sidestepped away from the edge. The tip of Urwan's blade sliced his shoulder, and sticky warmth oozed down his arm. He ground his teeth against the pain and moved out of reach. Sweat stung his eyes, and he shook his head with droplets spattering. Stepping on his shield, he brought its edge up to his hand. He shifted to escape another thrust of the broad sword.

Urwan pursued, closing in with fury, his ugly face contorted in an inhuman grin. Their swords clashed and caught in a test of strength until, with a bellow, the garn flung him backwards.

Rand slammed to the ground, losing both sword and shield, but rolled in time to miss being impaled by Urwan's blade. He took up his sword in a desperate rush.

With a mocking smile, Urwan held up Rand's shield. It looked pathetically small before the garn. Urwan tossed the shield outside the fighting area, and another brawl erupted. The garn lifted his blade into the air and gave a war whoop, much to the crowd's delight.

Acting on instinct, Rand dashed beneath Urwan's raised arm, and embedded his sword beneath the garn's arm pit.

Urwan screamed as blood spurted. His sword plummeted downward.

Rand was already vaulting away, but the flat of the falling blade slammed his arm. His sword spun out of his hand, and he scrambled to retrieve it. The garn bent to pick up his fallen blade. They straightened together.

Rand's head spun, and he heaved a breath, trying to steady himself.

The garn lunged.

21

VICTORY AND DEFEAT

Mara emerged from a tunnel of strongwood branches into the golden heart of the inner garden. She traipsed the dewy paths carrying a lute with a purpose that involved Kai. He sat gazing at the falling water in the fountain pool with such intensity she thought he hadn't noticed her.

"Good morning, Mara," he spoke without turning his head.

"Traelein tells me you play the lute." She glanced at her maid, waiting at the edge of the garden.

Kai's eyes had shone almost silver while he watched the water but now darkened. "Once."

"Will you again?" She held the instrument out to him.He accepted the lute but made no move to strum it. "I've lost the desire."

"But I want you to teach me." The words came out in a rush, and she looked away with heat blooming in her cheeks. Her outburst had been selfish and brazen. "If you will," she added to make amends.

He lifted an eyebrow. "Why do you want to learn?"

She wanted to survive on her own, like the son of Ellendia who traveled as a minstrel, but she wouldn't give her hopes away. "Must every wish have a reason?"

"A fool trusts another who answers with a

question." He chided her with a smile.

Her lips curved in response. "Would you use an ancient saying against me?"

"Oh, so you know it?"

"The Elder are not strangers to Kindren expressions. But won't you give me a song? I've soaked these ridiculous slippers in the grass to beg for one."

"I've an idea you'll haunt me lest I do." He softened the sharp words with a smile. Frowning, he bent his head to tune the instrument while his fingers plucked the lute strings.

She perched at the edge of the pool to wait, a pleasant task with a mist dancing above the water and the fragrance of new roses scenting the air.

Kai lifted his head. "What will you have?"

"Something inspiring."

A frown marred his brow, but then it cleared. "Perhaps you will find that quality in my tribute to Maeven of Braeth, your father's mother."

"Tell me of her."

"She ruled Faeraven alone after her husband, Lof Shraen Timraen, was killed. You remind me of her at times." Music rippled from his fingers on the strings. He gazed into the distance, as if seeing more than the garden before him, and sang.

"Once upon a morning
Rode a maid most fair
On a prancing palfrey
Golden light upon her hair,
Oh, milady of beauty and grace.
"In the middle of day,
She took for her own
A noble bridegroom

And arose to the high throne.
Oh milady of beauty and grace.
"Came then the gloaming,
When light forsakes the sky,
And a deceitful heart
Trades truth for a lie.
Oh milady of beauty and grace.
"In the marches of night
Find comfort and peace
In your bridegroom's arms
As mortal cares cease,
Oh milady of beauty and grace."

The last strains faded into silence. Kai set the lute aside. "I haven't the heart for more."

Nor had she the will to press him further. "Then I must content myself with the music you have given.."

"I'll try and play again for you another day."

He wanted to be alone, and she should let him, but sympathy held her fast. "The maiden you mentioned to Emmerich -- who is she?"

He gave her his silence, the reply she deserved for such a personal question.

"I'm sorry," she stammered with quick regret. "I shouldn't have asked."

He nodded toward the bronzed statue above the fountain. "Have you heard how Talan conquered his wingabeast?"

"I know parts of the tale."

"Long before he became Lof Shraen of Faeraven, Talan was a wild youth who pursued the wingabeasts into the Maegrad Paessad—the impenetrable mountains in the north of Whellein."

She nodded. Everyone knew about the haven the wild wingabeasts returned to after their midnight flights. "He must have been determined."

"Talan was Rivenn's son." He seemed to think that explained the matter, and perhaps it did. "From his early days, Talan dreamed of riding one of the wingabeasts he saw flying across the sky. No one thought it possible, but Talan proved it could be done, nearly losing his life in the process." He stood. "Her name is Shae."

She stared at him, at a loss, but then understanding dawned on her. "If I may ask, what happened to her?"

"Have you heard of the DawnSinger?"

"Who has not? Her song carried on the wind, bringing healings throughout Elderland."

"Shae sang the mael lido, the death song meant to provide safe passage for the dead from this world into the next."

"And this is what makes you sad?" Her face heated with the realization that she'd asked another private question. Kai didn't seem to mind, fortunately."She sang her own death song." He tossed a fallen leaf in the pool and watched as the currents spun it.

"Did she...die, then?"

His eyes took on a faraway look. "She dwells in the corridor between worlds. By trading places with Emmerich, she made a way for him to enter Elderland."

"Can she return?"

He focused on her once more. "Have you heard of Gilead Riann?"

"Only as a place of myth."

"The Gate of Life is very real, although it is not always found. After Shae went through the gateway, it vanished." His voice caught on his last words. "I'm not sure of her safety."

"Can nothing be done for her?"

"Only Emmerich can answer that."

Everything came back to Emmerich. "Will you ask his help?"

"The Lof Shraen has sent a skilled tracker in search of Emmerich. I must satisfy myself with that."

"But surely—"

He held up a hand. "Elcon has need of me here, and I will not break faith with my liege lord."

"Do you never wish for the freedom to make your own choices?"

"Your youth speaks through you, Mara." He smiled, but with sad eyes. "Yes. I have yearned for such freedom. I am surrendered to duty, however."

A browning scuttled by beneath the water, its fin breaking the surface. The fish rolled and dived. Kai's leaf vessels rocked in its wake. Mara would normally smile at such a sight, but now she scowled. "The more I learn of duty, the less I like it. Why should it direct our lives?"

He smiled. "We no longer speak of my affairs, I think."

She lifted a shoulder. "As Elcon's daughter, I must keep my duty, or so I am told."

"Does that surprise you?"

"I can name no one less suited to become heir to a kingdom."

"Do you think so little of yourself?"

His inquiry gave her pause, but she shook her head. "I see myself clearly. I know little of social grace, and nothing at all of ruling."

"These can be learned by the willing."

"There is that to consider as well. Surely I may have some say in my own life."

Kai laughed. "Spoken like a true daughter of Rivenn."

CR

Rand's knees trembled but thankfully held. He tightened his grip on his sword to keep it from wavering. Betraying any sign of weakness would bring a swift attack from his opponent.

Urwan snarled at him from across the fighting area. One arm hung useless and blood coursed down his side. He had to be weakening, but a single stroke from his blade might still do its evil work. Urwan showed jagged teeth that could rend flesh and barreled toward him, limping on the foot Rand had attacked.

Energy shuddered through Rand at the sight, freeing him from lethargy.

Urwan charged, gaining speed. Rand vaulted sideways, but the garn spun toward him, the great sword whipping the air.

Rand yielded, all the while deflecting blows.

Urwan pressed his advantage.

With no way of escape, Rand backed to the ropes.

Hands grabbed at him. The mob must have broken through the barrier. Lurching sideways to shake them off, he narrowly missed the tip of Urwan's sword. He rebuked the blow, but the impact jarred his arm into his shoulder. His sword flew, end over end, and landed between the ropes. The crowd thundered its approval, and angry shouts broke out from those brawling over his sword.

With his weapon lost to him, only one chance remained. He dropped and rolled. Hooking his boots around the garn's injured foot, he yanked with all his might. Urwan went down but somehow kept his weapon. Before the garn could regain his feet, Rand leaped up and stomped his sword hand.

Urwan released the blade with a bellow.

The breath rasped in Rand's throat. Sweat stung his eyes. He hoisted the mighty sword and held the point to his opponent's throat.

The garn's eyes widened in sudden recognition of death.

The sword pierced flesh as the heat of battle carried Rand through.

The garn spasmed and died.

The mob hissed and cheered.

With the world swinging, Rand raised the bloodied sword above his head. His arms shook from the strain as if palsied, and he fought the urge to heave. His father would proclaim him a warrior at last, but this victory tasted like defeat.

૱

Cold water hit Rand's face, wrenching him from sleep. "Arise, champion!" Draeg's friend, Lutz, held a dripping wooden bucket above him.

Rand pushed to his hands and knees. *Why had he made the floor his bed?*

Memory slammed back. He'd keeled over before reaching his cot and must have fallen asleep on the floor. But why was it night when it should be morning? He staggered to his feet, wincing as he jarred his shoulder, and glared at Lutz. "Why did you do that?"

"I was told to give you a bath." The guard guffawed.

Rand glared at him as water ran in rivulets down his neck. With his strength restored and a weapon in his hands, he'd run this tormenter through. His thoughts brought him up short. When had he become vicious?

The bucket thunked to the floor, and Lutz sketched a mocking bow. The tunic, surcoat, and leggings that he held in the crook of his arm swept the filthy puddle on the floor. He thrust the sullied garments at Rand. "You're to make yourself presentable, *champion*."

Rand accepted the garb with his good arm. "I'll need to remove this armor, and require water for drinking and washing—also a cloth to dry myself. Douse me again, and I'll see you punished. I suggest you remember that as a member of the elite forces I outrank you."

Staring at him as if he'd sprouted a second head, Lutz backed toward the doorway. "I'll fetch water from the well," he murmured and fled.

Rand smiled to himself. He'd made a start at regaining his freedom. Whether by intent or neglect, the guard had left the door unbarred. Rand chaffed to leave the cell but stayed put until the guard returned. A short while later, he strolled into the great hall of Pilaer, in appearance a conquering champion.

Torches burned at intervals, sending grotesque shadows crawling up the whitewashed walls and making the figures in tapestries jump. A bruin and several elks turned on spits in the massive fireplaces in the hall's outer wall. Between them, arched windows gave onto the tangled greenery of a long-abandoned garden and glimpses of the outer curtain wall. A rowdy tune started up in the minstrel's gallery along the inner wall.

His father, seated at table at the end of the chamber, looked up from gnawing a roasted kaeroc leg and beckoned him forward. Rand climbed the steps to the dais elevating his father's table. "My son, you have proven yourself today." His father swept his arm in a gesture of invitation. "Sit beside me and partake of the celebration feast."

Rand had no appetite, but he seated himself at the table in a carved chair cushioned in red velvet. On his father's other side, Draeg applied himself to a joint of elk.

Rand lifted the cup of mulled cider a servant set before him and drank with thirst, then signaled for a refill.

Freaer raised his own cup. "I wish to reward you for an excellent showing in battle. Name your desire."

Rand all but choked on his cider. "My mother's freedom." The words jerked from him.

His father frowned. "That is not possible. You must ask something else. Would you have gold? Or perchance a comely maiden has taken your eye."

"If you will not free my mother, at least let me visit her."

"Very well, but first you must prove yourself." His father turned away to address Draeg. "As your reward, you may accompany Rand on his assignment."

Dismay, quickly masked, crossed Draeg's face.

Rand swallowed his own disappointment. Even if he could not yet free his mother, he had hoped to comfort her. He broke off a portion of roasted fowl from the platter before him. He must eat. He'd need strength for whatever new test his father devised. He would have preferred to slip away from the feast early, but guardians of Pilaer rose from their tables to proclaim toast after toast in tribute to his prowess. Or so they said. It proved a drinking game that ended in bawdy choruses with the object of their 'admiration' forgotten.

Servants had long since removed the remnants of the repast, but ale still flowed. The fires burned low even as the noise level rose. Surely no one would miss him if he made his escape. He had no taste for the debauchery to come. He levered to his feet.

His father caught his arm. "Must you leave? The daughters of Amora are about to dance for your pleasure."

Mother had not protected him from much, but she *had* taught him to avoid the tender mercies of the daughters of Amora. More than one Kindren had found himself in the dungeon after being driven by drink and lust into acts he could not afterwards recall. "Forgive me, but I am weary."

His father released his arm. "Go then, if you must. I will send for you in the morning."

Rand retreated from the chamber, walking a little taller after realizing no guard followed him. He skirted the outer bailey to avoid the sward where he'd fought Urwan. He passed beneath an archway and paused on the drawbridge to the inner bailey, breathing in the freshness of salt-tinged air. Water diverted from the faen rippled like black silk beneath him. The tide, covering the ugliness of the mud flats, lapped against the shore, tempting as a seductress.

Perhaps he should escape into the faen, forget his identity, and never return. Why should he stay? Believing he could redeem his mother was probably foolhardy anyway. Even if he managed to find her, she might resist rescue.

The night wind chilled his face. He turned his back on the faen and set off. How long ago it seemed since he had occupied the bed in his chamber. He let himself in at the door and swung about to latch it quickly behind him. Across the corridor, his mother's chamber door stared at him.

No. He would not allow himself to be swayed from his purpose. As long as a chance remained of saving his mother, he had to try.

22

Freedom and Imprisonment

Across from Rand at the strongwood table in Pilaer's war room, Draeg slouched in his chair, obviously suffering the effects of last night's debauchery.

At the table's head, their father rubbed his hands along the arm rests of a high-backed chair carved in the shape of a gryphon with furled wings. Light tumbling into the chamber through high windows turned his hair gold but also revealed the redness of his eyes. "My armies are ready to march on Torindan, and when they do, Elcon will try to send his wife and daughter to safety through the escape tunnels." He pinned Rand with his gaze. "You will assassinate them there."

"You want me to kill them both?" Rand couldn't help the note of horror that crept into his voice.

Draeg snickered.

A line formed between their father's brows. "I blame your mother for this softness. Mark my words, Rand. Fail in this duty, and she will pay the price alongside you. Do you understand?"

"Yes." The 'duty' expected of him had become even more onerous, but no good would come of pointing that out.

"Good." His father narrowed his eyes, as if reading something he didn't like in Rand's face. "Draegmor will ensure you complete your assignment."

Draeg sat straight in his chair, his startled expression making it clear that, whatever assignment he had expected had not been this.

"That's not necessary." Rand spoke past a constriction in his throat.

His father's smile didn't reach his eyes. "Oh, but I insist."

"I will do my best." Rand inclined his head, the very model of submission. He kept to himself what doing his best meant when he no longer served his father.

"You will do more than that if you wish your mother to live," his father snapped. He glared at Rand as if privy to his innermost thoughts.

Uneasiness walked over Rand, and he hid himself more deeply, lest the shil shael betray him. "And if I succeed?"

His father quaffed from his drinking horn and wiped his mouth with the back of his hand. "I will allow you to decide her fate."

Rand gnawed his lip, unable to reply. His father named the very thing for which he'd yearned since he'd understood his mother's sorrow. He would have smuggled her out of Pilaer long ago had she allowed him the liberty. With the choice removed from her, he could help her with his father's blessing. The only problem with the plan was that it came at the cost of Mara's, and now her father's, life.

"I would speak with the Lof Shraen." A voice announced from the doorway.

"Olaeg, why do you disturb me?" Father demanded.

"Forgive this intrusion, I beg." The captain of the

guard entered, followed by four guardians of Pilaer escorting a prisoner. "I thought you should know that we've captured a prisoner—a warrior from Torindan." The guards stepped back, their swords pointing toward a Kindren garbed in the green and gold of Rivenn. He stood tall, walked with quiet dignity, and scanned the room with piercing light eyes.

"*Bow* before the Lof Shraen!" Olaeg barked out.

"I will not honor this pretender but only to the true Lof Shraen of Faeraven." The prisoner's nostrils flared as he made his declaration.

Olaeg and the guard behind the prisoner exchanged glances. The guard reared back. Flesh pounded flesh. The prisoner fell to his knees, groaning and clasping his side.

Olaeg grinned. "That's better. Rise and I'll slit your throat."

The prisoner lifted his head in a defiant gesture that sent light spinning through his streaked brown hair. He made no attempt to rise, however. Rand could understand. A prisoner had to choose his battles.

Rand's father gestured the guards back and inspected the prisoner. "I remember you from Torindan. You were once a humble tracker, as I recall. You are...Eathnor. Don't bother to deny your identity. Your face gives you away. Now state your mission."

His father's cunning showed plainly to Rand, for as far as he could tell, the prisoner had not given any reaction.

"I will not." The prisoner spoke the words without flinching.

Olaeg looked again to the guard who had struck him.

Rand's father slashed his hand in a cutting gesture,

and moved closer to the prisoner while the guard eased backward. "You have courage, I'll grant you that. You defy me while I control your life...or decide your death. Beating you would not bring so much as a whisper of your errand. How disappointing for you that I already guess it. You have been sent to rally the shraens foolish enough to pledge their loyalty to Elcon. Oleg, confine him in the tower, but don't mistreat him."

The guards closed around the prisoner and herded him away.

"He won't tell you anything." Draeg pointed out in a bored voice.

"From what I recall of him, he would die first and leave me none the wiser. No. Another use for him suggests itself, one that will help us lay claim to Torindan."

℣

Elcon paced before the hearth in his meeting chamber. Never before had he disliked Dorann's penchant for silence, but the tracker seemed slow to divulge his news. To be fair, he had only just arrived. "Tell me, did you find Emmerich?"

Dorann gave a swift nod. "That I did."

"Where did you find him? No, tell me first what he said."

"About Torindan or regarding Kai's question?"

Elcon restrained his impatience. "I want both answers, but start with Torindan."

"You are to ask King Euryon for aid."

"Euryon? What do I want with Euryon when

Emmerich has only to whisper and armies flee?"

Dorann shrugged. "He did not explain himself."

"That sounds like Emmerich. But I'll ask him myself. Where is he?"

"In the Vale of Shadows."

"The Vale of Shadows!" Elcon made an effort to lower his voice. "You went to that fearsome place?"

"It was there I found him."

"Did he not return with you?"

"He'll not come."

"*What?*" Elcon could hardly credit his hearing. "Does he understand the urgency?"

"I explained it to him, but he told me he fights a different battle."

Elcon halted his pacing before Dorann. "What does he mean by that?"

Dorann met his glare with a calm expression. "I don't know."

"What good is a savior who will not come when bid?"

"Lof Shraen, might it..." Dorann ducked his head, and a red lock tumbled onto his forehead. "Never mind."

"Speak your thought."

"I only wondered if he might come if you ask rather than, well–"

Understanding dawned. "Are you trying to tell me to stop ordering Emmerich around?"

Dorann's face turned red. "Well—"

"You are right, I fear. I didn't realize. But come, tell me how he answered Kai's question."

"Emmerich would only say that he has come to put the worlds right."

"And what of Shae?"

Dorann's forehead creased. "Believe me when I say that I beseeched him on her behalf, but he told me nothing about her."

"Nothing?"

"Only that she gave herself willingly and remains by choice."

Elcon frowned. "I wanted a better answer."

"Emmerich instructs us to entrust her to Lof Yuel's keeping." Dorann's tawny eyes darkened to amber. "That's difficult to do, sight unseen."

Elcon paced to the hearth and gripped the mantle. "Faith often clothes the unseen." He turned back to Dorann. "Meanwhile, we must ensure a home awaits her. I mislike sending you back into the Vale of Shadows, but it seems I neglected to *ask* Emmerich to come to Torindan."

"I will return. Would you have me also carry a message to Euryon, King of Westerland?"

"I'm not convinced he will help us. He never has before."

"Begging your pardon, Lof Shraen, but it seems wrong to reject Emmerich's advice because you don't like it."

A rap on the outer door spared Elcon from making a reply. Recognizing the voice in his outer chamber, Elcon flung open his meeting room door. "Craelin, we're in here."

The first guardian entered the meeting room and made a hasty bow. "Lof Shraen, I bear the sad news that Eathnor—"At sight of Dorann, he broke off and sent an uncertain glance to Elcon.

Dorann rose to his feet. "What's happened to my brother?"

"Go on, Craelin. You can't leave Dorann

wondering."

"He's been taken by Freaer's guards."

"How did this happen?" Elcon snapped out the words as Dorann protested.

"Four of them surrounded him while he slept in the smallwood of Muer Syldra at the edge of Graelinn's grasslands." Lines of strain settled around Craelin's eyes. "If Weilton hadn't woken early and gone to water the wingabeasts among the weilo trees, he might have been taken, too. He tracked them, looking for a chance to free Eathnor, but with such an urgent message to deliver, he could spare little time."

"What will they do with him?" Dorann asked.

Craelin shook his head. "I wish I knew."

"Lof Shraen, I need to leave." Dorann sketched a hurried bow.

"Wait." Elcon halted the tracker with his voice. "Where are you going?"

Dorann looked back with his hand on the door latch. "To find my brother."

"No."

Even with Dorann's back turned, Elcon could see his flinch. "I remind you that you've just given your word to carry my request to Emmerich."

The tracker spun to face him. "Can't someone else go in my stead?" His glance flicked to Kai.

"No one else knows the wild lands as you do." Never before had Elcon so vehemently hated the demands of rulership, but Torindan's needs had to come before ties of blood.

CS

Pilaer rose above the drowned lands like some fierce beast of prey, ready to spring on an unsuspecting victim. Rand blinked and the image dispelled, leaving in its place a ruin haunted by shadows of nothing.

The guard, Lutz, rode ahead of him, leading the prisoner's horse. Bound to the saddle, Eathnor stared straight ahead, displaying little emotion. They had left him strong enough to carry the false information he and Draeg would feed him.

Draeg rode ahead without turning his head, keeping his own company. Rand agreed with his half-brother on this point. He'd rather Draeg kept to himself.

Their horse's hooves clattered across a rotting bridge just above the place where Weithen Faen met Maer Syldra. The southern sea was little more than a huge bay that separated lands in the north of Elderland from the wilder south. Rand squinted past the shifting waters to the curve of distant shore marking the edge of Triboan, stronghold of Elderland's garns. The foul creatures were contained in the north by the sea, faen, and canyons and in the west by the efforts of the Kindren.

The early sun warmed Rand's face as they followed the beaten road, little more than a path, cutting toward the canyonlands through the salt grass at the edge of the faen. Although narrow, the road's holes had been patched, the loose stones removed, and the collapsed portions rebuilt. Even the worst of the undergrowth that had once clawed at those reckless enough to attempt passage had been cut back. The restoration had taken time and labor, but now the garrison and elite forces could cross the faen in swiftness.

They stopped for the night in a meadow where the waters of Weild Aenor tumbled from the mouth of the canyonlands and frothed into the sea. Rand rode to the bank and let Taelant lip water as he gazed at the mesmerizing flow, thankful Draeg had called a halt to their journey for the day. Tomorrow would be soon enough to cross deep water without a bridge.

"Stop lolling about and water my horse." Draeg's snarl roused Rand. "And after you finish, gather firewood. Mind you are quick or I'll thrash you."

Rand pulled on the reins but met resistance. With his own horse still thirsting, he could not comply with Draeg's demand at once. He turned with a sinking feeling to say as much.

With bound hands, Eathnor led Draeg's dark brown horse to the bank of the weild. Lutz trailed him much as he had Rand during his captivity at Pilaer. Eathnor looked up, and their gazes touched.

Draeg had found another scapegoat, at least for now. Rand had no doubt that his half-brother would turn on him with little provocation, though. His bonds didn't show like Eathnor's, but he was as much a prisoner.

23

TREASON AND LOYALTY

Wind snagged in the tree tops above Kai, setting the leaves sighing. Light and shadow shifted on the path, giving the illusion that he walked underwater. Spending time in the inner garden comforted him. How strange to think war would soon destroy it's peace.

He reached the pool, startling a flock of wingens into flight. The birds bunched and separated, forming patterns in the air. Kai sat on the pool wall and carressed the strings of his lute. Music brought him joy but also sorrow. He played anyway, his fingers wandering the strings in a spontaneous melody that captured the mystery of a garden at shadowfall. As Maeven's quaint term for twilight sprang to mind, he smiled. He pictured Maeven as she'd looked when arriving at Torindan to marry Timraen. She'd been a beautiful maiden with red-gold hair glinting in the sun. Pledging himself to her service when he became a guardian of Rivenn had been no hardship. After her death, he could have shaken off the yoke of servitude and stand in for his older brother as heir to Whellein. That would have pleased his parents. Despite the proof his father had shown him, he still could not think of Daeven as dead. He'd wanted to investigate his brother's disappearance for himself. Bowing his knee to Elcon after Maiven's death had cost him the chance, but he would not take back the choice.

His fingers stilled on the strings as his thoughts returned to Shae. If she ever returned, he would look for the freedom to devote his days to her happiness.

The sound of footsteps snapped his mind to attention.

Garbed in the jerken, leggings, and boots of a tracker, Dorann strode along the path from the keep. "Elcon remains firm in his decision to keep me from my brother, even in the face of my mother's pleas." Anger throbbed in his voice.

Kai frowned. "I'm sorry."

"Yes, well. Everyone is sorry but no one *does* anything. Elcon forbids me to try, and for what? I'll tell you what. To salve his conscience."

Kai had never heard the tracker string together so many words at once. "Careful what you say about Elcon."

"Of course." Dorann's gaze drilled into him. "I should have remembered you are his guardian."

"I meant that you will regret hasty words spoken in temper. Come, now. Do you think I know nothing of what you feel?"

"What can you know of it? *Your* brother isn't suffering or dead."

"That's where you are wrong."

Dorann stared at him. "What do you mean?"

"My older brother probably suffered."

"What happened to him?"

"Daeven yearned to see something of the world before settling down to the responsibilities of Whellein's heir. The ship he boarded wrecked along Muer Maeread. His body was never recovered."

Dorann's brow creased. "The Coast of Bones

earned its name, I've heard, from the wreckers, those savage souls who lure ships with false lights onto the rocks nearest shore in order to loot them."

"That was the sad fate of the Kestrel, my brother's ship."

After a silence, Dorann cleared his throat. "Sorry for what I said."

"Forgiven." Kai gave a nod. "I didn't mean to shame you, only to let you know I understand something of what you feel."

"What am I to do?" Dorann seated himself beside Kai. "The Lof Shraen holds me to my promise to carry another message to Emmerich."

"I thought Emmerich might return with you."

"He does not come or go on demand."

"I...see." Elcon could exhibit his father's impatience. "Well, you must carry out the Lof Shraen's wishes, even when they counter your own."

The cords in Dorann's neck stood out. "Abandoning my brother goes against the grain. And for what? Emmerich may still refuse to come."

"Still, you must try. If Torindan falls, your mother and father could suffer, and many others might die."

"I need no reminder of that." Dorann glanced away, but not before Kai glimpsed the sheen of tears in his eyes. The tracker gusted a sigh. "I will go to Emmerich."

Kai hesitated to intrude into Dorann's grief, but he had questions of his own. "What did Emmerich say about Shae?"

"Only that we must leave her fate to Lof Yuel."

"I had hoped he knew of some way to help her."

"As did I." Dorann's clipped words served as a reminder that he, too, loved Shae.

With an effort, Kai pushed away his disappointment. "We must trust Lof Yuel and obey duty. That's all that remains to us." If only it didn't hurt so much.

CR

Rand started awake, blinded by darkness, mute from shock. A fell creature probed the edges of his mind, wheedling, coaxing.*Lof Yuel, save me.*

Turning his mind to the quiet place within had always blocked Draeg's soul touch. It hid him now from his father's.

The cold dread that had weighted him slid away and his sight returned. He could make out patches of moonlight and the effervescent surface of the weild, The moonlight glinted in a nearby pair of eyes.

Rand's heart thudded against his chest.

The eyes blinked and chains clanked. The dark shape of Eathnor turned away.

Rand let out his breath on a sigh. That he'd woken a tracker should come as no surprise. He settled down again, but the weild churned loud in the night, preventing a return to slumber. Starlight burned into his eyes, and the moon lit the clouds it rode like a ship in troubled seas.

Morning arrived none too soon, and he dragged out of his bedroll to rummage in his pack for food.

Draeg rolled from his bedding and went down to the weild. Lutz trailed a few steps in the same direction but did not follow.

Rand chewed a strip of jerked elk, noticing that the tracker watched him with hungry eyes. Had anyone fed the prisoner last night? On impulse, he held out a strip to the tracker.

Eathnor needed no other encouragement but clutched the jerky between his bound hands and sank his teeth into it at once.

Lutz started back, but after giving Rand the perplexed look he'd adopted ever since their confrontation in the tower chamber, he made no comment about his act of mercy.

"Thank you." Eathnor spoke with his mouth crammed full. His voice sounded rusty, as if he'd not used it in a long while.

Rand nodded in reply. He uncorked his elkskin water bag and offered it as well. Eathnor gulped the water down with such greed Rand wondered how long it had been since he'd had anything to drink. He hadn't paid attention while they traveled. Knowing firsthand what a prisoner of Pilaer suffered, from now on he would look after this one. He searched for a scrap of comfort to offer the tracker. "You will be home soon."

"Only if Elcon agrees to trade Benisch for me." Eathnor's light eyes gazed into the distance then snapped back to Rand. "If he refuses, what will become of me?"

"For what it's worth, I doubt Elcon will refuse a chance for your return." He and Draeg had persuaded Eathnor he would be exchanged for a distant cousin rotting in Torindan's dungeon. The wretch had remained imprisoned throughout the span of Rand's life, a thought that made him shudder after his experience in Pilaer's dungeon. "A sad fate, to die in such a place with no one caring."

"Ah, but Benisch put himself there by trying to murder Lof Raelein Aewen while she was with child."

"He tried to kill Mara in her mother's womb?"

"Freaer urged him to it, as Benisch told us. We got that much sense from him. He fancied a share in the rulership of Faeraven."

Rand could scarcely fathom Benisch's naivety to believe his father would have allowed him a share of power.

Eathnor's eyes pierced his. "You speak of Mara as someone you know."

The time had arrived for truth. He leaned toward the tracker. "Listen well. Lutz is out of earshot but only for so long, and there's little time before Draeg returns. Trading you for Benisch is a ruse. The battle plans Draeg and I will let you overhear are false. Don't believe them.Forces allied to Freaer will not approach solely from the north. We will allow you to escape and carry the lies we feed you to Elcon. "

Eathnor's eyes narrowed. "Why tell me this?"

"Stop staring at me like that or you'll give us away." Rand twisted the toe of his boot into the dirt at his feet, trying to look as if engaged in idle chatter. "Pilaer's forces will skirt the desert to reach Torindan, with a flank attack striking from the south and west."

"Why should I trust you?"

Rand hesitated, but then spoke the simple truth. "Because I love Mara more than life."

"You are Mara's love?"

He shook his head with regret. "She thinks little of me, but I still mean to save her."

"And just how do you plan to accomplish this feat?"

Rand kept an eye on Lutz, already walking back. "I'll help Elcon defeat Freaer, but first I need to escape from Draeg."

"That part's easy. Set me free, and I'll help you vanish into the canyons."

Rand eyed the tracker. "Your words come too readily."

Eathnor's light-eyed gaze didn't waver. "You ask for trust but don't give it yourself."

Lutz's proximity spared Rand from replying. "Quiet, now. The guard is near, and I'd as soon not have my throat slit for treason."

∞

Kai stepped past the maid at the door and into Mara's outer chamber.

From a chair beside the window, Mara rose to greet him. "What's wrong?"

"Must something be amiss for me to visit you?" He held up his lute. "You asked me to teach you to play."

"Yes, but I hardly thought you would."

A smile tugged at his lips. "I'm sorry if my reply was...less than gracious. Your request surprised me, but I'd be delighted to teach you."

She inclined her head with a formality he'd never seen her display. "Thank you."

He gave her the lute and immediately had to squelch the urge to laugh. "You must hold your instrument like the friend it is. Don't treat it like a stranger ready to rob you in your sleep. Here now, curve your fingers so the tips rest against the strings. That's it!"

Mara stumbled through the lesson with tortured persistence. Kai kept his patience but the tap at the door that interrupted them came as something of a relief. Traelein admitted Anders, who acknowledged Mara with a cursory nod before turning to Kai. Frown lines grooved his face. "Forgive me for interrupting, Kai, but the Lof Shraen has need of you."

Kai bowed to Mara. "I'm sorry to cut your first lesson short."

"It's all right," she assured him. "I can practice what you've shown me. I hope the matter Father summons you on is not grave."

"I join my hope to yours." He bowed to her.

In the Lof Shraen's outer chamber, Elcon sat in a carved chair at the edge of a mat woven with silver unibeasts dancing in a strange contrast to the Elcon's serious expression. Before Kai could finish sketching a bow, he had vaulted out of his chair. "Dorann's wingabeast has returned without him, clawed by some forest creature."

Kai sucked in a breath. He had expected news of Freaer's approach, or a meeting with Craelin, perhaps to learn that Elcon wanted his company—but not this. An image of Dorann as he'd last seen him, defiant but willingly humbled, flashed in his memory. "Surely he can not be dead."

Elcon paced to the window and looked out for a time without speaking. "I blame myself. He didn't want to go, but I sent him back into the Vale of Shadows." He faced Kai. "He seemed so tough, as if nothing could ever break him. I let myself believe nothing would."

"If anyone can enter the Vale of Shadows alone and live, it is Dorann. Whatever mishap has caused his wingabeast harm may not have touched him." Kai didn't believe the words he spoke. Why should Elcon?

"I hope you are right. Meanwhile, I can only assume there's a message still to deliver to Emmerich."

Kai didn't hesitate. "Send me."

"We settled this before, or so I thought. I'll not rob Mara of your protection, although I hope not to call upon it."

"I'd return with all haste."

"No, I tell you. I've made up my mind. I'd rather seek Emmerich myself."

Kai reined in his frustration. "That would not be wise."

"Even with a company of guards to protect me?"

"You might all perish."

"I'll take that risk."

"Just how far will you go to redeem your guilt?"

"You speak too plainly." Elcon rapped out the words.

Kai fought for composure. "Forgive me, Lof Shraen, but sacrificing yourself will not save Dorann."

"Your words wound, Kai, but I'll admit they also hold merit."

Kai had never suspected Elcon of understanding his own failing. He went on in a gentler tone. "Perhaps you should give this more thought. I can think of a Kindren who would seek Dorann with all his heart."

"Name him."

"Craelin had to restrain Jost from going to Pilaer to rescue one of his sons, an act that would surely have brought his death. I suspect he will readily go after the other."

"How do you know he hasn't started after Eathnor regardless?"

"Craelin confined him in the guardhouse for his safety."

Elcon subsided into his chair. "It seems I must yield to a father's love for his child."

24

FREEDOM AND SERVICE

Rand could barely make out the outline of Draeg's horse, just ahead, as mist rose from the ground like wraiths from their graves. He could see nothing of Lutz and Eathnor, who brought up the rear. The mist eddied ever more slowly until it thickened, muffling the roar of water in the place where Weild Aenor and Weild Rivenn met. Going on held risks, but he made no protest. Spending the night in the haunted meadow of Paiad Burien appealed less.

Tales of the battle site known as the field of blood had circulated at Pilaer since he could remember. Here garns had ambushed the last Shraen of Braeth, who had died alongside the flower of his fighting forces, including his only son and heir. Betrayed from within, the stronghold of Braeth fell in a day, and none had the heart to rebuild it. Specters were said to haunt both the ruined hold and the ancient battleground. He'd banished the shadows of Pilaer with strength of mind and courage, but he'd rather not face Paiad Burien by night.

Storm clouds had gathered all day, and now utter darkness descended with the rain. Even when Lutz rode ahead holding a lanthorn with flames that guttered, their pace slowed to a crawl. Rand urged Taelant forward into the dim light that tunneled around Draeg. Rand glanced behind to Eathnor. Draeg had tied the reins of the tracker's horse to Rand's saddle, a fact that made him attentive. Tethered as they were, if either horse fell from the path into the raging waters, the other would follow.

A sudden outcry came from Lutz. The lanthorn light swung in a wild arc and extinguished. Lutz's screams mingled with his horse's shrieking. Both sounds ceased abruptly.

Fear crawled over Rand's skin. "What happened?"

"Can't you imagine?" Draeg snapped. "Lutz has gone for a swim. I never liked him much, anyway."

Rand shuddered. He had wished Lutz ill more than once but never by such a horrible fate. "We should turn back."

"And make our beds with the specters?" The panic edging Draeg's voice brought the memory of his widened eyes and flaring nostrils while he fled the shadows of Pilaer in their early days.

"Would you rather join Lutz in a watery grave?" Rand kept his voice level.

"Nonsense, *Misbegotten*." Lightning arched across the sodden sky, throwing Draeg's smirking face into relief. "I have every faith in you."

Rand blinked rain out of his eyes. "What do you mean?"

"You must lead the way now. Light another lanthorn."

Rand raised his voice to be heard above a clap of thunder. "Have you considered that if I take the ride in front with the prisoner's horse tied to mine you will bring up the rear yourself?" Somehow, he couldn't imagine Draeg doing that. "I doubt a lanthorn will light in this downpour, regardless."

"You'll not persuade me to go back, no matter

what you say," Draeg said in a shrill voice.

Rand called upon the same tone he'd used to calm Draeg after an encounter with the shadows of Pilaer. "I don't want to turn around either, but this far from Paiad Burien, we can safely wait out the storm."

"All right, then, but you go first."

Rand dismounted in another flash of lightning, more comfortable guiding them off the path by testing the ground on foot. The sky lit up again, revealing boulders and rain-flattened grasses huddled against the canyon wall. "This way!" He turned to call. Thunder shook the ground.

Draeg had already dismounted and now forged ahead with more speed than caution.

Drawing the dagger he'd used during his fight with Urwen, Rand severed the ropes tying Eathnor to the animal. The sky flared again, and he slipped his blade between the tracker's wrists and cut the cord that bound them. Eathnor's startled face looked down into his, and then darkness swallowed them.

Rain lashed Rand's face. Thunder boomed. The horses stamped and snorted. Holding their reins, he ran beside Eathnor toward the canyon wall. It bent outward overhead, but offered little shelter as the rain drove sideways. Rand crouched, hunching over in an instinctive posture to wait out the wretched night. Hunched over in a sea of thunder and rain, darkness and light, he lost all sense of time.

The rain eased at last, but the wind still buffeted him. Draeg sat against the canyon wall with his head bowed, either fast asleep or too miserable to watch his reluctant companions.

"Come with me." Eathnor breathed near Rand's ear.

He repressed a start.

Draeg muttered and stirred but did not wake.

Rand hesitated, his heartbeat loud in his ears. All the times his half-brother had mocked him, beaten him, and maligned his mother ran through his mind. He saw again her tear-stained face, and then an image of the murdered youth hanging from the sacrificial pole. His jaw tensed, and his fingers gripped the hilt of his dagger.

He could kill Draeg with the flick of his blade. A sick feeling shot through him. He shook so violently that he nearly dropped his dagger. His shoulders slumped. Draeg deserved to die, but not by a brother's hand.

A horse nickered and hooves stamped. Rand sprang into action and soon rode his horse away from Draeg behind Eathnor's onto the path, now gleaming blue in the moonlight. Mist hung like a low cloud above the roaring weild. Overhead, a gibbous moon floated on wispy rafts.

He spared a pang for Draeg, sleeping alone and unguarded, but hardened his resolve. . Draeg had more than earned any consequences, should they come his way. He needed to rid himself of the hope that his half-brother could ever be different. It sapped his resolve. He knew the truth. Draeg would torment them without mercy if he tracked them down.

૭૨

Footsteps echoed through the allerstaed, and Elcon looked up from kneeling at the prayer rail.

"I'm sorry to disturb you, Lof Shraen," Kai said.

"Graelinn sends an urgent message."

Elcon rose to his feet. "Freaer's forces will have begun to move. Has another guardian gone to Emmerich?"

"Dithmar has, but it will be days before his return."

"And so, whether Torindan stands or falls becomes a matter of timing." He stood and looked about the chamber. "I've stayed away from the allerstaed far too long. *Why* must I wait for trouble to drive me to it?"

"It seems a common failing. Did you pray for Torindan?"

"Yes, and for Faeraven, but I came for a more selfish reason—to seek my own peace."

"And have you found it?"

His gaze flicked away from Kai's. "Perhaps I don't deserve peace."

"Does anyone? And yet, Lof Yuel may smile upon us yet."

Elcon tilted his head as he considered Kai's words. "I've always admired your faith. It makes my own disbelief stand out."

Kai laughed. "I'm not convinced you are as doubtful as you wish to seem."

"How well you know me. I should say instead that believing sometimes asks more than I care to give."

He started for the strongwood doors beneath the central archway at the rear of the allerstaed, and Kai kept pace. "Surrendering your will is the challenge. I have struggled with that myself of late."

"It becomes a wearisome business."

"Yet faith rewards the devoted."

"I'm glad of that. I have an idea I'll need to call

upon what remains of mine soon."

☙

Mara thrust the lute away from her and ran a hand over the knotted muscles at the nape of her neck. Her fingers ached from strumming, plucking, and pressing the strings, and her mind wearied of remembering the finger positions Kai had shown her. She sighed. Learning to play an instrument demanded a lot from a person. Tomorrow would be soon enough to try again.

She stood up from the bench before the fireplace in her outer chamber and stretched her arms upward. The kinks in her back eased. She'd wanted to play the lute to find a way to live after she left Torindan, but now the urge to create music drove her as well. Where that came from, she didn't know. She'd always sang when going about her duties at the inn. Others had remarked on her voice, but she'd never thought herself musical.

From her tall window, she looked over the inner garden. The day had dressed itself in golds and greens and the aching blue of a rain-washed sky. The storm that had woken her early had passed, leaving behind fresh puddles already drying in the wind. While gazing upon such serenity, she found it hard to believe death could be marching toward Torindan. On a not-so-distant day smoke would foul the air and the screams of the dying replace the harmonies of birds. This people and the war they fought did not belong to her. Why should she remain and risk death?

Mara's mouth went dry at the thought. She should leave now, while there was still time to escape. Traelein would help her escape Torindan. She closed her eyes until the panic that gripped her eased.

How could she leave her father when she was beginning to love him? Arillia had softened to the point where Mara almost dared hope for true acceptance. Neither of them could take Mam and Da's place in her heart, but they occupied one of their own.

She belonged at Torindan with more certainty than she ever had anywhere before, and it was finally beginning to feel like home. If only it could survive a siege, she could go on building a new life within its walls.

Maybe she shouldn't run away to become a bard, after all.

A knock interrupted her musings, followed by soft footfalls. Her outer chamber door swung inward, and Traelein curtsied with delicate grace.

Arillia graced the doorway, part of her hair coiled in plaits around her head and the rest flowing down her back beyond her knees. A delicate wingabeast wrought of gold, its wings spread like fans and its hooves shod with diamonds, rested in one of her hands.

"Lof Raelein." Mara curtsied also. "You honor me. Pray come in. Can I offer you a seat?"

Arillia shook her head. "I can't stay long, but I thought you might like this ornament to wear in your hair."

"Thank you. It's finer than anything I've ever owned."

"Jewels should bedeck a lof raena as lovely as you. We must make certain of it. It is only a matter of time before admirers vie for your favor and bards sing ballads in your honor."

Mara's smile faltered.

Arillia frowned. "What troubles you?"

"I'm sorry to disagree, but my future may not hold jewels and admirers and ballads."

Arillia sank onto a bench beside one of the windows and patted the cushion beside her. "Come and let us speak plainly."

"All right." Mara joined Arillia.

The Lof Raelein's gray eyes fixed on her. "I am told you know of the siege."

Mara clasped her hands in her lap, warning herself not to fidget. "Father told me of it, and now I can think of little else. What if Torindan falls?"

Arillia's hand settled over hers, its warmth soothing. "We must not let fear rule us."

She bowed her head. "I have nothing to put in its place."

"Where is your courage? If we lose heart, Freaer will already have won."

Rand dreaded to think what would happen if Draeg found them. Eathnor had lit Rand's lanthorn, a difficult feat in the dampness for anyone but a tracker Taking turns lighting the way, they had traveled without ceasing, although mud under the horse's hooves made progress slow. When the wind and sun at last dried the path, leaving only puddles, Rand urged Taelant to a greater speed. But weariness dogged him, and he fought to keep his eyes open, jerking upright in time to save a fall from the saddle.

Eathnor seemed unaffected, so Rand made no protest throughout the long hours.

Late in the day, shadows lengthened and mists drifted down the canyon walls. Rand reined in his horse and followed Eathnor off the path to search for a place to rest along the banks of Weild Aenor.

"Here!" Eathnor called back to him.

Rand caught up to him in a place where boulders dotted stony banks.

Rand slid from Taelant's back while Eathnor dismounted. After watering their horses, Rand pulled several packets of elk jerky from his saddlebag. He tossed one to Eathnor, and the tracker caught it with deft skill. Rand sat beside him on a boulder and untied the coarse cord from a bundle of jerky wrapped in kaba leaves.

Eathnor glanced sideways. "Thank you for feeding me yesterday morning. It meant a lot."

Rand gave a nod. "I've known hunger." He tore into the jerky. They ate in silence while the horses cropped the grasses along the bank and a breeze brought the scent of water.

Eathnor stood and stretched. "The boulders will shelter us from view this night, but we should take turns sleeping, all the same."

"We can't delay long. Draeg will stop at nothing to find us."

"I gathered as much." Eathnor propped a booted foot on the boulder and clasped his knee. "He is your brother?"

"Of a sort. We are born of different mothers but the same wretched father."

"But wait. Freaer is your father?"

"That is my misfortune." Rand acknowledged the bitter truth.

"Name your mother."

"Chaeldra of Merboth."

"Chaeldra!" Shock showed on Eathnor's face. "We thought her dead."

"I've not seen her since her imprisonment, but as far as I know, she lives, at least after a manner of speaking. But how do you know of her?"

"Are you certain you want my answer? It isn't pretty."

"She has spoken many times of past regrets. Tell me or I will imagine far worse."

"I doubt you can. I'm glad she feels remorse. She should, for having poisoned Lof Raelein Maeven."

Rand sucked in a painful breath. "Are you certain?"

"Yes."

"No wonder she refused to leave Pilaer. She had nowhere to go." Sorrow ached through him. He would no longer call the Kindren who had tormented her by the name of father. "Even when Freaer rejected her, she remained with him."

Eathnor plucked a blade of grass from a bunch at his feet and nibbled the end. The rushing of water mingled with the thud of stones turning in the weild's bed. Eathnor cast the blade away. "Did you grow up at Pilaer, then?"

"I did."

Eathnor gave a low whistle, and the horses raised their heads to stare at him with liquid eyes. "I don't envy you. I've experience of the wraiths of Pilaer. They run at you, but when you strike at them, multiply."

The wraiths of Pilaer had become the least of Rand's worries. "In my early days, I learned that if I didn't strike at them, they'd go away. They couldn't hurt me unless I let them."

"You were wise as a child."

"I survived. But tell me something." Rand settled again on the boulder. "Now that you know I'm the son of Chaeldra and Freaer, why should you trust me?"

"That's a question I'm asking myself, and no mistake." Eathnor gazed into the frothing waters. "I can't explain it, except to say that I sense nothing to fear from you."

The dying screams of the innocent creatures whose lives he had ended and Urwan's final gargling gasp echoed in his memory. What did Eathnor know of him? For that matter, what did he? "I hope I may honor your faith in me." The words sounded stilted, insincere.

The tracker's eyes narrowed. "I expect more than hope, just so you know."

CR

Elcon tossed a pebble into the pool, rippling the pattern created by the falling water. That had been his life—flowing ever the wrong way, pushing against the current, seldom at rest. He'd ascended to the high throne of Faeraven far too young. What did an untried youth know of rulership?

His father had done everything right. At a young age, he had led the Kindren to victory against the garns of Triboan in the Last Battle of Pilaer, pleased his people by choosing Maeven of Braeth as his Lof Raelein, and established the high hold at Torindan.

Why had the father succeeded while the son failed? He tilted his face toward the pewter sky, as if to find an answer written there.

Here in the quiet before dark fell he could admit the truth. When his mother had bequeathed Sword Rivenn to him, she had said he would make his own history. That had been true, but not in the way she'd meant. Would he forever be known as the Lof Shraen who had destroyed Faeraven?

No. He would not let a lie consume him, not this time. Freaer sought to destroy Faeraven, not him.

A whistling cry split the air. A white ghost hovered on gossamer wings above the garden. Its ungainly flight and long tail feathers marked the creature as a kaeroc. He caught his breath at its beauty, transfixed until the rare bird disappeared beyond the trees.

If only Mara had seen it with him. How much they had missed together. Might they capture something of what had been denied them? And would Aewen's memory release him now that he'd made good on his promise to find their child?

He hadn't, really. Mara had found him. He'd taken the innkeeper's word that his child lay in the grave with her nurse. Whoever's infant that had been, if an infant indeed lay buried there, it had not been his. He hadn't needed to see the star sapphire band, one of Aewen's cherished possessions, Mara had offered as proof of her claim. Her resemblance to her mother spoke the truth.

"Lof Shraen."

Elcon started and fought to gather his scattered wits.

Kai straightened from his bow with a smile. "Forgive me. I caught you much in thought. Should I go away again and leave you to them?"

"Don't do that." Elcon waved a hand, inviting Kai

to sit beside him. "Your company soothes me."

Kai's mouth quirked into a faint smile.. "I don't know why since I have so little peace myself. How odd that your mother said the same."

"Mother said much more of you, praising your faithful service, and I count myself fortunate to have you at my side again. I hope you will bend your knee to Lof Raelein Syl Marinda in my place."

Kai frowned. "Why speak of this now?"

"My mind is made up. I will pass the Scepter of Faeraven and the Sword of Rivenn to Mara before Freaer's forces reach Torindan."

"You plan to lead the guardians into battle."

Elcon tossed another stone into the pool. "If I survive, I will remain Lof Shraen of Faeraven. But if I die, Mara will have an irrefutable claim. In that event, you must take her to safety and help her ascend to the high throne of Faeraven. There is every reason to acknowledge her as my heir."

"Except Mara's wishes."

"It is the burden of rulership to choose the good of your people over your own will. Mara is aware of that and will accept her duty."

"That is my understanding, too. However, I'm not certain she will do so readily."

"I will give her as much time as I can."

Elcon didn't need to say what they both knew, that little time remained.

25

DEATH AND VICTORY

Rand blew steadily until the tinder smoked and caught, then eased back in the soft grass to wait for his fire to take hold. The wind that ever followed the river breathed through the stand of keirkens behind him. With the afternoon sun on his shoulders, flitlings chirping in the trees, and the horses cropping soft grasses, he could almost believe he dwelt in a gentle world.

At the top of the small hillock above the river bank, Eathnor, stripped to the waist and with his leather leggings tied above the knee, stomped toward him. The tracker carried a mess of fish strung on a line. "We'll eat hearty this night and have plenty to dry, as well."

Rand drew his dagger and set about gutting the perckens. "I wish we didn't have to risk sending up smoke." Tonight, he'd burn the entrails and bones to hide any sign of their feast. Tomorrow he'd scatter the ashes and stones ringing their fire.

Eathnor picked up a fallen branch. "We've traveled days with no sign of Draeg. Might he have turned back?"

Rand considered the possibility, but ended by shaking his head. "I know him too well to delude myself he would." He helped Eathnor tie the perckens along the branch.

"We may well have outpaced him."

"Let us hope for that."

Their task completed, they set the pole with fish dangling on tripods made from lashed branches with whittled ends pushed into the soft ground.

Hands on hips, Eathnor surveyed their handiwork. "Either way, we have little choice but to stop. Your rations were not meant to feed two, and we can't continue to drive the horses without mercy."

"You're right, of course, but I'll not rest easy until we reach Torindan." Rand did not miss the irony of his words.. The last place he'd expected to find rest was the stronghold of his father's enemy.

Eathnor crouched and poked the fire with a stick, making it crackle as sparks flew. He glanced up, his light eyes piercing. "I'll speak for you when we do, but I can't promise you'll escape the dungeon."

"Thank you, and that's a risk I'll take." Rand sat on a boulder and broke off a wand of grass to twirl in his fingers. "What else can I do? By escaping with you, I've branded myself a traitor to my father's cause. That's a title I embrace but one that bans my return to Pilaer. Perhaps I can reveal enough of my father's forces and weaponry to give Torindan an advantage. That is, if Elcon believes what I say. I can think of no reason he should."

"Perhaps you deliver yourself to your father's enemy for another reason as well." Eathnor leaned back on his hands and watched the fire as it flared and smoked with dripping fish oils. "I once loved as deeply."

"What happened?"

He shrugged. "Her family welcomed my advances until I became a guardian of Rivenn. After that, they rejected me. They wanted a tracker who could put meat on the table, not a soldier who might leave her widowed with children to feed."

"How did she feel?"

"She wept in my arms but allowed her father to decide the matter." Eathnor stood and flung the stick away. "He gave her to another in marriage."

"I'm sorry."

Eathnor perched on the boulder beside Rand. "If I had it to decide again, even knowing how it would turn out, I'd still choose to become a guardian. It sounds hard, but I can only walk the path before me, not that of another."

Rand narrowed his eyes, blurring the frond he twirled. "We have something more in common, it seems."

༄

The cushioned chair by the fire in her father's meeting room dwarfed Mara. She twisted her hands in her lap and looked away from her father. "You ask too much! How can you expect me to surrender my future to a people I barely know?" The frankness of her words made her face heat, but she wouldn't call them back.

"You must look beyond yourself to duty." Her father drummed his fingers on the armrest of his chair, but then sat back against its cushions. "I want all of Faeraven to know my choice of heir. Accept the Scepter of Faeraven and the Sword of Rivenn to preserve the alliance of Faeraven and, should I fall in battle, none could contest your claim."

"Don't wish such a fate upon yourself." Mara

frowned at the thought that she sounded as superstitious as Traelein.

"A shraen must consider all possibilities. I may survive the attack and continue to rule, but perhaps I won't."

"And what of the Kindren? They resisted a Lof Raelein of Elder blood. Why would they accept her half-blood daughter?"

"Whatever else you may be, you are a descendant of Rivenn—and my only child and heir. None can replace you. The Kindren will come to recognize you as their only hope."

There it was again—the thing that trapped her. If she refused this responsibility, she would disappoint her father and risk the alliance of Faeraven. She wanted to bolt from her chair and from the chamber. Instead, she fixed her gaze on her father. "I need time to consider."

"You ask for the one thing I cannot give you, daughter. My spies report that Freaer's forces gather at Maeg Streihcan, the Broken Mountain rising above the Plains of Rivenn. By accepting the sceptor and circlet, you can give the Kindren the heart to go on if both I and Torindan fall."

"And if I do not?"

"Freaer will destroy the Kindren and corrupt all of Elderland. And don't think you will escape. He would make a point of hunting you down. You'd be murdered, or worse."

"Worse?"

"Sometimes death can be a release."

A chill ran over Mara. She folded her arms against it and attempted a laugh. "What a gloomy future you foresee."

His face saddened. "I won't withhold the truth from you, Syl Marinda, although revealing it breaks my heart. You weren't raised a lof raena, but the title belongs to you nonetheless. Denying your own will for the greater good is the burden and privilege of rulership. Don't learn this lesson by a difficult route, like your father."

He spoke of his marriage to her mother and the sufferings it had brought. Pity closed her throat. Could she allow him to go into battle, possibly to die, without feeling Faeraven could rise again without him? Whether she accepted the scepter and circlet might not matter if Torindan fell, but what if it could?

She'd have to set aside her plans to run away from Torindan, but they seemed selfish now. She'd already proven that yielding to emotion above duty brought sorrow. Here, then, was a chance to atone for her mistakes. As her father had pointed out, she couldn't escape her own identity.

Don't let fear rule you. Kai's words returned in memory.

Pushing out of the chair, she sought the warmth of the hearth. One of the marble gryphons supporting the mantle gazed at her with blank eyes. She pulled air into her tightening lungs. "All right, Father. I'll do what you ask, even though it pains me."

His chair scraped back, and his fingertips pressed her shoulders in a light caress. "In time you may count serving your people more a blessing than a curse."

She blinked away a mist of tears. "I will hope for that."

"Tomorrow afternoon, we'll proceed."

She spun to face him. "So soon?"

"I can think of no reason to wait."

What of the fact that she needed time to adjust? But he'd told her he had none to give. She bowed her head. "You are right, of course."

In the outer chamber, Traelein rose from a chair beside the door with a questioning look. Mara gave no indication of her emotions while in the corridor, but once inside her chambers gave a shuddering sigh.

Traelein turned a worried face toward her. "What is it, milady? How may I comfort you?"

Mara struggled to calm herself. "I'm to be named my father's heir."

"I don't understand. Why do you weep where another would rejoice?"

"Because I am a fool." Her voice sounded bitter to her own ears.

"I have offended you."

"You haven't. I've suffered a shock, that's all."

Traelein's brow puckered. "Perhaps you are taken ill and should lie down and rest. Shall I assist you?"

"No!" She refused to faint into bed like some pampered princess. "You are more than kind, but I only want a little time alone."

"As you wish." The door clicked shut behind Traelein.

Relief washed through Mara on a quiet tide. Now she could grieve without the burden of reassuring her maid. She sank into a chair, ready to let her tears flow, only to discover they had deserted her. Clutching a cushion, she stared into space.

In some ways her father and Mam were no different. Without any thought to what she wanted, each had made plans for her future. She choked on a laugh.

At least she'd never have to marry Rohan.

CR

The shrilling of horses and thud of hooves thrust Rand from sleep. A face, blued by moonlight, hovered above him. Eathnor. He sat up but caution kept him silent.

The tracker scanned the sky, the tension of his posture telling its own story.

Rand shifted to his knees and reached for his dagger.

The flapping of wings punctuated the stillness, a sound Rand recognized. Although the sky lightened toward dawn, it was too early for a welke to leave its roost. Only training and a rider on its back would cause one of the raptor birds to fly at such a time. Glimpsing a welke rider had made Rand shake with dread since his early days. Only Pilaer's fiercest and most skilled warriors earned the privilege of riding the raptor birds.

A winged nightmare hove into sight, inky against the gray sky above the blackened keirken trees lining the weild. The urge to flee gripped Rand in sharp talons, but he held himself in stillness. Even the smallest movement could awaken a welke's vision. The rider did not suffer the same limitations of vision. Rand and Eathnor had sheltered against the canyon walls beneath a jutting shelf of rock and could hope to avoid detection.

That the welke rider hunted for them seemed obvious. Draeg must have returned to Pilaer to report them missing. His father could not have been pleased. He might even have vented his irritation on Draeg, not that he would do any real harm to the son of Amora. A sudden thought made his mouth go dry.

He knew of one his father *would* willingly harm.

He curled his hands into fists. It seemed he won every crust of freedom at a cost in innocent blood. Would his mother pay the price this time?

The welke moved north along the weild and dwindled out of sight.

Rand released a shaky breath and might have spoken, but Eathnor pulled him deeper into shadow.

"Don't relax, just yet." Eathnor murmured beside Rand's ear. "There may be more to come."

"True. My father has never tolerated his will being thwarted."

"We'll have to find a better place to hide, and the sooner the—"

The riffling of flight feathers carried to them on the night wind.

Rand went still as did Eathnor, beside him.

A dark shape flew over the canyon wall. Rand pressed against the rock wall with his skin crawling. Why did the welke hover so near their hiding place? Eathnor had spoken quietly, but a welke's sensitive hearing might have picked up the sound of his voice.

Wings spread, the welke glided downward and became a shadow passing over the ground on its way toward the weild. Rand had almost found his breath again when the raptor bird swung back toward them. The welke soared at their height but so close to the canyon wall that the rider on its back would not see them below the overhanging rock. The creature neared, filling his vision. Rand's heart pounded so loudly it seemed certain the welke must hear.

The giant head jerked sideways. The raptor bird

peered toward them with hooded eyes above a sharp beak. If it caught their scent, it would find them. Rand held his breath to bursting, but he couldn't do anything to stop his shaking. His mind traveled beyond the constraints of reason into the borderland of terror.

The welke glided past, the ragged feathers at the tips of its wings rippling. The raptor bird flapped into the sky and out of sight beyond the canyon wall.

Rand released the air he'd held and pulled in another lungful.. His knees went weak, and his legs shook. His voice stuck in his throat.

Eathnor touched his arm in urgent warning. With a sick feeling, he followed the direction of the tracker's gaze. Another welke skimmed the canyon floor. Its shriek reverberated along the canyon walls as it sailed toward them with deadly purpose. Metal scraped, followed by the glint of moonlight along the rider's sword.

Rand's fingers cramped around the dagger he'd all but forgotten. It would do little good against a sword but at least offered some sort of protection. Eathnor had none. Without giving it more thought, he stepped in front of the tracker.

Eathnor tugged on the back of his jerken, and a quick backward glance revealed the dagger gleaming in his hand. He'd underestimated his companion.

Rand stepped aside.The welke dove at them.

Rand wanted to jump aside but couldn't make his legs work.

"Watch out!" Eathnor's shoulder rammed him sideways.

Rand went down, keeping his dagger by some miracle.

The welke rider leaned sideways, thrusting his sword at Eathnor. The blade ripped a gash in Eathnor's shoulder. He cried out, pitching against the canyon wall. Blood ran from his wound.

The welke bore down on Rand. It seemed a long time before the talons reached him. A strange malaise gripped Rand. How sad that this would be his death.

At the last instant, the welke swept toward Eathnor, instead.

Rand's inertia broke. The point of his dagger pierced the rider's leather leggings. Blood spurted.

Roaring, the rider turned on him with savage fury and sent his sword whistling through the air.

Rand sidestepped, the wind of the blade's passing fanning his face. Instinct carried him into a move that had protected him more than once from Draeg.

The sword thrust toward him. He deflected it with his dagger, but the blow jarred his arm and spun his weapon out of his hand.

Eathnor launched himself at the welke from the side, drawing blood. The welke wheeled toward him, snapping its beak. Eathnor jumped out of range. The rider leveled his sword straight at the tracker's heart.

The welke screeched and slumped to the ground without warning, its mouth frothing as it writhed and moaned. The rider careened backwards out of the saddle, slammed into the canyon wall, and slid to the ground with his head at an odd angle.

Eathnor pushed away from the blood-spattered canyon wall with a grimace. A dark stain seeped through the shoulder of his torn surcoat, and his hand shook on his dagger as he approached the rider. His posture eased. "He has no breath."

Rand straightened. "The welke is dead as well."

"I wish I knew how. I barely nicked it."

"I lost my dagger." Rand caught the glint of metal in a patch of heather. "There it is."

He stepped into the sunlight and reached for his dagger.

A welke flapped into the sky above him.

26

Colors of Rivenn

Mara rose to greet her father, who entered her outer chamber clad in a blue surcoat embellished by a golden gryphon with claws ready.. His manservant followed with a length of blue silk over his arm.

Her father swept her with a glance. "This day you must put on the colors of the House of Rivenn."

Mara glanced down at her plain tunic, then at the delicate silk as the servant placed it in Traelein's arms. "What a beautiful color."

Her father opened his hand, revealing star sapphire droplets edged by diamonds suspended from a gossamer chain. "This necklace belonged to your mother. Wear it in tribute to her."

With careful fingers, Mara lifted the necklace to the light. "It's lovely."

"Your beauty puts it to shame, my daughter."

Her face warmed. "Thank you."

He smiled with the gleam of moisture in his eyes. "I'll leave you to prepare."

Mara closed her hand over this most precious of gifts. When had her mother worn this necklace? Her father would tell her if she asked him. Perhaps telling her about her mother would remove the haunted look from his eyes.

Traelein helped her into the kirtle then fussed over arranging her hair to best display Arillia's wingabeast ornament. Wearying of her maid's attentions, Mara welcomed Kai's arrival with a small guard to escort her to the presence chamber.

She entered by a side door, at once longing to escape as cheers greeted her. At the Inn, she'd waited on crowds who seemed as hungry, but for the food she brought them. She hadn't expected such a welcome, but the Kindren remaining at Torindan were those who had remained loyal to her father despite his marriage to her mother.

With the Crown of Faeraven on his head and holding in his hand the jeweled golden scepter that denoted high rulership, her father sat on the carved and gilded throne of Rivenn.

Arillia, bedecked in blue velvet and wearing the gem-encrusted circlet of Elder on her head, sat beside him on a smaller but no less magnificent throne.

Mara had given Arillia little thought until now. She'd borne no children but must once have hoped to provide an heir for her husband and for Faeraven. What might it cost her, even if only in ceremony, to surrender the circlet of Elder to the daughter of her rival?

Arillia might be the one person present who shared her reservations about today's events.

Her father and Arillia rose together. One of the priests came forward to lead Mara up the steps onto the throne dais. Father drew the sword from the scabbard at his side and with both hands lifted it before him. Light falling into the chamber through the high windows gleamed along the steel blade and sparkled in the rubies, diamonds, and emeralds embedded in its hilt. "With this Sword, forged by Kunatel in the Viadrel burning at the heart of Maeg

Waer, Timraen of Rivenn freed his bride, Maeven of Braeth, from the garns at Pilaer. This twain-edged Sword divides joint and marrow, spirit and soul, bringing judgment and destruction, but protection to those who seek it. It breaks magics and guides the lost to safety. Kneel, Syl Marinda of Rivenn." She obeyed, and her father laid the flat of the sword on her head. "In this sword find birth, death, and life. Arise."

The priest behind Mara stepped forward and offered his hand to her.

Father lowered the great sword and extended it by the hilt.

Heart pounding, she accepted the weapon.

He turned her to face the crowd. "Hold up Sword Rivenn!" he whispered near her ear.

Mara obeyed, to the crowd's shouting and applause.

Her father's eyes shone like the glimpses of the Western Sea that had glimmered on the horizon during her journey to Torindan. Arillia smiled beside him. Following Kai's earlier instruction, Mara gave the sword into the priest's hands.

Her father raised the scepter, and she caught her breath, stunned by the majesty of the rampant gryphon spreading goldenh wings and curving its claws around the star sapphire orb at the scepter's tip. "Syl Marinda, daughter of Elcon, open heart and hands to Faeraven, the ancient alliance of *ravens*, lands joined of necessity and choice."

"I receive and will keep the alliance of Faeraven." She recited the ceremonial words Kai had taught her. Her father placed the Scepter of Faeraven in her hands, and she raised it amid fervent cheering. Peace and a sense of rightness overwhelmed her, bringing sudden clarity. She belonged to Faeraven, after all.

CR

Rand froze in indecision.

The welke flapped nearer.

"Have you lost all reason?" Eathnor's call penetrated through the drumming in his ears. "Leave the dagger!"

More than anything, he wanted to obey the voice of reason, but they needed every weapon against this foe. He bent to snatch up his dagger, the hum of bees in the heather loud in his ears.

"*Run!*" Eathnor shouted.

Rand launched himself toward the overhang where Eathnor brandished a dagger in one hand and a sword in the other. Rand's feet pounded the ground, but the wings flapped nearer. He spun about. If he fought well, Eathnor might have a hope of surviving.

The welke screeched, unsheathing wicked-looking talons. The rider brandished his sword.

Rand hauled his arm back, gauging the distance he'd need to throw his dagger to embed it in the welke's chest. Eathnor rushed past in a blur, the dead welke rider's sword leveled. Rand barely stopped his throw in time. Swords met with metal clanging metal. The welke shot beyond Rand but wheeled to return with talons stretched. The rider pointed his sword at Eathnor, who stood, white-faced and panting. His shoulder bled anew, and the sword he grasped seemed about to slip from his hand.

Rand threw himself into the welke's path.

"Out of my way!" Eathnor bellowed behind him.

With a jerk of the reins, the rider turned the welke broadside and leaned out to strike.

Rand dived beneath the welke's claws and came up on the opposite side before the creature could react. The raptor bird turned its head, but before it could peck him, Rand leaped on it. His dagger penetrated flesh. The welke screamed. Blood spattered.

A blade sliced Rand's arm.

Staggering backward, he tripped over his own feet and crashed into the ground, driving the breath from his lungs. He scrambled to his knees and tried to gain his stance. The edges of his vision darkened. The ground tilted. He fell to hands and knees.

A battle cry pulsed the air. Eathnor vaulted over him.

Rand pulled air into his lungs. and lurched to his feet.

Blood streamed from the welke's side. The raptor bird continued to bear its rider, seeming little effected by its wound. Rand could not say the same for himself. His shoulder blazed with pain, blood loss drained his strength, and his reactions were slow and clumsy. Eathnor's condition was no improvement on his own. Life at Pilaer had taught him certain practicalities. He could admit the truth. Unless they found a way of escape, he and Eathnor would soon die.

He scanned the canyon wall, and a darker patch in a shadowy indent snagged his attention. It had to be...yes! The mouth of small a cave gaped a short distance away. They'd missed it in the darkness last night.. If only he and Eathnor could enter the cave, the welke wouldn't fit through the entrance to follow. They would still have the rider to contend with, but with shelter on three sides of them.

The welke rider's cursing recalled Rand. With his injured arm hanging useless and bloodied, Eathnor seemed able to do nothing but wait for the welke rider's next strike. Rand shook free of his inertia and slipped behind the welke, looking for another chance to attack it.

The welke levered to face him, claws critching. The rider flailed, obviously inexperienced to be unbalanced by a sudden move.

Surprise arrested Rand, giving the raptor bird the chance to peck at his gashed arm. He cried out and leaped away. The rider's sword cut the air where he'd stood.

"A cave!" He shouted to Eathnor, his chest so heavy he could barely drag out the words.

Eathnor stared at him, seeming planted in place.

Rand gestured with his head toward the cave. "Go!"

Eathnor's eyes glinted, and his jaw tightened. Rather than retreating, he rushed forward again.

Leaving him to fight while he fled must not have sat well with the tracker. The cave would have to wait then. Rand wouldn't willingly leave a companion to die while seeking his own safety. He fought in tandem with Eathnor, taking turns running in from opposite sides..

The welke ripped into Eathnor's shoulder with its beak. He yelled and backed up, his sword thudding to the ground. The rider leaned toward Eathnor, muscles surging to deliver a killing blow.

Rand's dagger sliced the welke's windpipe, cutting off its shriek. The raptor bird collapsed, pinning him under its bulk. He struggled to free himself from the welke's carcass.

Eathnor and the rider faced one another. Eathnor had recovered his sword somehow but could barely lift it. Lines of strain etched his face, and his chest rose and fell in panting breaths.

A blow from the welke rider sent Eathnor's sword spinning through the air.

Eathnor drew his dagger from its sheath and circled the welke rider, turning ever to face him with a mocking smile on his face.

The blood lust on the rider's face reminded Rand of that shown by the crowd during his warrior training. Images of all he had seen and done at Pilaer flashed before him. He drew his dagger and gave a blood-curdling cry as he rushed at the rider.

The rider swung about and whacked Rand in the side. He turned at once to meet Eathnor's charge.

Rand's armor had protected him, but the shock of the blow brought him to his knees.

Eathnor's dagger pierced the leather covering the rider's shoulder. The rider howled as blood welled.. The rider recovered his stance, but swayed and slid to the ground. He clutched his stomach, writhing as his mouth foamed. The breath rattled in his throat a final time and came no more.

Eathnor pushed at the rider's body with the toe of his boot. "Same as the welke. Some sort of sickness?"

A horrifying thought occurred to Rand.."Let me see your dagger."

Eathnor laid the weapon in Rand's palm with a questioning look.

Rand ran his thumb over the hilt he'd carved with a gryphon. "Tell me, how came you to carry my dagger?"

"Is it yours?"

"I'd know it anywhere."

Eathnor shrugged. "I lifted it from Draeg while he slept."

Rand sucked in air. He'd lost his blade after trying to use it to assassinate his father. Draeg must have taken it from the guards. "The blade—I poisoned it."

"What?"

"It's a long story, and one I'd rather keep to myself."

"Nice blade, but you can have it back. I'm thankful I didn't nick myself with it, and it's just as well you cleaned the fish last night."

"You could have let me see it sooner."

"I didn't want you to know I carried a weapon."

Rand could guess why. They traveled together, but didn't trust one another very far. It seemed time to start. He extended the other dagger by the hilt. "Go on. Take it."

Eathnor's light eyes gleamed. He accepted the dagger. "Thank you."

Rand sheathed his dagger and, using his good arm, collected the swords of the fallen riders.

"We've a new visitor."

The strain in Eathnor's voice brought Rand's head up. Another welke rider flew above the weild from the north. Rand's hand tightened on the weapons he carried. "Will they never stop?"

"We'd better hide while the rider remains distant. I'm loath to play host again." Eathnor relieved him of one of the swords. "Now, tell me. Where is this cave? You brought it up when I was a bit…occupied."

"Not far. Just there." He pointed the way and let Eathnor walk before him. The blood staining Eathnor's surcoat had spread, and shredded flesh hung from his wounded shoulder. Rand's own arm throbbed dizzyingly.

Eathnor poked a stick into the cave, and receiving no response, ducked into it.

About to follow, Rand turned his head at the flap of wings. How had the welke rider traveled so quickly? He dove into the cave and rolled away from its mouth as a sharp beak pecked the air where his legs had been. Rand fetched against Eathnor, cringing as a screech echoed through the cave.

"Mind your manners." Eathnor pushed him to the side. "Your cave is a bit cramped."

The ceiling was too low to allow standing, but Rand scrambled into a crouch. "Best I could do on short notice, and it's already saved our hides."

Eathnor crouched beside him. "Yes, but we'll have to fight in this position."

"We'll be able to see and the rider won't. Have your eyes adjusted?"

Rand blinked. "Is there more to see than darkness?"

A shadow blocked out the light at the cave's entrance. "Come out and you may be spared," a gravelly voice called.

"Why do I doubt that? Say, there's an echo in here." Eathnor shifted backwards and away. "Hold on."

"Hold on?" Rand's voice rose on a note of panic. "Eathnor? *Eathnor!*"

Shadow shifted at the entrance and formed into the shape of a head and shoulders. Faint light limned the edges of a blade. Rand's skin prickled, and he gripped his sword with sweaty hands.

The rider crawled into the cave with his sword

before him, but from the way he groped along the wall with one hand, he couldn't yet see.

An arm caught Rand around the waist and hauled him backward. Rand pushed away from his assailant.

"Quiet." Eathnor whispered near his ear.

Rand let the tracker guide him through the darkness with a hand on his arm. He crawled on his belly through a narrow tunnel behind Eathnor while at every instant expecting a hand to catch his heels or a sword to thrust after him.

Unable to see, he felt his way. A breeze chilled his face in a place where water dripped. Eathnor pulled him to his feet but kept a restraining arm about his shoulders. He understood why when a rock at his feet dislodged, followed for a long time by the clatter of stone against stone. They skirted a narrow ledge before stepping onto firmer ground. Prisms danced along the cave walls, giving enough to light their way.

Eathnor released his arm.

A wall of rough stone blocked their way, but a hole cut by the rivulet running beside them showed in the light wavering above the surface of the water. Eathnor's hand pressed his back. "Time for a bath."

Going into the water was the only way forward, but he hesitated, daunted by the small opening. "Might there be another exit?"

"Maybe, but this is the one we've found."

The echo of a soft footfall behind them ended Rand's deliberation. He plunged into the stream, gasping at its coldness.

Eathnor waded into the water behind him. "When you're ready."

Gathering his courage, Rand ducked through the opening. He walked hunched-over until the stone ceiling above him vanished. Blinking in sudden light, he stumbled to a stop.

He stood on a small ledge with water falling a long way into a pool that frothed. Eathnor emerged from the cave, and Rand put out his arm. "Careful. There's no way down."

"We'll have to jump."

"It's a long way."

A splash sounded from within the cave.

Eathnor looked over the edge. "They way I see it, we've but two choices."

How did he manage to sound so calm? Rand sighed. "I can guess what's coming."

"Defend ourselves or jump."

"Only the best fighters become welke riders." Rand reminded him.

"There are two of us."

"Both wounded."

Eathnor jutted out his chin, a gesture made less impressive by his pallor. The tracker's courage could not be plainer, but he could have no idea of the resilience of a welke rider in hand combat. Rand knew. He had witnessed their training.

They only had one option, and he wouldn't argue about it with a strong-headed tracker half-dead on his feet. Eathnor trusted him, more or less, a fact that might make this easier. In a move Rand had found useful in confrontations with Draeg, he darted behind the tracker and shoved him off balance.

Eathnor lost his sword over the side and, flailing, followed it into the pool. His head bobbed up again, and he swam toward the edge.

Rand hesitated at the drop. He could wish for someone to push him over, too.

The welke rider stepped into the light, all the goad he needed. He cast his sword over the edge and launched himself into the air. The fall seemed to take a long time, but then he struck the surface with a blow that set fire to his injured arm. Water closed over his head, and he sank for a long time into the cold darkness that rose to meet him. Wrenching himself free of the malais that gripped him, he pushed toward the surface. His surcoat held him down. His lungs burned, screaming for air, and still he did not gain the surface. He could see the light of day above him, tantalizingly near but too far.

27

INJURY

Elcon halted his pacing and composed himself before turning to greet his visitors. Kai's flared nostrils betrayed his fear, and the face of Dorann's father, Jost, drooped with sorrow.

"Lof Shraen." Kai straightened out of a bow. "We found Dorann alive but injured."

"What happened to him? How did you find him? Where is he now?" Elcon paused to draw breath.

Kai opened his mouth but hesitated as if uncertain how to respond.

Elcon reined in his impatience and made the inquiry that mattered most. "Will he recover?"

Kai spread his hands, palms up. "None can say but Lof Yuel. Praectal Daelic tends him, now."

Jost cleared his throat. He stood square and strong, an older version of his sons. "Lof Shraen, if I may speak—"

"Yes, yes." Elcon came to stand before him. "Give me the tale at once."

"I found my son in the mountains and carried him back on my pony. He'd been mauled by a shaycat."

Elcon tried to imagine Dorann bested by any creature and couldn't. "But he seems so capable, especially in the woods."

"Even the strongest of trackers is no match for a shaycat. They move about, silent as ghosts, hungry for prey. It's a wonder Dorann lived. Had he not bound his own wounds before fainting, I doubt he would have."

Elcon clasped his hands behind his back. "Did he speak of Emmerich?"

Jost scrunched one of his eyes. "The name passed his lips more than once while he was delirious. I couldn't understand what he said."

Elcon tamped down his frustration. "You'll want food and drink and a comfortable bed."

"My thanks, Lof Shraen. However, I must leave my son in the care of the good praectal and return home for his mother. Erinae will want to know at once what's become of her son and to join me at his side."

"Of course." Elcon inclined his head. "You can both stay here at Torindan as long as necessary."

As the tracker's father departed, Elcon strode to the window. He gazed at the fitful clouds of a gathering rainstorm. "I should go to Dorann."

"He may not be able to tell you what you wish to know." Kai spoke from behind him.

"Agreed, but I want to pay my respects. Dorann lies at death's door because of my stubbornness."

"Will you blame yourself for this?"

"Who else? I didn't like what Emmerich told me, and so I returned a demand in the guise of a supplication and sent Dorann into danger for nothing."

"As you said, he seemed capable," Kai said in an unsteady voice.

Elcon laid a hand on Kai's arm. "Come with me to his bedside. The presence of friends may lend him the strength to rally."

଼

The pain in Rand's body told him he hadn't died. From the hardness of a saddle swaying beneath him and the chafing of the bonds contraining him, he must be tied across a horse. Had he been captured? He opened his eyes, but at the dizzying sight of the path sliding by, closed them again. Blackness sucked him down in a whirlpool.

The ping of a hoof against stone roused him. He pried his eyes open and turned his head.

A familiar figure rode ahead, leading the horse that carried him.

"Eathnor." His voice came too softly, and he gathered the strength to call again.

Eathnor glanced back at him. "So, you wake at last. Hold on." He turned off the path toward the river.

Rand's horse stumbled, and he gritted his teeth against the pain in his shoulder. "Why did you tie me?" he asked when his horse came to a stop.

"Sorry, but I thought you might slide off." Eathnor dismounted.

Rand frowned in concentration, casting back in memory. "What happened?"

"Do you recall pushing me off that cliff and jumping yourself?"

"Yes, but why am I alive? I thought I drowned."

"You did, but I fished you out and revived you. Do you remember vomiting water?"

"Thankfully, no. And the welke rider?"

"He decided not to jump." Doran worked at Rand's bonds. "I found another cave to hide in, just in case he came calling."

"How long did I sleep?"

"Most of the day. I hid until I was sure the welke

rider had given up, and then moved on. I'd have let you rest longer, but the wind carries the sound of marching. Forces from Pilaer aren't far behind."

Draeg would no doubt ride among them. The cord around Rand's waist gave, and he slid until his feet touched the ground. His legs supported him, but he held onto the saddle while his head cleared. "We need to reach Torindan soon."

"It's almost nightfall, but we should continue after watering the horses. We're better off traveling by dark anyway."

The subdued light could have belonged to dawn or dusk. Rand pushed away from the saddle to stand alone. "Careful there." Eathnor put out a steadying hand. "You'll be weak."

"I'm all right." Rand spoke with bravado, but he didn't pull away from the tracker's support. "Thank you for saving my life."

"You did the same for me."

"You tended my arm, I see. Have you dressed your own wounds as well?"

"I have. My brother, Dorann, has more skill at healing, but I know a little something, too. I made a poultice of greenings for our wounds. It should draw away poisons."

"You captured the horses, too."

Eathnor laughed. "That wasn't difficult with the lush grass in a side canyon distracting them. Speaking of food..." He pulled a packet of dried fish from Rand's saddlebag and passed it to him. "Try to eat while I see to the horses."

"I'm thirsty."

Eathnor untied the thongs securing Rand's water bottle to the saddle. "Swallow the rest of that and I'll fill it again."

Rand drained the bottle and wiped his mouth with his arm. "Thanks, but I can fill it myself."

Eathnor grinned. "You're recovering."

Rand's legs shook as he followed Eathnor over a small hillock and down to the banks of the weild. A log afforded him a place to rest and with his appetite recovered, he tore into the dried fish.

The bank behind Eathnor slanted into the weild at a gentle angle. The surface shone like glass and the pebbles below it glowed like gemstones. The horses waded to their knees and flicked their ears as they lowered their heads. A fish jumped and splashed while the blue dragonfly that had been its quarry darted away on gossamer wings.

Rand would have liked to linger, but they needed to press on. With his hunger sated, he refilled his bottle. He turned back to find Eathnor with an intent look on his face. Rand opened his mouth to ask what was wrong.

The thud of approaching hoofbeats reached his ears.

CR

Elcon curved his hands into fists. It had been a long time since he'd felt this helpless. Dorann lay still, bandages covering the side of his head, a shoulder, and his arm.

From the other side of the bed, Kai gazed down at his stricken friend.

"I've given him a draught, Lof Shraen. He'll not wake." Praectal Daelic spoke from the doorway of the guest chamber above the gatehouse.

Elcon nodded. "Spare nothing to restore him."

"If that may be done, I will do it. He's bled a lot, and his wounds gather poisons. He may not survive."

Elcon wished Daelic's prognosis offered more hope. His shoulders slumped. "I'm certain you will care for him well."

"Thank you, Lof Shraen. That is my intent." Daelic withdrew.

Elcon had meant to stand watch over Dorann until his father returned, but now an urgent errand pressed him. "Kai, stay with him."

From the look on Kai's face, he could not have assigned a more welcome task. Elcon studied the silent figure in the bed, and then pushed through the doorway into the torchlit corridor. His steps led him to the allerstaed, where moonlight slanted through the clerestory windows. "Lof Yuel!" His shout gathered echoes. "Tell me what I must do to turn your judgment from Dorann to me. Why should he be the one to pay for my guilt?"

Silence.

He knelt at the prayer rail and bowed his head in utter defeat.

A quicksilver touch brushed his mind and withdrew, an island of comfort in a sea of grief. He rose and looked around, but the allerstaed kept its mysteries.

⊗

Rand crawled through the grass swaying on top of the hillock above the weild. He drew his dagger, and beside him Eathnor did the same. They didn't have long to wait.

Two mounted figures garbed in the red and gold of the guardians of Pilaer hove into sight on the path. All birdsong stilled, leaving only the thump of hooves and huffing breaths of their horses. The riders scanned the terrain, one glancing straight at Rand.

His spine tingled, and he crouched lower in the grass.

The horsemen spurred their horses, and the thud of hooves faded.

Rand sat up. "Who were they?"

Eathnor came up beside him. "Advance scouts in search of the night's camp, or else they search for us. In either case, the army won't be far away." He frowned. "I'd hoped for more distance."

"You'd travel quicker without me." Rand stated the obvious truth. "You should leave me behind."

"I'll not do that." Eathnor shook his head.

"Why not?"

"Let's just say you've grown on me. Come, we should be going. We'll need to follow the banks of the weild and avoid the path as much as possible. Otherwise, if the scouts return this way tonight, we could meet them without warning."

Along the banks, travel came more slowly and finally stopped altogether. Boulders blocked the way in a place where the weild combed through rocks and formed rapids that made riding through the water too risky. They had little choice but to follow the path, but the sound of marching drove them back to the weild.

Sunset blossomed above the canyons like a flower unfurling petals edged in gold. The night wind breathed through blackened keirkens that twisted as if bending to drink from shadowy pools.

Rand came up beside Eathnor and joined him in surveying a bluff gilded by the sun's dying rays. The water ran against its base, allowing neither Kindren nor beast to pass. "I suppose we'll have to backtrack."

"More's the pity." Eathnor glanced at him. "You sound weary."

"Don't concern yourself." Rand sat taller in the saddle, although his eyes remained open only by an act of will.

"We should reach Torindan by morning."

Was he really that close to Mara? Fresh energy surged into Rand. "Then, by all means, let us go on."

They found a place where the horses could gain the path by a steep climb.

The sun went down but its glory lingered at the horizon. A full moon rose to light their way.

Rand resigned himself to the arduous journey. They had little time left to reach Torindan. Whatever it cost him, he would not slow their progress.

Eathnor motioned him to stop.

Rand reined in his horse with frustration, and then he, too, heard the crackle of a fire and the voices rasping. Smoke wafted into the air. Had their way not been blocked by the bluff, they would have ridden into the scout's camp. Lof Yuel must watch over them yet.

Skirting the camp without being heard seemed an easy task, for the scouts, arguing in some sort of squabble, weren't particularly quiet.

Rand stiffened. One of the voices belonged to Draeg.

28

DAUGHTER AND HEIR

"Father!" Mara's cry wrenched Elcon from sleep. She bent over him, her forehead creased. "Why are you lying there? Are you ill?"

"What?" He frowned. "I must have fallen asleep at the prayer rail." The night had passed, and now faint light slanted into the allerstaed through the clerestory windows. He sat up and ran a hand over his face.

"Tell me what troubles you."

"I shouldn't rest my burdens on you."

"Even when I am willing to accept their weight?" She extended her hand to him.

"I'm not convinced you should." He pushed to his feet without her help.

"But I am your daughter and heir!"

Elcon smiled, but with a touch of sadness. In her fervor, she had never looked more like her mother. "I need no reminder."

"Then let the one comfort you and the other share in important matters."

He couldn't hold out against his daughter's pleading. "All right. You will know this in time, anyway. I've failed my people."

She stared at him. "Surely not."

He sighed. "How I wish that could be true."

"I can't imagine your doing anything so terrible."

"It is what I failed to do that condemns me." He

pushed to his feet and reached out a hand to help her rise. "At the last siege of Torindan, the DawnKing sent by Lof Yuel had only to lift his arms to cast the enemy into darkness and confusion I wanted this new battle to end by the same means, but Emmerich refused to come at my call. Instead he instructed me to seek help from the one person I am loath to stand before."

"Who do you speak of, Father?"

"Euryon of Westerland. He denied my entreaties in the past. Why should he listen to me when he has reason to despise me? I robbed him of his daughter." He shook his head. "I didn't want to humble myself and ask Aewen's father for help, so I sent Dorann into peril for no good reason. Emmerich still won't come but only repeats that I should send to Euryon for aid."

She touched his arm. "It's not too late, then. Let me carry your message to Westerland."

He stared at her. She had a look of her mother in a strong mindset. "Why would you do that?"

"Perhaps he will come at the request of his granddaughter."

"We are on the very eve of war. It's far too dangerous." He would not repeat the error in judgment that had taken Aewen's life with his daughter.

"I have pledged to serve the Kindren as Lof Raena of Faeraven. What is my safety in the face of that? Send Kai with me, along with an archer. I know I can do this."

"Such concern for Faeraven is to your credit, but Euryon may not listen to you."

"He won't hear me at all if I do not go."

"I will ponder the matter."

She arched her brows. "There's no time for delay.

You must decide at once."

"Faith, but you remind me of myself! But I'll not rush a decision that puts your life at stake. Leave me now and let me take it to prayer."

She held her ground. "Let me stay and join my prayer with yours."

He touched her cheek. "You seem to have inherited the strongmindedness of both your parents. You may stay, but tell me why you are unaccompanied."

"I did not come alone but sent my maid away at the door so I might speak to you in privacy."

She was hiding something. "What brings you to the allerstaed so early?"

She hesitated. "You may think my sanity in question."

"Go on."

"Sometimes it seems that souls…touch. Last night I felt your sorrow in this place and this morning followed it to you."

That explained the quicksilver touch that had comforted him. "Is this what you fear I'll call madness?"

"Will you not?"

"I have neglected to teach you of your heritage. Souls can and do touch, at least among the children of Rivenn."

"This is…normal?"

"Within our family, yes. It is called the shil shael, the soul touch Lof Yuel gave to our ancestral father, Rivenn, when the garns held him captive in Caerric Daeft, the cavern of death. He used it to warn his family to escape. Afterwards, the shil shael passed to some, though not all, of his children. Don't fear it, child. The shil shael is a blessing from Lof Yuel."

"Then I will not despise it, but at times it frightens me."

"By its own right, the soul touch is beautiful, but darkness can corrupt even a thing of beauty."

"I've sensed darkness."

"What do you mean?" He spoke more sharply than he'd intended.

Her eyes flared. "Sometimes it's as if evil itself has a soul that seeks to enter my mind."

"That is how Freaer intrudes. Whenever this happens, you must hide yourself in Lof Yuel."

"I have learned how to do that. The effort tires me, however."

"How well I understand. Freaer buffeted my mind without mercy during the first siege of Torindan. Fending him off wore out my strength, but I endured. I suspect he may attack in the same way again. This time he may target you as well.."

Her eyes widened. "Me?"

"I'm sorry to frighten you, but I don't want to leave you unprepared. I have so little time to teach you these things." He touched her hair. "How I wish we could have had more time."

She pulled away. "Don't talk like that."

"We must face the truth. I may not return from battle." He lowered himself to kneel at the prayer rail.

"You will *not* die and abandon your throne to me."

His lips curved at her tone. "I will bear that in mind. Now, come and pray."

Her mouth parted as if to say more but instead she knelt beside him and bowed her head.

He let his gaze linger on her silken eyelashes, the curve of her jaw, and the hair tumbling past her shoulders in a glossy waterfall. How Aewen would have loved their daughter.

If only...

He closed his eyes, shutting out the familiar sorrow.. Regrets could not change the past. Even if they could, he would not want them to. All the paths he'd walked, whether joyful or bitter, had brought him to his knees before Lof Yuel, holding his daughter's hand in prayer.

CR

Mara bowed her head and closed her eyes, the very model of submission, although inwardly she chafed. Why must her father linger in prayer when he needed to act? He'd suffered enough shame. She could save him from more if only he would let her. She was not some delicate flower to coddle. Besides, who could say if remaining at Torindan would prove more wise than leaving it?

Her father's explantaion of the soul touch had set her mind at rest. She frowned. If the shil shael belonged only to the children of Rivenn, Rand must be related to her by blood. Her father would know how, but she wasn't proud of running away with Rand and would rather leave that particular episode in the past. She could manage such a thing more readily if he wouldn't haunt her thoughts.

Her father took her hand in a strong grip. Tears caught at the back of her throat. That he could die in battle was too much to be borne. Gripped by the possibility, she set her mind to prayer at last.

The rear door banged open, and the guard Kai had

introduced as Craelin strode in. He bowed before her father and straightened with a furrowed brow.

"Is something amiss?" Her father rose and helped her to her feet.

"Lof Shraen, something has happened." Craelin cast a glance to her before continuing in a subdued voice. "I beg an audience."

"You may speak in my daughter's presence. As only this morning I have been reminded, she is heir of Faeraven."

Craelin inclined his head. "I must inform you that Eathnor has returned."

"I welcome the news. How did he escape?"

"In the company of Randolph of Pilaer."

"Rand is here?" Mara blurted. Two gazes swung to her, one blue, the other green, and her cheeks warmed. How ridiculous. She'd already given herself away.

Her father frowned. "Do you know him, Syl Marinda?"

She lifted a shoulder. "Only as a tracker."

The gleam in her father's eyes told her he did not believe the indifference she pretended. "Would you count him trustworthy?"

What could she say? That he had helped her run away, and then abandoned her in the wilderness? That he'd returned to the inn but had left without speaking to her? What did she really know of Rand? Perhaps he *was* a thief, for he seemed to have stolen her heart. "I'm not certain."

"Eathnor vouches for him," Craelin said. "But he wears the garb of one of Freaer's wretched guardians, so I had him chained."

"This grows ever more curious." Her father came

to stand before her. "My daughter, how do you know this tracker from Pilaer?"

"I had no idea he came from Pilaer." She might have asked Rand where he hailed from but had taken him on faith for no reason she could now name.

"With all respect, Lof Shraen," Craelin interrupted. "Eathnor waits in your meeting chamber."

"Summon Kai."

Craelin bowed and withdrew.

Her father turned to her. "We'll find out what message Eathnor brings before deciding the fate of the prisoner from Pilaer."

What had she done? She would welcome any other duty but the one before her. Mara walked beside her father to his chambers, regretting with every step having urged him to include her in his affairs.

They entered the meeting chamber, and Eathnor rose to make his bow. Crumbs of bread and the dregs of what might have been ale in a drinking horn were all that remained of the food he'd consumed. Dirt sullied the gryphon on the front of his surcoat, and blood stained the shredded fabric at one bandaged shoulder, but his hands and face were clean.

Her father embraced the tracker, and then stood back. "I'm grateful to find you alive."

"Thank you." A smile flitted across Eathnor's face. "I share the same opinion."

"Craelin and Kai should arrive soon. They will be eager to welcome you." He guided Mara to the high-backed chair beside his at the head of the table, and Eathnor sat down again.

Her father leaned forward. "Tell me, how did you escape?"

"I didn't. The Kindren now chained in the

gatehouse freed me."

"Ah, yes. Craelin mentioned him. Are you certain this Kindren did not deceive you into believing in his friendship?"

The question struck Mara like an arrow to the chest. Rand had seemed a friend she could trust, but his actions had told a different story.

"I would stake my life on his truthfulness." Eathnor's gaze never faltered but met her father's squarely.

Mara couldn't speak for Rand as forthrightly. He had lied when he'd promised to take her to Torindan, then abandoned her in the wilderness.

Her father leaned forward in his chair. "Why did you bring him here?"

"He wants to ally himself with you. He is willing to become a traitor to Pilaer."

"A traitor?" Her father narrowed his eyes to green slits. "Why is it you trust him?"

"I have two reasons. The first is that he saved my life at great risk to his own."

"That speaks in his favor. And the second?"

Eathnor glanced sideways at Mara. "Forgive me for speaking of personal matters, but his regard for your daughter recommends him."

CR

"Awake with you!" A rough hand dredged Rand from the depths of slumber.

He bolted upright and might have risen but for the irons cutting his hands and feet.

Where am I?

"The Lof Shraen sends for you." The guard bending over him wore the green and gold of Rivenn. Memory slammed into him. They'd ridden through the night to reach Torindan. No wonder he'd slept soundly despite his bonds.

Metal grated on metal, and the shackles weighting his legs fell away. The guard stood back with a grunt. "Come, you."

A second guard waited outside the strongwood door, and together they each took one of his arms.

"I can walk unaided."

Laughter followed his protest. "Ah, but ours is the privilege of escorting you."

They hurried him into the keep and accompanied him into a circular stairway that wound upward in one of the corner towers. They emerged and proceeded down a long passageway into a side corridor and halted before a carved door. One of the guards knocked, and the door swung inward. Rand gained an impression of polished wood, blue velvet, and gilded furniture. The guards dragged him through a second door into a chamber with a strongwood table down which a handful of Kindren sat, among them Eathnor. Beyond an initial glance at them, he saw no one but Mara.

Seated beside her father, she looked rested and pampered, a beautiful lof raena. The color in her cheeks and parted lips gave away her strong emotion. He could guess what she felt at the sight of him. Well, he deserved it.

The guardian, Craelin pushed back his chair and strode to him. "What, no bow for the Lof Shraen? And stop gaping at the Lof Raena like one devoid of wit!"

Rand pulled his gaze from Mara and fastened it on

her father. Lof Shraen Elcon pinned him with a stare from eyes the same green as his daughter's. Rand wavered on the edge of capitulating. He could never go home again, but bowing to Elcon made his alienation from his father complete.

"Well?" Craelin glared at him while the silence pulsed with tension.

It had to be done. He went to one knee. "I pledge my oath of fealty to Elcon, Shraen of Rivenn, the only Lof Shraen of Faeraven. May Lof Yuel ever walk beside you."

The tears shining on Mara's cheek made no sense. Why would she weep for him? He had expected her to berate him for his treatment of her and beg her father to cast him into the dungeon where she need endure the sight of him no longer. He might have weathered that, but he couldn't withstand her pity.

"Rise!" Elcon gripped the arms of his chair and leaned forward, his face red. "You make yourself a traitor to Pilaer and expect me to trust your word of honor!"

Rand obeyed. "Lof Shraen, my life and my service are mine to give. They now belong to you."

Craelin, who had gone back to his chair, narrowed his eyes. "Does fear of the dungeon prompt your surrender?"

"I don't dread imprisonment of the body, but one eager to enslave every heart, mind, and soul in Elderland. His forces draw near. But even that hasn't swayed me."

"Enough of this!" Elcon roared. "Speak plainly or not at all."

"Lof Shraen, I seek only to stand before Lof Yuel with a right mind and a pure heart. I will tell you what

I know of my father's scheme against Torindan."

"Why should I believe you?" Elcon scoffed.

"Shall I remove this pretender to the dungeon?" Craelin asked.

Elcon looked from Rand to his daughter. "That would be best."

"Wait!" Eathnor's voice rang out.

"Father, please!" Mara cried at the same time. All eyes turned to her. She looked back at Rand, and he read an emotion in her face he'd never hoped to see. Rot in Torindan's dungeon though he might, he would comfort himself with this last image of her.

"Forgive my outburst, Lof Shraen, but this Kindren has come to you at great risk to himself." Eathnor spoke in quieter tones. "I am convinced he will tell you the truth."

"All right, since you speak for him. I will listen." Elcon eased backwards in his chair.

Rand released his breath and, fortified by Eathnor's encouraging nod, broke the last tie of loyalty to his father. "Last night the guardians of Pilaer camped in the canyonlands of Dorienn Ravein but a few day's march from Torindan while Garreth of Tallyrand leads northern ravens loyal to Pilaer across the plains of Rivenn. Freaer sends an assassin to breach Torindan's walls by use of a forgotten sallyport. He intends to take your life and that of the Lof Raena."

Elcon folded his hands on the table. "How do you come to know these things?"

"I heard them in Freaer's own chambers. He may try to change his plans after learning With you and your heir dead, defeating Torindan would only require him to draw out the guardians of Rivenn and cut them off with a flank attack from southern ravens. Lenhardt of Morgorad leads them."

Elcon stared at him without speaking, his lips pressed together..

"Lof Shraen—" Craelin stood.

Elcon held up a hand for quiet. "Tell me by what method you gained access to Freaer's chambers. Why did he make you privy to this information?"

"Because…" Now he would have to tell them the thing he wished to forget and had hoped not to speak. He couldn't look at Mara while he uttered the truth that shamed him.. "I am his ill-gotten son."

29

GATHERING STORM

Mara stared at Rand, tragic as one condemned to hang. She should despise him. Why did she ache to comfort him?

Exclamations rang out around the table. Her father stood. "No matter how richly Freaer deserves betrayal, it's unnatural for a son to turn against his own father."

The guards watching from behind Rand moved forward to flank him.

Eathnor jumped to his feet. "Lof Shraen, if I may speak—"

"Will you yet champion him?" Craelin's voice throbbed with disbelief. "Sit down, tracker."

Eathnor opened his mouth with an expression on his face that indicated he might counter this command.

"Don't land yourself in trouble on my account," Rand warned.

A progression of emotions swept across the tracker's face, but he subsided into his chair. Color drained from his face, hinting at what the effort had cost him.

"What harm will it do to let Eathnor have his say?" Kai intervened..

"Very well." Elcon took his seat. "Go on."

"Lof Shraen, I knew Rand's identity when first I spoke for him," Eathnor said. "Having traveled with and fought beside him, I can say that he is nothing like his father. He wants to help Torindan for the Lof Raena's sake but also because he hates evil. That he has the substance to reject his father's plans should be a mark in his favor."

Mara pushed aside her desire to believe Eathnor's testimony, but Rand had shown he cared nothing for her. She should tell her father all she knew of him, but somehow couldn't bring herself to speak.

Her father frowned. "I'm not sure I can credit your words, knowing the terror wrought by Freaer's other son."

A murmur of approval arose from those present.

Eathnor remained silent until it quieted. "This is not Draegmor."

Her father eyed the prisoner. "What can you tell me about yourself, son of Freaer?"

Rand squared his shoulders. "I once wanted my father's favor, but no more. He refused to acknowledge me and allowed Draeg to make my life a living nightmare."

Craelin peered at him. "Is that why you turn against him? To seek revenge?"

"If I wanted revenge, I could have taken it before this. No. My father's wretchedness brings me sorrow more than wrath. There's a sickness of the soul at Pilaer. I won't say it didn't affect me, but that's why I can't abide it. If my father ever dwelt in the light, he remains in darkness now."

Mara didn't want to think about what Rand had suffered. Letting herself soften towards him would hurt too much.

Her father lifted a brow. "If your aim is not revenge, what gain does betraying Freaer bring you?"

"I want no gain, only to avoid learning what will

become of Elderland under his rule."

"I can't fault that desire." Craelin spoke grudgingly.

Mara fought hard to dislike Rand, the only protection against her own treacherous heart. He sent her a look of longing that tore down her every defense. Almost, she could let herself suspect he had abandoned her in the wilderness for some reason other than meanness of spirit.

"What do you think, Syl Marinda?" Her father's question intruded into her thoughts.

She started. "I—believe him." As she spoke the words, she knew their truth.

Rand flinched. "Will you defend me, too, Lof Raena?"

Her father's gaze traveled over her face "Do you advise me to free the prisoner?"

She pushed away the temptation to reject Rand as he had rejected her, extracting her own revenge. "I do."

Craelin stirred, but Kai laid a hand on his arm. "Why not let him prove himself?"

"Unchain him." Her father nodded to Eathnor. "I release the prisoner into your custody. Do you accept this responsibility?"

A broad grin spread across the tracker's face. "Willingly."

"Randolph of Pilaer," her father addressed the prisoner. "You have won your freedom, but on one condition. Go anywhere near my daughter, and you will find yourself in chains. Understood?"

Rand bowed his head. "Yes."

How could her father have demanded such a thing, and how could Rand have agreed to it? It was all Mara could do to hold her tongue, but a lof raena shouldn't berate her father before his counsel. She wasn't much of a princess, but she knew that much. Mara bit her lip. Had Rand professed love for her only to gain his freedom?

"We have attended to duty." Her father turned to Eathnor. "Now I must give you the sad news that Dorann is under Praectal Daelic's care."

Eathnor sat straighter. "What's happened?"

"A shaycat mauled him"

"I beg your leave to go to my brother, Lof Shraen."

Elcon inclined his head. "You'll find him in one of the gatehouse chambers. While you are there, ask the praectal to take a look at that arm."

Eathnor shoved back his chair and strode to the door. He looked back to Rand. "You'd better come with me."

Mara ignored the glance Rand cast her way before following Eathnor through the doorway. Why should he look at her with pleading eyes when he had rejected her all over again?

Her father returned to the high-backed chair at the head of the table. "Craelin, do you remember the sallyport in Torindan's walls? Shae mentioned it, as I recall."

"Yes, Lof Shraen. We searched but never found it."

"We must try again to find this breach."

"We should assign guardians to the Lof Raena," Craelin suggested.

Her father sighed. "That is best."

"And to watch over you."

"I'll not have my every step dogged when Kai can protect me."

"Kai may soon require assistance in that task." Craelin pushed to his feet. "If you'll excuse me, I'll attend to the duties you've set for me." He made his bow and at her father's nod, quit the chamber.

Mara shivered in the draft that entered through the doorway.

"Whatever it takes, I will keep you safe." Her father gave her a reassuring smile, but his brow remained furrowed.

She had no doubt he would try to keep his promise, but he might lack the ability. "Father, have you decided whether to send me to Westerland?"

"Kai, pray wait for me in my outer chamber." Her father dismissed the one person she'd hoped would be an ally.

"As you wish." Kai gave her a sympathetic smile before leaving the chamber.

Once the door clicked shut, her father continued. "Circumstances decide the matter, I'm afraid. I won't risk you on the open road with war gathering and an assassin ready to take your life. You are better protected within Torindan's walls."

"But— "

"Enough!"

She shrank at the harshness of his tone.

He went on more quietly. "I will not lay your death at my door beside your mother's. I sent her away when I should have kept her close. I will send another messenger to Euryon."

"Who?"

"Eathnor and Dorann's father."

"Will you take him from his wounded son's side?"

"Few others have the skill to reach Westerland by the shorter route through the wild lands. Euryon may give us help, provided I haven't left asking until too late."

CR

Rand walked beside Eathnor along the path at the edge of Torindan's inner garden. Strongwood branches formed a tunnel above them and water falling from the fountain danced in the light. All creation sang, and his soul joined in. Mara had defended him. He would never have more from her, but she'd given much more than he deserved. He could almost let himself believe she loved him in return. He curbed the foolish thought. He'd come to save Mara, not to claim her for himself. He considered himself honor-bound to obey Elcon's command to stay away from her.

"You are silent." Eathnor's voice recalled him.

"I have much on my mind."

"I can well imagine."

"I'm glad Elcon released me into your charge."

"As am I. You may discover the need of a friend beside you."

They passed beneath the archway into the outer bailey. The gatehouse stood before them, and the tracker fell silent. Concern for his brother would naturally drive all else from his mind. Rand had once hoped for such closeness with Draeg, but he could only guess what that would be like.

"Weilton!" Eathnor hailed a Kindren with eyes light as his own and garbed in the green and gold of a guardian of Rivenn.

"Eathnor! We'd given you up for dead."

"I'm happy to prove you wrong. Do you know where my brother lies?"

"You'll find Dorann two doors beyond your own

chamber."

"How does he fare?"

"For a time he lingered near death, but I am told he rallies."

Some of the strain went out of Eathnor's face. "That's welcome news."

"The sight of you won't fail to comfort him."

Eathnor knocked on the door Weilton had named, but burst into the room before any could answer.

The red-haired Kindren in the bed looked up from a bowl of broth, eyes wide in a pinched face.

Staring at Eathnor as if seeing a specter, an amber-haired beauty dropped the spoon she held to Dorann's mouth.. "My son!"

Dorann swung his legs out of bed, and the bowl flew, splattering broth.

Eathnor rushed to his brother and gathered him in an embrace. "Watch yourself. You don't look as able as you seem to think you are. Now lie back and tell me how a shaycat bested you."

Dorann sank into the tick with a smile on his face. "And I'd like to know why Freaer's guardians found you sleeping."

Eathnor laughed. "Your tongue has taken no injury, at least. Mother, this is Rand of Pilaer. My mother, Erinae."

Rand hid his surprise. Her unlined face and ungrayed hair gave her the appearance of a mere maiden, too young to be Eathnor and Dorann's mother. She nodded to him, but her eyes were all for Eathnor. "It's good to have you home, my son."

"I'm thankful to find you well." Eathnor embraced his mother, wincing even as he smiled.

Rand looked away, his throat thickening. He had

never experienced such a homecoming. He probably never would. His own mother was lost to him, maybe always had been. In a sense, her life had ended before his birth. What part could someone like him take in such a tender scene? He edged toward the door.

Eathnor and his mother broke apart, smiling at one another, but then she plucked at his torn sleeves. "What's this? Are you injured?"

"It's nothing."

She narrowed her eyes. "How came you by this injury?"

"I doubt you'll want to know, Mother."

"Maybe not. But Praectal Daelic should look at it."

"That's certain. He can tend Rand's arm, as well."

Erinae's gaze, alive with sympathy, swung to Rand. "Wait and I'll find him."

Rand perched on a bench beside the bed. He would do as she bid, though weariness was catching up with him. Leaning his head against the wall behind him, he shut his eyes to ease their aching while the brothers carried on a quiet conversation.

The praectal's arrival roused him from a half-slumber. Dorann drank a healing draught and surrendered to sleep.

Rand endured the torture of the praectal cleaning his arm and packing his wound with a stinging poultice.

Eathnor, a fresh tunic covering his newly-bandaged shoulders, embraced his mother a last time and led them from the chamber. In the long corridor where light streamed from high windows, he turned to Rand. "Hungry? I could eat a bruin."

"I've had little food, but my bed holds greater appeal."

"Since I'm to watch over you, be good enough to let me visit the hall."

Rand laughed. "All right, but then I must sleep."

They settled at a table in the great hall, and servants brought them food and drink.

Dorann broke bread from the loaf before him and offered a piece to him.

Rand savored each bite and gratefully accepted a portion of cheese. Days on end of jerky and dried fish had sustained their travels but could not compare to the delights of this simple meal.

The Lof Shraen and his golden-haired Lof Raelein sat at the table on the dais at one end of the chamber. Mara seemed to have stayed away from table, but then she entered through the main archway, trailed by two guards.

Rand drank in the sight of her.

She kept her eyes averted from him as she passed, the set of her jaw telling him he had offended her.

His appetite vanished, and he put down his crust of bread.

He glanced sideways at Eathnor, haunched over his food. If only the tracker would finish so they could leave. When he'd promised to stay away from Mara, he'd not considered the sweet agony that gazing upon her would become.

Elcon kept a guard around her, but she was still too vulnerable for his liking. If she were his, he'd secret her away until all danger passed. A smile touched his lips. He knew without being told that Mara would object to being thus protected.

ᏯᏒ

Mara took the portion of bread her father offered her but couldn't quite summon a smile. He didn't seem to notice. With war at Torindan's gates, he must have other things to consider than his daughter's emotional state. She took a bite of bread and tried to chew. Seeing Rand just when she wanted to forget him didn't help her digestion. She should eat to keep up her strength, however. Having never experienced a siege, she had no idea what lay ahead, but she had no doubt that the fabric of life at Torindan would fray.

Her gaze collided with Rand's, catching until she wrenched away. The bread stuck in her throat, and she reached for her cup to wash it down with a swallow of cider. She couldn't help her feelings at how readily he'd agreed to keep away from her.

What else could he have done? He'd been in no position to bargain.

She pushed her errant thoughts away. He could at least have objected. That her line of reasoning was not entirely rational did not escape her, but this wasn't about logic. Why did there seem nowhere to look save at Rand? She pretended a deep fascination in the minstrels' gallery. Did they play with more fervor than usual? Perhaps news of the coming conflict had spread throughout Torindan. How strange to sit at table making merry as if nothing would change.

30

VISITATION

Wake. A voice breathed across Kai's mind, wafting away the vapors of sleep. He sat up and stared into the darkness. A diaphanous figure in a shaft of moonlight watched him.

"Shae." He spoke softly to avoid disturbing others asleep in the gatehouse.

She walked through his chamber door.

He stumbled out of bed and flung open the door.

Shae hastened along the corridor. The torches had burned out, but she shimmered in an unknown light. At the top of the stairs leading outside, she beckoned for him to follow.

Caution restrained him. Something seemed different about her this time. "Why should I go out there with you?"

She gave him an aching look. *Kai, don't you trust me?*

"You could be some dark phantom luring me to danger."

You must listen to the small, still voice of Lof Yuel.

How could he hear anything from Lof Yuel with his mind in turmoil? "Where do you want to take me?"

You wish to find the sallyport.

"How do you know this?"

Please! My strength fades. Her figure dimmed.

"Wait, there." He returned to his chamber and

pulled on his boots with hands that shook. On the way out, he caught up his cloak and sword.

She stood where he had left her, more insubstantial than before.

He followed her down the stairs.

Waiting for him to reach her in the outer bailey, she lit the darkness like a shaft of moonlight. *Kai.* She smiled and lifted a hand as if to touch his cheek, but her smile faded as she turned away.

"Shae..." He reached for her, his hands passing through air.

She waited beside the archway to the inner bailey.

Kai hesitated, but the temptation to pursue her tugged him too strongly. He had to hurry to catch up.

She stepped off the path and glided beneath silvered strongwoods into deeper shadow.

Confusion assailed him. Whyst could kill evil spirits, but if one came to him disguised as Shae, dispatching it would require more strength of mind than he possessed. However, if he didn't continue, he'd never know the truth. With both mind and heart committed to his course, he stepped off the path. Winter's breath lingered at night as yet, and he shivered in the predawn chill despite his cloak.

Movement came from behind him, and he spun to meet the intruder with sword leveled.

"Careful, there!" A voice carried out of the darkness.

"Randolph of Pilaer." He kept his sword raised. "What brings you creeping behind me?"

"I woke and opened my window to the night air. That's when I heard voices outside."

Kai prodded the story for holes and could find none. But that didn't mean he had no suspicions. "Is the night air the only reason you opened your window?"

"I wasn't trying to escape, if that's what you're wondering. It sounded like someone needed help, so I came out."

"Noble of you."

Rand huffed. "Believe me or not, as you choose."

Kai! Little time remains.

From the turn of Rand's head, he had heard Shae. "What was that?" he hissed.

"*Who* was that, you mean."

"I grew up in Pilaer. I know the voice of a wraith."

Kai frowned. How well he remembered the wraiths of Pilaer—shadows that ran at him, fed on his fear, gathered power from his efforts to destroy them. He couldn't imagine growing up in a place infested with them. He started off. "Shae is no wraith."

"Why do you follow her?" Rand kept pace.

"She knows where the sallyport you mentioned lies." Branches met overhead, closing him into dense shadow. He emerged into a clearing. The moonbeams straggled down from the sky seemed all the brighter for the darkness he had just left.

Shae hurried down the overgrown path beside the inner curtain wall, so pale she appeared little more than a vapor that might dissipate.

Here. The word brushed Kai's mind.

Already vanishing, she pointed at the wall.

He rushed to the spot she had stood and bowed his head.

"Who was she?"

Rand's question brought Kai back from his despair. "One bound by chains of love."

"Can you free her?"

"That is not mine to do."

"There is more here than I understand."

"That is true for me as well." Kai lead the way toward the wall. "Since you are here, you might as well make yourself useful. Help me search." He ran his hands over the hewn stone wall. "There must be some sort of lever."

"I wish she'd shown it to us."

"She may not have known of it." Shae had learned of the sallyport when Freaer carried her into it against her will, but there was no need to explain any of that.

An extended search turned up nothing.

Rand rubbed the back of his neck. "Could someone have sealed it shut?"

"That's doubtful. We'll have to wait for daylight." Kai crouched low and explored a gap at the base of the wall. A smooth shape met his fingers. "I found it!" Pushing, and then pulling, didn't budge the handle. He added more strength, trying again with the same results. "It must have rusted shut."

"Here, let me try." Rand shoved against the lever, the muscles of his good arm bulging. He shook his head. "I can't move it."

"We'll have to rouse Craelin. He should know of this."

"I'd rather not go with you, if it's all the same."

After the first guardian's hostility toward Rand, Kai could understand his reluctance. But he shouldn't leave Rand, with his loyalty unproven, alone at the sallyport. "I'm sorry, but I must insist."

"I'd sooner face a pyrek in the desert." Rand strained against the lever with renewed vigor. He sat back. "It yielded—not much, but it did move."

"Here, step aside and I'll take a hand. It pains me

to stand by while you struggle with one arm useless at your side. Did Praectal Daelic not tend you?"

"He did, but I didn't put on my sling before coming out. The voices sounded rather—urgent."

"You must have heard me talking with the guards. I'd like to know how you thought you could rescue anyone with that injury."

"It wasn't a matter of thinking, but I've held my own with worse."

"In between fending off the wraiths of Pilaer? What sort of life have you lived, Randolph of Pilaer?"

"Call me Rand."

Kai applied himself to the lever. An opening cracked in the wall, and damp air rushed into his face. The crack widened like a gaping mouth. Beyond lay a hidden chamber within the curtain wall, with steps leading downward into the motte

Rand whistled. "Pilaer also has such a weakness in its walls."

"Really? Craelin will be interested in its location. We should find him at once."

A roar came from outside the stronghold's walls, making Kai's heart pound. A fireball launched into the sky, streaming a flaming tail, so bright it turned night to day. Kai crouched by instinct, shielding his eyes, and Rand did the same. The fireball thumped somewhere in the outer bailey. Dread rippled through Kai. Dragonsfire had ended more than one siege before it began. He grasped Rand's uninjured arm. "Hurry!"

Another burning orb hurtled upward, its roar swallowing his words. It flamed overhead, but he couldn't tell where it landed. Screams tore through the air.

The march of booted feet echoed in the sallyport.

Kai spun about, ready to run.

CR

Mara woke in a cold sweat. Something was wrong. She could feel it. Sitting up in bed, she threw back the covers.

Traelein rushed in without knocking. Her candle flared and guttered in stray drafts. She stared at Mara with wide eyes and parted lips, the very image of terror. "Milady, it's begun!"

Bright light flared at the edges of the wooden shutters shielding the windows.

Mara clutched her throat, robbed of speech.

Traelein wrung her hands. "Oh, what shall we do? They'll burn us alive!"

Mara went to Traelein and gripped her shoulders. "We must not panic." An explosion erupted outside. Mara flinched as agonized screams pulsed in its wake.

Traelein cowered against the wall.

"Help me dress." She called to her maid. "If I'm to be made a corpse, I'd rather meet my fate wearing more than a chemise."

"Don't say such things!" Traelein stared at her with frightened eyes.

"I'm sorry, I didn't mean to alarm you." She'd forgotten Traelein's superstitions, but they had more to fear than the spoken word.

Traelein helped her to dress with clumsy hands. Mara's thoughts spun in circles. Where was Rand right now? Her father? Arillia? Kai? Each face flashed before her as she mentally recited their names. If even one life precious to her ended she could not bear it. She would not let herself dwell on the possibility of losing her own.

Torindan's catapults responded, the clunk they made as they recoiled bringing the comforting knowledge that Torindan was fighting back.

A lull in the fighting stretched her nerves to breaking point, and she rushed to open the shutters.

"No!" Traelein gripped her arm with the strength of panic, but then fell back. "Forgive my boldness, Lof Raena, but I feared for your safety. A stray missile could strike you."

Mara gripped her maid by the shoulders. "Perhaps you should leave the chamber." She spoke in a gentle but firm voice.

Traelein's forehead creased. "I'll not leave you. Please don't ask it of me."

"Your loyalty speaks well of you. All right, then. I'll be quick as I can, but you must let me look out. I'll go mad if I can't see what is happening." She cracked the shutter only enough to show her the horrifying scene outside. Flames consumed one of the kitchens and another fire raged across the sward toward the inner garden. "How can green grass burn so readily?"

"It's dragonsfire, milady." Traelein said in an awed voice from beside her.

Mara had heard the term before, always spoken of with awe. "What is it?"

"I'm not entirely sure, but none can stand against its fury. Even water does not extinguish its flame. It seems an uncanny thing, begotten in darkness."

"That may not be far from the mark." Only the soul of evil could devise such a weapon.

The catapult in the outer bailey propelled a flaming ball across the wall. Shrieking rose from outside the stronghold.

Mara pulled in a breath. "We have it, too." The thought did little to comfort her. Even an enemy should not suffer so horrible a death.

A whistling sounded and grew to deafeaning. Light and heat flared through the shutters. Glass shattered. The floor vibrated beneath their feet.

"May Lof Yuel save us!" Traelein cried.

31

COURAGE AND COWARDICE

Elcon shut the door as servants rushed down the corridor. Some carried buckets of water toward the blaze, while others ran away from it, screaming. He caught Arillia close. "Your chambers are on fire."

"Oh, no!" Arillia gripped his tunic. "I hope my maid has escaped."

"It's not likely, I'm afraid."

"Poor Lyneth."

"You would have perished with her, had you not come to my bed last night." He kissed her forehead. "Go with Anders and hide in the allerstaed. I'll send Kai to watch over you."

"Let me better clothe myself."

Garbed in a simple tunic, her hair tangling down her back and color staining her cheeks, she had never looked more beautiful. "Your clothing is gone, Arillia, and there's no time to find replacements. Put on your slippers. They will have to do. I'll ask Syl Marinda to bring a cloak to cover you."

She gazed at him with sorrowful eyes. "You're sending me away."

"I must. I let my fears keep you and Mara with me longer than I should have."

"Come with me, I beg of you."

"Arillia." He sighed. "We've been through this many times."

"Don't ask me to leave you. If you remain at Torindan, then so should I."

A new argument presented itself. "Can you not see how vulnerable that looking after you would make me?"

"Very well." She heaved a breath. "I will yield, for your sake."

He gave her a swift kiss. "Thank you."

The sorrow in her eyes nearly broke his heart. "You must return to me."

"I have the same desire." He turned from her. "Anders!"

੒

Rand remained standing before the sallyport, frozen in place, as Kai backed away.. "Draeg approaches, leading the best of Pilaer's warriors."

Had Draeg's emotions not shouted of desperation, his use of the soul touch would have betrayed it. He'd always avoided using the shil shael, for his fear of the spiritual realm prevented him from mastering it.

Their father must have threatened even his favorite son.

"Come away." Kai's voice penetrated Rand's thoughts. "We must run to alert Craelin."

Rand shook his head. "That will give Draeg time to reach Mara and the Lof Shraen. He'll not spare either of them." Rand kept his voice low, but it throbbed with emotion. "Don't ask me to abandon Mara to my half-brother's mercies."

"It seems I have no choice but to trust you. Go and warn Craelin, and I'll protect the Lof Shraen and his heir."

"I'd rather reverse our duties."

"Protecting Elcon is my duty, and he placed Mara in my charge as well."

Much as Rand hated to admit it, the plan held merit. Kai would be the better fighter, and he had access to Elcon and Mara. There was just one flaw. "Craelin won't believe me."

Sword tips glinted from the stairway within the sallyport as the march of boots grew louder.

"If he has eyes and ears he will, but if we argue any longer, he won't have the chance. *Run!*"

Rand launched into motion, keeping pace with Kai until the path split. He veered toward the smoldering sward and sprinted through the archway into the outer bailey. Servants, members of the garrison, and guardians shouted as they ran about. Flames shot out of windows in the kitchens, and a brigade passed buckets of water drawn from the well. Craelin was nowhere to be seen. Fighting a surge of panic, Rand put himself in the path of one of the guardians, who halted. "What's amiss?"

"Where is Craelin?" Rand measured out the words.

The guardian shook his head. "I haven't seen him."

Rand left the guardian and made short work of the stairs to the gatehouse battlements. Order reigned here, with archers stationed at every opening. Arrows flew, a perverse flock of birds with a bite that could kill, and he threw himself down to avoid being impaled. He rolled, gasping with pain from his shoulder, and fetched against the battlements. He landed at a flame-haired archer's feet. The archer peered down at him, gaspng in pain from his injured shoulder. "What are you doing up here?"

"Looking for Craelin," Rand said between his teeth, "to deliver an urgent warning from Kai."

The archer's expression clouded with mistrust. "Why does Kai send you to speak for him?"

"You have to believe me."

A hand gripped Rand's good arm from behind and pulled him to his feet. Rand swung around. Ash smudged the face before him, but he recognized Craelin's glare. "I doubt Kai would trust you with a message."

"He had no choice. The Lof Shraen and Lof Raena are in peril, and he went to protect them."

A fierce light entered the first guardian's eyes. "You'd better be telling the truth."

"Why would I lie about something so easy to check?"

Craelin's expression softened, but only slightly. "Well? What is this message you supposedly bring?"

"Warriors have breached the wall through the sallyport. They will have entered the keep by now."

Craelin nodded to the archer. "Lock him in his chamber while I verify his story."

"Come with me," the archer prompted.

Rand fell into step beside him, thankful he hadn't drawn his bow. He kept silent while they descended the stone steps, alert for an opportunity to break free. They reached a landing, and the archer turned aside toward Rand's chamber.

Rand vaulted partway down the next flight.

"Stop!" the archer warned.

The hair on the back of Rand's neck stood on end. He kept going, flinging himself in an erratic pattern as arrows thudded against the walls.

❦

Elcon's outer door stood ajar. Kai pushed it open wider. *Empty.* The inner chamber door also hung open. Nothing stirred within. A quick look into the dressing room, Ander's chamber, and the meeting room yielded the same results. He returned to the corridor and, holding his sleeve over his nose and mouth, dashed through the acrid smoke toward Mara's chambers.

Footsteps echoed behind him.

He pressed against the wall, but warriors from Pilaer might have already seen him. The thought galvanized him, and he sprang for the nearest doorway. *Locked.* He tried the next with the same results. A latch farther down the corridor gave beneath his hand. He slid inside a darkened storage chamber, leaving the door cracked.

A warrior so like Freaer he could only be his son shoved into the Lof Shraen's chambers. Before long, he emerged and crept along the corridor. He tried a locked door and gestured with his head. Two fighters in the colors of Pilaer applied their shoulders to the door. Wood splintered, followed by rushing feet.

Sweat broke out on Kai's brow. *They would find him.* He hung his sword over pegs above the door. With no other hiding place, it would have to do. In the dimness, it might escape notice. Feet scuffled outside the door. Kai heaved himself into an empty grain barrel and pulled the lid in place.

The door slammed. Footfalls and muffled voices penetrated to Kai. Barely drawing breath, he waited for discovery.

CR

Mara banged the shutters and latched them. "The fire cannot be far off." She spun about and met Traelein's frightened gaze. "We should quit my chambers at once."

"Yes, milady." Traelein's voice held panic, and she seemed ready to bolt.

As they entered the outer chamber, the door from the corridor burst open. Her father rushed in and held out his hand. "You must flee. Bring nothing but a cloak for you and your servant, and one for Arillia."

"Where will we go?"

"To the allerstaed, where there is a way of escape. You were right all along, daughter. I ought to have sent you to Euryon when you suggested it."

"Who knows what might have happened?" She went to him, and he enfolded her in his arms.

Footsteps accompanied the crashing and splintering of wood, and they broke apart.

"What was that?" Mara peered through the doorway behind him, but the smoke made it hard to see.

Another crash made her jump.

"Warriors from Pilaer." Her father faced the corridor, a deadly luster running along the blade he drew. "Hurry, there's little time. You and your servant must both show courage. You'll need to pass by the fire before it closes off the corridor to the allerstaed. Put your cloaks over your mouth and nose."

She held back. "Won't you come, too?"

"If it may be done, I will. Now promise you'll run quick as you can without looking back, whatever happens."

"I promise." The words caught in her throat, and she had to blink away tears. "Make haste, Traelein." She tied her cloak about her and stepped into the hallway.

Shadows grew on the wall as warriors swarmed toward her. Her heart pounded, and her mouth went dry. The urge to shrink back into her chamber and cower behind a bolted door overtook her.

She flung herself toward the flames.

ભ

Where had all the servants putting out the fire gone? Elcon could hardly fathom that they had all deserted the keep. Had any remained, they could have stood beside him now.

A window broke behind him, adding fuel to the fire. He couldn't tell if his daughter had moved past the flames before they surged. Her maidservant stood at an opening in the window with glass shards at her feet, gasping in air. What had she done? The fear widening her eyes explained why she had remained behind.

"You must follow your mistress." He called to her. Even now, it might not be too late to pass the flames.

She retreated into Syl Marinda's chamber and slammed the door shut. The bolt thudded into place.

He pounded on the door, calling to her. Silence answered him. He turned away with sadness. If the warriors found her, she might rather have died by burning. He would shield her as long as he could, but against so many he had no hope of survival.

A warrior stopped just short of him and waved the others back. "Elcon, son of Timraen, I am Draeg, son of Freaer, come to end your miserable life."

"At your cost." He flung out the challenge.

Draeg smiled. "Brave, or foolish, words." He sliced the air with his sword.

Elcon deflected his thrust, the clang of metal cutting through the calls of gathering warriors. Blow followed blow, swift and telling. Draeg's skill with a blade could not be faulted. Elcon had returned to practice of late but was no match for a hardened warrior. His opponent left him no option but to yield, and he retreated with the fire's heat searing his back.

The splintering of wood came, and a scream vibrated from the direction of Syl Marinda's chambers.

Draeg checked at the sound.

He must think they'd found Syl Marinda. The thought goaded Elcon to lunge, and he thrust his blade at his opponent's chest with penetrating force.

Draeg sidestepped, and his blade whipped through empty air.

Elcon stepped in again, finding his mark.

Draeg shrieked and fell back, blood oozing from a gash in his surcoat.

Elcon braced for the backlash, which came with more fury than precision. Elcon met Draeg fully but found himself driven back by the strength of his opponent's rage. Smoke stung his eyes. He couldn't see...

Cold steel sliced his side.

32

IN THE ALLERSTAED

Mara's lungs begged for air. The corridor tilted, and she slammed into the wall. Choking, she clung to crevices in the stone and sucked air into her burning lungs. She pushed away from the wall and staggered onward. The smoke thickened around her. A fit of coughing carried her once more to the wall. She couldn't catch her breath this time. The archway to the allerstaed seemed a long way off.

Traelein hadn't followed. Fear must have held her back. What would become of her?

She couldn't think about that now, not while her legs refused to obey her will. She dropped to hands and knees. Her skirts hampered her attempt to crawl, snarling about her legs, dragging at her. The door to the allerstaed waited, just out of reach, so near she wanted to weep. A curious numbness assailed her. Blackness edged her vision. She fell into utter darkness.

∞

Rand slowed and caught his breath before opening the side door to the keep. The archer might pursue him still, but that was the least of his worries. He'd carried out his errand, although whether he'd convinced Craelein remained to be seen.

Drawing his dagger, he started along the corridor. Crashing sounds and the clash of metal from the floors above guided him to the stairwell in the corner tower. As he climbed, the ruckus increased in pitch.

He turned out of the tower at the highest floor. Light streamed in bars along the corridor, but he crept forward in the shadow that lay beneath the windows. Huddling close to the wall for concealment, he advanced toward the warriors from Pilaer forcing their way into chambers, room by room. Draeg must have ordered them to be thorough in their search for Elcon and Mara. No screams followed their intrusions. Those who dwelt in the keep must have vacated it after the dragonsfire struck. He couldn't count on Mara having escaped, however., Searching for her with the shil shael yielded no results.

The door beside him swung inward. Before he could react, a hand clamped over his on the dagger and an arm hauled him backwards into a darkened chamber and pinned him against the wall. "Taking on a band of warriors alone will earn you certain death." Kai rasped close to his ear.

"Better that than remaining idle." Anger drove his reply but caution lowered his volume.

"I understand your frustration, but we should attack together and guard one another's backs." Kai released him. "Have you no other weapon?"

"I arrived with a sword, but the guards returned only my dagger." If any poison lingered on the blade, it might change the odds in his favor, but that seemed a distant hope.

Kai pressed the hilt of his own dagger into Rand's free hand.

Gratitude flooded him, as much for the mark of

trust as for the blade. It wasn't much of a weapon, but he had faced Draeg with less.

A woman's screeching raised the hair on his arms. *What were they doing to her?* He couldn't know it came from Mara, but his stomach lurched anyway. Whoever she was, some poor creature was suffering. He'd have to stand forth.

Apparently of the same mind, Kai took a sword down from above the door. Shoulder to shoulder, they moved along the corridor toward the small band of warriors riveted by something beyond them. He thought it might be the fire until the scrape and ching of swordplay reached him.

The screaming came from behind a gaping doorway where a small group gathered. From the map of the keep his father had made him memorize before leaving Pilaer, that could only be Mara's chamber.

"Steady." Kai urged, reminding him to step aside from emotions that would hinder his ability to think.

They started toward the doorway. As they neared, a warrior at the edge of the group peered into the shadows hiding them. His cry of discovery blended into the crowd's roaring. He leveled his sword, but Rand vaulted over the blade. His feet smashed into a broad chest. The warrior toppled, and his sword clattered to the floor. Rand tucked one of the daggers he carried into his boot sheath and snatched up the fallen sword.

The screams from the chamber ceased abruptly.

Rand broke into a sweat.

Warriors turning away from the doorway ran at them.

Kai shifted into position behind Rand. They stood back-to-back with blades leveled.

The warriors circled them, calling to those further down the corridor. Some left the sword fight to join them. Others rushed toward the flames, beating at them with blankets. Why were they bent on putting out the fire? Unless….

The only credible answer settled the sickness churning his stomach.

Mara must be escaping through the secret passage in the allerstaed.

"Halt!" The shouted word silenced the mob, which parted. Down the passageway thus formed strode Draeg. His eyes glittered in meeting Rand's. "This fight belongs to me."

Emotion choked Rand's throat as he waited for his half-brother to strike.

Draeg held up his sword, from which blood dripped. "I've just taken the life of my father's enemy,. I'll take you on, *Misbegotten*, and your defender also."

Rand swallowed against a sour taste. However this ended, he wouldn't like the outcome. "Does it matter to you at all that we are brothers?" Even as he asked the question, he knew its uselessness. Their kinship had never mattered to Draeg except as a reason to make him suffer.

"The garn you slew was more brother to me." Draeg sneered. "You were nothing but an embarrassment. You brought shame to my father, pining for his enemy's daughter. Oh, yes, I guessed about that. Well, know this. She has no hope of living. While you lie cold and dead, she'll be mine."

Rand ignored Draeg's lies and focused on the truth. "Mara lives?"

Not for long," Draeg sneered. "once I've dealt with you."

"She's done nothing to deserve death."

"You've always been soft. I'll never know why Father thought to make a warrior of you."

"We agree on that point, at least."

Draeg's brow furrowed. "You've changed."

"Is it unthinkable? I've discovered I have a soul."

"One I'll soon part from your body." Draeg whipped his sword through the air and ended with it pointing at Rand "Stand ready."

Kai charged.

Draeg brought his sword around in time to deflect the blow.

Kai danced in again, sword flashing. Their blades locked.

In a show of strength, Draeg forced Kai back. He moved into place for a deceptive maneuver Rand knew well.

"Careful!" Rand warned Kai. He rushed into the fray.

Draeg shifted to counter Rand's blow, then spun as if to thrust at Kai.

Kai wasn't fooled, but stopped the real strike when it came.

Draeg grunted in surprise or annoyance, possibly both. He fell back.

Kai followed, allowing him no rest.

Rand took up Draeg's other side, preventing him from sidestepping. Together, he and Kai drove their opponent backward. Behind Draeg, a body sprawled. Elcon lay still and white with blood oozing from his side.

Kai let out a moan and came at Draeg, raining blows. Draeg met him with seeming ease. Kai's strikes slowed, and he retreated.

Draeg pursued.

Rand stepped forward to intervene

Draeg swiveled to confront him..

Rand leaped aside, barely in time to avoid the tip of his half-brother's sword.

Kai moved in again.

Draeg feinted, and this time Kai took the bait.

Rand couldn't let this happen. He sucked in a breath and lunged, acting from instinct more than plan. His blade slid through Draeg's surcoat and found its way between the coat-of-plates beneath it. He pulled the blade free, his stomach twisting as if he, and not Draeg, had taken the wound.

Draeg dropped his sword and caught at his side, Blood flowed between his fingers. "Well done...little brother."

"You were about to stab Kai."

"Why explain?" Draeg went to his knees. A fit of coughing doubled him over.

Rand knelt beside him. "Lie quiet." He tore a strip from his sleeve and wadded it to press against the wound.

Draeg clutched his arm. "You have killed me. Will you now...show me kindness?"

"You are my brother." Tears slid down Rand's cheeks.

Draeg pulled him down and murmured beside his ear. "I'd not grieve you."

Rand jerked back. "You can't make me hate you."

"No?" Draeg's laugh turned into a wheezing cough. His mouth worked, and Rand bent over him again. "Father gave me the honor...of torturing your witless mother to her...last breath."

"You lie to torment me." He jerked back, but his

half-brother tightened his grip.

"Father...called for her blood..." Draeg's smile gave way to a grimace. "...before you left Pilaer." He gasped out the last words and fell back with staring eyes.

Rand closed his half-brother's eyes and dashed away tears from his own.

The faces of Pilaer's best warriors shifted into focus.

Rand turned his head to find Kai crouched beside Elcon, pressing a cloth to his wound. He seemed to have forgotten the fight at hand.

A solid wall of muscle clad in armor rushed at them.

Rand scrabbled for his fallen sword and lurched to his feet. "Kai!"

The warriors pressed in, their faces fierce. The stench of sweat and smoke clogged the air.

Kai came up beside Rand, his face a mask of fury. A sword flashed, and Rand brought his blade up to deflect it. Kai moved to fight behind him.

Three blades came at Rand, but he deflected each one. Clashing metal behind him testified that Kai remained at his back.

An arrow zinged, and a warrior toppled. The others halted in obvious confusion.

The battle cry of Faeraven roared through the keep. Warriors charged down the corridor to meet the guardians of Rivenn. A few hurried past the fire, now subdued, and continued past the turning for the allerstaed. They either had lost their way or didn't know of the passageway in the allerstaed. Only a remnant still challenged Rand and Kai. As Torindan's forces approached amid the clangor of battle, these broke and ran.

Kai bent again over Elcon "He's alive, but I fear moving him."

"He may die in the fighting unless we move him, but we must first stop his bleeding." Rand ripped ripped a strip from the bottom of his **jerken**, and as Kai lifted Elcon, wound the makeshift bandage around him.

Elcon's head lolled sideways, and he opened his eyes. "I can walk on my own."

"Lof Shraen, you are not strong enough." Kai protested.

"I *will* stand." Elcon clenched his jaw and with sweat glistening on his forehead propelled himself upright. "I must go to the allerstaed. I must...make certain that my wife and daughter escape."

"Allow me to assist you." Kai moved in to support him.

"If I may, Lof Shraen." Rand took Elcon's other side.

Elcon threw his arms over their shoulders and swayed between them.

They started down the corridor to the allerstaed.

Rand gulped air before walking into the suffocating heat. Flames flicked toward him, biting like welkes hungering for flesh. His lungs burned for air that did not come. The need to breathe pressed him harder with every heartbeat, and he knew an urge to drop his burden and run. The scorching heat lessened beyond the flames, but the thick air choked Rand.

Despite Elcon's brave words, he sagged and would have fallen without them. They emerged from the worst of the smoke in front of the carved double doors that gave onto the allerstaed.

"Wait." Kai halted. "Someone's lying there."

"Syl Marinda!" Elcon cried in a faint voice.

Mara, her face smeared with grime, lay on the stone floor with her eyes closed and one hand reaching toward the allerstaed.

Rand shifted Elcon's weight fully to Kai and flung himself down beside her. Her pulse still beat. He lifted her into his arms. Breathing came more easily inside the allerstaed. He carried Mara across the nave, moving from light to shadow and back again, and laid her beneath the altar. How frail she looked. Wrenching his gaze from her, he went to help Kai.

They lowered Elcon onto the dais beside his daughter. With their lashes fanning over pale cheeks, their faces looked much alike.

"Lof Shraen?" Kai called.

Elcon made no answer.

Kai checked his pulse. "He's only fainted. That might be just as well, for it will spare him the pain of the journey."

Mara moaned, and Rand shook her with a gentle hand. "Wake up, Lof Raena."

Her eyelashes twitched, then fluttered open. A spasm of coughing gripped her.

Rand propped her against him, raising her shoulders to ease her breathing.

Kai felt along the side of the altar, a look of concentration on his face. "Ah, here it is." Behind the altar a trap door levered open. Kai leaned into the hole now exposed. "Come up at once." He reached down.

Arillia appeared, her hair tumbling in a golden curtain about her shoulders.

Anders came next, carrying an unlit lanthorn and a tinder box.

Mara's coughing bout ended, and Rand turned her in his arms. Her eyes widened, and she pushed away from him.

"What's happened to Elcon?" Arillia's question rang out.

Rand caught the sound of Mara's indrawn breath. He ached to comfort her, but she'd made it clear she wouldn't welcome his embrace. Besides, he'd promised her father to keep his distance. Pressed by circumstance, he'd forgotten that.

Arillia rushed toward her husband's prostrate form, but then held back as if fearful of harming him with her touch.

"He lives." Kai assured her.

Tears glazed her eyes. "Who did this to him?"

Rand waited with sadness for Kai's answer. Once Mara knew his half-brother had wounded her father, she would despise him all the more.

"Lof Raelein." Kai held out a hand to her. "For your safety, we must leave at once."

She arched a brow. "And Elcon?"

Kai squared his shoulders. "We must take him to safety."

"Let me carry him." Anders went to Elcon.

Footsteps echoed behind the double doors. Rand couldn't guess at their owners. Had Torindan's forces won through, or might some of Pilaer's warriors have found their way here?

Kai closed the trap door to the priest's hole and took up the lanthorn and tinder box Anders had abandoned.

Rand stood and offered a hand of assistance to Mara. She glared at him, but after trying to rise on her own, took it. She swayed, and he reached out to steady her. This time she didn't pull away from his touch, but he didn't delude himself it could be from anything other than need.

Kai gestured that they should follow and led them to the rear wall. He fumbled behind a tapestry, and a secret door in the paneling gaped ajar. Musty air exhaled into the chamber. Kai placed the lanthorn and tinder box just inside the aperture and hurried to assist Anders with Elcon.

Rand escorted Mara into the dank passageway.

Voices sounded in the corridor, whether of friend or foe, Rand could not tell.

Arillia refused to go into the opening until Anders had carried her husband through.

The outer doors crashed just as the secret panel clicked behind Kai. Darkness shut them in, so heavy it pressed Rand's eyes.

From behind the thin membrane of wood concealing them from the allerstaed came thumpings, then a mighty crash could only be the altar overturning. That the newcomers came from Pilaer now seemed certain. No guardian of Rivenn would treat the place of prayer with such disrespect.

But the warriors' actions made no sense. From what Rand could tell, Torindan's forces outnumbered Pilaer's. Unless the odds had somehow changed, why would these warriors take time to destroy the allerstaed instead of fleeing?

A chilling certainty came over him. They knew about the secret passageway. They either sought to escape or meant to carry out Draeg's loathsome mission.

A hand gripped his arm. "The lanthorn." Kai whispered.

He must be standing where Kai had placed it. He shifted to allow Kai past. Stone scraped and a spark flew, bright in the darkness. More scraping, and Kai's face flickered in and out of the light from a tiny flame. Part of the flame moved upward, and the lanthorn's wick hissed as light flared.

They stood in a womb of rough stone with dampness glistening about them.

Kai brought down the horn cover, so thin as to be transparent, to shield the flame.

Knocking sounds vibrated along the paneling.

They stared at one another.

Arillia took the lanthorn from Kai, freeing him to help Anders carry Elcon. As one, they started down the hewn steps.

CR

Mara moved through a haze of pain, her stomach churning. Her throat ached, and a headache jarred her. The stone stairs went on endlessly through darkness that shifted whenever the lanthorn swayed in Kai's hand. Water dripped from an unknown source. A precipice plummeted on one side of the stairs, while a natural cave wall enclosed the other. Where the ceiling might be, she couldn't say.

No sounds of pursuit came from behind.

Her steps slowed despite her will as weariness dogged her. Coughing overtook her, and she halted, forcing them all to pause.

Rand turned to her. "Pray allow me assist you."

Whatever her feelings, she needed help. She turned to Rand in tacit agreement, and he swung her into his arms. Surrendering her last shreds of pride, she rested her head against his chest. He started off, and she closed her eyes as she swayed in his arms. They moved faster now, but it seemed an eternity before Rand carried her out of the darkness.

He put her down on the hillside and steadied her to stand alone.

Arillia and Anders watched over her father in the lee of an outcropping.

Below them, a walled path connected a watergate giving onto the river with two defensive platforms built of wood farther up the hillside behind the stronghold. A flock of tiny birds winged above the river, chirruping.

How strange that the sun warmed a perfect spring day. Night should cloak evil deeds in darkness, but today battle cries blighted the air, and from beyond the curtain walls a burning pyre sent smoke and ash into a clear sky.

Something moved at the edge of sight. A wingabeast with a saddle but no rider climbed into the sky. As she watched, more of the graceful creatures flew out from the hold, only four bearing riders. "What does it mean?" She spoke her thought aloud.

Kai, standing on the path, squinted upward. "The battle goes against Torindan. Guaron would only free the wingabeasts to keep them out of other hands." His whistle sounded loud from so near but would be lost beneath the clangor of battle. A silver wingabeast must have heard it, however, for it changed course to land on a wooden platform.

The four riders directed their mounts to follow, and one of them whistled down several more of the creatures. Gathering the reins of the riderless wingabeasts, the riders led them after the Silver along the path toward Kai. As they neared, Mara recognized the features of Guaron, keeper of the wingabeasts. Another was Eathnor, the tracker she had met in her father's meeting chamber. The other two were unknown to her. From the bow he carried, one was an archer. The other wore rough garb and a bandage on his head.

Kai started out to greet them, and Rand pulled her into the lee of an outcropping beside the path where Arillia and Anders watched over her father.. "Remain here."

He seemed to think she had the energy to do anything else. Not to be ordered about, she stepped from behind the outcropping to watch as he moved off after Kai.

"Lof Raena, you should remain hidden." Anders cautioned her.

The echo of footsteps from the cave stilled her protest.

A cry went out along the battlements.

33

The ground reverberated with the thud of hooves, and now two wingabeasts writhed on the path, shrilling in obvious agony. The rest of the small herd descended toward Mara, huffing and snorting, wings unfurling in anticipation of flight.

Warriors burst from the mouth of the cave but stood blinking in the light.

Arillia threw herself over her husband.

Anders stood forth, holding a dagger that looked pathetically inadequate against their swords.

The wingabeasts thundered by before Mara could muster the wit to pull back.

An arm caught her around the waist. Her feet left the ground. A scream forced past her throat. Whoever held her captive rode the wingabeast from its side. "Stop fighting Mara." Rand's voice carried above the thud of hooves.

"But my father—"

"Would prefer not to watch you die. Now be still. I'd hate to drop you."

"That…might be better…than crashing into that gate."

"Hold on." He pushed her up, and she climbed into the saddle.

He swung up behind her as their mount launched upward. The watergate passed below, so close it seemed she could touch it. Dizziness swept over her in a wave, making her instantly regret looking down.

"Stop leaning." Kai's arm tightened around her.

She opened her mouth to complain about his bossiness but speech fled as the sky tilted. The wingabeast climbed in a spiral that leveled out above the water.

Rand's arm squeezed her waist. "What were you doing back there, anyway?"

"I was about to help Anders. He needs help."

"Not from you."

"Why won't you go back and fight?"

"I'm a little busy keeping you alive, if you hadn't noticed. Your father wouldn't want you anywhere near those warriors. Don't worry. Neither Eathnor nor Kai will leave them."

" The others caught up with them, and Rand's prediction thankfully proved true. . Kai rode the silver wingabeast which had answered his whistle. Eathnor carried Arillia. Her father sagged before Anders. The archer and injured tracker rode alone. Where was the wingabeast keeper?

She had no time to inquire, for shadows rippled over the ground. Two black birds of such enormous size they had to be welkes flapped toward them, carrying riders with swords gleaming in the sunlight.

"Scatter!" Kai shouted.

❦

Rand had never ridden a wingabeast before. However, he'd learned a few riding tricks in his warrior training. He pointed the Black they rode westward, reveling in the power of its wing strokes. A glance behind revealed one of the welke riders had split off and now closed the distance between them. "Hold tight, Lof Raena."

Necessity had always served an excellent teacher, one that didn't desert him now. He guided his mount lower until they flew just above the forest canopy. Diving still lower hid them below the tree line. Under the forest cover, he backtracked along the serpentine path cut by Weild Aenor and brought the wingabeast down on a rocky ledge veiled by shadow.

The welke rider passed within view, soaring westward and out of sight.

He headed eastward with the water flowing beneath them and scanned for a better hiding place. When the welke rider figured out his ruse—and Rand had no doubt he would—the ledge would become a death trap.

He rejected a cave as too obvious, almost missing an overgrown track in the bluff above it. Overgrown and reposing in heavy shade, the path led away from the edge and disappeared into thick forest.

He swerved the wingabeast, shearing close to the cliff. Mara trembled but thankfully didn't scream. He'd allowed too little time to slow their flight, and now branches whipped them. They landed farther along the path than he'd intended.

The glance Mara sent him gave her opinion of his riding. Without thinking he covered a welt on her cheek with his hand. "I'm sorry."

The wingabeast beneath them snorted and stomped, reclaiming his attention. He patted the creature's sweating neck. A welke's screech shook the air, and a long shudder ran down the wingabeast's flank. Rand guided the wingabeast forward, and it responded at once.

A green tunnel closed over them, shutting out the roar of the weild. They hadn't gone far when he had to dismount to clear underbrush from the track, but afterwards the forest canopy thickened, its shadow keeping the ground clear of growth. The shade and a refreshing breeze brought a welcome coolness. Birds scolded them in passing. In the springtime, the tiny creatures guarded nests.

No sounds of pursuit followed them. The birds kept singing, which indicated they didn't sense a threat. The track descended into a glade where a stream cascaded around rocks. The wingabeast would need water, and they should take a small rest before going on.

Rand dismounted and reached up to help Mara out of the saddle.

Ignoring him, she slid to the ground on her own. Her hair had escaped its plaits and now tumbled about her in wild abandon. Under other circumstances he'd have been hard pressed not to kiss her. He steadied her and stepped away.

The Black lowered its muzzle to drink from the stream.

Rand rummaged in the saddlebag and pulled out an elkskin full of water. The wingabeast keeper must have outfitted the Black for a rider who never came. Rand frowned at the memory of the wingabeast keeper running back to the shrilling creatures outside Torindan's wall. An arrow had pierced him. Rand extended the water bottle to Mara, and their fingers brushed as she accepted it.

She tilted her head back, and the muscles of her

throat moved as she took long swallows.

He drank in turn, then tore another strip from the hem of his jerken and wetted it in the stream.

Seated on a large rock, Mara watched his approach.

Noticing her puckered forehead, he smiled to ease her. "The welt on your cheek needs cleansing." He'd half-expected her to reject his help, but she remained still as he washed dried blood from her cheek.

Wings flapped in the sky, and Mara turned a frightened gaze on him.

Rand caught up the wingabeast's reins and pulled Mara into forest cover. Stepping in front of her, he waited with a hand to his sword hilt.

A shadow rippled across the stream. Ragged wings and leather armor gleamed with dark luster against the pale sky.

Rand held his breath and prayed that both Mara and the wingabeast would remain motionless.

The welke and its rider vanished beyond the tree tops.

Rand drew in air and let it out in a long sigh. He turned to find Mara trembling. Unable to resist the desire to comfort her, he drew her into his arms. She looked up at him with parted lips. He lowered his head, ready to succumb.

Trust shone in her eyes.

He groaned and pulled away.

Several heartbeats passed, and then she touched his arm. "Thank you."

Did she thank him for restraining his ardor?

"You placed yourself between me and danger."

Speaking of love would be so easy right now, but he shook free of the impulse. In her present vulnerable state, it would be unfair. "I owed you that much."

"I should have thanked you before this. You could have saved yourself and left me at the watergate."

No, he couldn't have, but he didn't tell her that.

She cast her gaze downward. "Why did you abandon me in the wilderness?"

"I'm sorry, Mara. If I could do it again differently, I would."

Her head came up. "But *why* did you do it?"

He'd been trying to save her from his confusion, but how could he explain something he didn't fully understand? "I had...an important reason to return to Pilaer, and I wasn't thinking clearly. I thought you would return home." He needed to end this conversation before he revealed things he wasn't ready to say and that she probably wouldn't want to know. He lifted her by the waist and into the saddle, and for once she didn't fight him. The bewilderment on her face almost proved his undoing.

Mastering himself, he levered himself onto the wingabeast's back and reached past her to gather the reins. "Come, Lof Raena. We've a journey to complete."

Thank you…

for purchasing this Harbourlight title. For other inspirational stories, please visit our on-line bookstore at www.pelicanbookgroup.com.

For questions or more information, contact us at customer@pelicanbookgroup.com.

Harbourlight Books
The Beacon in Christian Fiction™
an imprint of Pelican Book Group
www.pelicanbookgroup.com

Connect with Us
www.facebook.com/Pelicanbookgroup
www.twitter.com/pelicanbookgrp

To receive news and specials, subscribe to our bulletin
http://pelink.us/bulletin

May God's glory shine through
this inspirational work of fiction.

AMDG

You Can Help!

At Pelican Book Group it is our mission to entertain readers with fiction that uplifts the Gospel. It is our privilege to spend time with you awhile as you read our stories.

We believe you can help us to bring Christ into the lives of people across the globe. And you don't have to open your wallet or even leave your house!

Here are 3 simple things you can do to help us bring illuminating fiction™ to people everywhere.

1) If you enjoyed this book, write a positive review. Post it at online retailers and websites where readers gather. And share your review with us at reviews@pelicanbookgroup.com (this does give us permission to reprint your review in whole or in part.)

2) If you enjoyed this book, recommend it to a friend in person, at a book club or on social media.

3) If you have suggestions on how we can improve or expand our selection, let us know. We value your opinion. Use the contact form on our web site or e-mail us at customer@pelicanbookgroup.com

God Can Help!

Are you in need? The Almighty can do great things for you. Holy is His Name! He has mercy in every generation. He can lift up the lowly and accomplish all things. Reach out today.

Do not fear: I am with you; do not be anxious: I am your God. I will strengthen you, I will help you, I will uphold you with my victorious right hand.
~Isaiah 41:10 (NAB)

We pray daily, and we especially pray for everyone connected to Pelican Book Group—that includes you! If you have a specific need, we welcome the opportunity to pray for you. Share your needs or praise reports at http://pelink.us/pray4us

Free Book Offer

We're looking for booklovers like you to partner with us! Join our team of influencers today and periodically receive free eBooks and exclusive offers.

For more information
Visit http://pelicanbookgroup.com/booklovers